Theaker's Quarterly Fiction #59

Edited by
Stephen Theaker
and John Greenwood

Theaker's Quarterly Fiction #59

Edited by
Stephen Theaker
and John Greenwood

Cover Artist

Howard Watts

Contributors

Charles Wilkinson
Chris Roper
David Penn
Douglas J. Ogurek
Elaine Graham-Leigh
Jacob Edwards
Jessy Randall
Lorelei Theaker
Michael Wyndham Thomas
Rafe McGregor

Contents

Editorial

Fiction

Red Nose Reviews

The Quarterly Review

Reviews by Stephen Theaker, Jacob Edwards, Douglas J. Ogurek, Rafe McGregor and Lorelei Theaker

Audio

Books

The Theaker's Quarterly Awards

Stephen Theaker

We launched the voting in the inaugural Theaker's Quarterly Awards at the beginning of January, and voting closed at the end of February. It was good fun, and we'll definitely be doing it again next year. Thanks to everyone who took part! Here are the results.

Audio

1st **The Brenda and Effie Mysteries: Spicy Tea and Sympathy, by Paul Magrs (Bafflegab Productions)**

2nd Doctor Who and the Ark in Space, by Ian Marter (BBC/Audible)

3rd Vince Cosmos: Glam Rock Detective, by Paul Magrs (Bafflegab Productions)

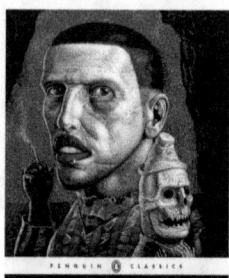

Books

1st **Songs of a Dead Dreamer and Grimscribe, by Thomas Ligotti (Penguin Classics)**

2nd The Last Weekend, by Nick Mamatas (PS Publishing)

3rd Slow Bullets, by Alastair Reynolds (Tachyon Publications)

Comics

1st **The Glorkian Warrior and the Mustache of Destiny, by James Kochalka (First Second)**

2nd Ms. Marvel Vol. 1: No Normal, by G. Willow Wilson and Adrian Alphona (Marvel)

3rd The Savage Sword of Conan, Vol. 14, by Charles Dixon, Gary Kwapisz, Ernie Chan and chums (Dark Horse Books)

Films

1st **Captain America: Civil War, by Christopher Markus and Stephen McFeely (Marvel Entertainment et al.)**

2nd Star Wars: The Force Awakens, by Lawrence Kasdan, J.J. Abrams and Michael Arndt (Lucasfilm et al.)

3rd X-Men: Apocalypse, by Simon Kinberg (Twentieth Century Fox Film Corporation et al.)

Games

1st **Trials Fusion Awesome Max Edition, by RedLynx (Ubisoft)**

2nd Rare Replay, by Rare (Microsoft Studios)

3rd Saints Row IV: Re-Elected, by Volition Software (Deep Silver)

Music

1ˢᵗ It Follows: Original Motion Picture Soundtrack, by Disasterpeace (Milan Records)

2ⁿᵈ —

3ʳᵈ —

Television

1ˢᵗ Doctor Who, Season 9, by Steven Moffat and friends (BBC)

2ⁿᵈ The Flash, Season 1, by Andrew Kreisberg and many others (Warner Bros Television)

3ʳᵈ Penny Dreadful, Season 2, by John Logan and chums (Sky Atlantic)

Issue of TQF

1st **Theaker's Quarterly Fiction #56, edited by Stephen Theaker and John Greenwood**

2nd Theaker's Quarterly Fiction #54, edited by Stephen Theaker and John Greenwood

3rd Theaker's Quarterly Fiction #57, edited by Stephen Theaker and John Greenwood

TQF cover art

1st **Theaker's Quarterly Fiction #56, art by Howard Watts**

2nd Theaker's Quarterly Fiction #55, art by Howard Watts

3rd Theaker's Quarterly Fiction #57, art by Howard Watts

Fiction from TQF

1st **The Policeman and the Silence, by Patrick Whittaker**

2nd Septs, by Charles Wilkinson

3rd Nold, by Stephen Theaker

Congratulations to all the winners and runners-up! To break any ties we referred to our reviewers' star ratings, where relevant, and if that didn't do the trick we invited Alexa to roll a dice. To claim their prestigious Theaker's Quarterly Awards, pictured below, winners should email us at theakersquarterlyfiction@gmail.com with an address to which we can send them.

In this issue

I think you will thoroughly enjoy this issue, if only because we have seven stories and not one of them is by me. Nope. None of these are pseudonyms (or at least not pseudonyms of mine), and none of this is filler, but you don't need me to tell you that because Charles Wilkinson, Elaine Graham-Leigh, Rafe McGregor, Michael Thomas, Chris Roper, Jessy Randall and David Penn have all appeared in our magazine with brilliant stories before. We're so grateful to them for returning. Which will get your vote in next year's Theaker's Quarterly Awards? Well, unless our voting system changes, there's no need to decide, you'll be able to vote for all of them, and I'm sure you'll want to!

Stephen Theaker is the co-editor of Theaker's Quarterly Fiction, and the father of two amazing super-friends.

The Devil's Hollow

Rafe McGregor

...There entered in at the east window of the church a dark unproportioned thing about the bigness of a football, and went along the wall on the pulpit side; and suddenly it seemed to break with no less sound than if a hundred cannons had been discharged at once; and therewithal came a most violent storm and tempest of lightning and thunder as if the church had been full of fire...

The Wrath of God
Reverend Fr. Austen, 1868

I

Shortly after the coronation of the great uncle of Europe, I took to frequenting the public bar of the Royal Hotel every Wednesday evening. The change of my routine was not motivated by a desire to acknowledge the passing of the austere era that had exhausted first my youth and then my good health, but to give my housekeeper, the aptly-named Mrs Knaggs, a night off during the week. For some reason I could not fathom, she had no objection to leaving me to my own devices on Saturday and Sunday evenings, but would under no circumstances attend her midweek bridge club if I was in residence. Being a naturally reclusive individual, I was initially concerned that my presence in the hotel would be misconstrued as a desire for company, but in four years I had only been approached on three occasions, exclusively by members of the Whitby Literary and Philosophical Society, the only society of which I was a member. In order to discourage company, I would arrive at the hotel at half-past six with a pile of newspapers, two to three copies each of *The Yorkshire Post*, the *Daily Mail*, *The Morning Post*, *The New York Times*, and the *Boston Herald*. I would take a table in the most secluded corner, next to the sash window overlooking the lower harbour, the East Cliff, and the ruins of Whitby Abbey. I would order a pot of coffee, light up my pipe, and study the periodicals until ten o'clock, by which time I could return home free from guilt. On most weeks the editor of the local *Dailygraph*, a flamboyant American by the name of Largo Delapena, entertained his colleagues, friends, and the curious at the next table but one, throwing a veil of chatter, clinking glasses, smoke, and good cheer across my sanctuary.

On the night in question, Delapena had arrived shortly after me, wished me good evening – for he was always immaculate in his manners – and indulged himself and his half-dozen associates in a manner of which our cheerful but somewhat dissolute monarch would have approved. Nothing extraordinary occurred until a couple of hours later, when a pale man of about forty years of age entered the bar-room, demanded a bottle of brandy from the steward, and sat down at the table across the sash window from me. He filled his glass to the brim, drank it down in one swift draught, refilled the glass, and lit a cigarette. While this may have been *de rigeur* for saloons in the American West or the Australian Outback, it was unusual behaviour for a gentleman in a luxury hotel at a seaside resort in Yorkshire. What's more, he certainly maintained the appearance of a gentleman, being a dapper little man in a smart black suit with cigarettes from Sobranie of London. I had no wish to intrude, however, so I reapplied myself to the trans-Atlantic news from Boston.

Three-quarters of an hour later, I happened to look up from a review of Mr Parry's *The Scarlet Empire* and noticed a cloud of smoke hovering above the alcoholic gentleman. He had already consumed half of his bottle of Armagnac, filled his ash-receiver, and was drawing heavily on a Black Russian. I studied him surreptitiously, from the corner of my eye, as I refilled my pipe. He was, as I had initially discerned, small of small stature, wan of complexion, and four decades old. He had pitch black hair and a generous but neatly-trimmed beard, although neither had felt the touch of a brush recently. His beard was slightly discoloured beneath his mouth, perhaps the beginning of a grey streak. His suit was complemented with a necktie, embroidered silk waistcoat, and impeccably-shined boots. From the absence of a hat, stick, and overcoat – and the readiness with which the steward had acquiesced to his demand – I deduced that he was a guest of the hotel. Much of his face was concealed by the beard, which made his pallor seem even more deathly than it really was. He was staring directly ahead, which should have brought me under his scrutiny, but his gaze was blank, eyes unfocused. I noticed that he was sweating and that his hand shook as he raised the cigarette to his lips. The perspiration and palpitation could have been either the cause or the effect of his alcohol consumption.

I finished packing my pipe, but did not light it, choosing instead to continue my clandestine surveillance of the gentleman over the top of the *Boston Herald*.

He smoked his Black Russian down to the gold filter, stubbed it out in the ash-receiver, and opened his cigarette case. It was empty. He cursed, retrieved a wooden box from his coat pocket, and removed a handful of cigarettes. He lit another cigarette with a permanent match and started filling the case. He stopped a few seconds later, before the case was full, smiled to himself, and laughed rather loudly for someone sitting on his own. When he had smoked his cigarette down to the filter, he dropped it in the ash-receiver, and poured more Armagnac from the bottle. He stopped when the glass was one third full and consumed the contents before he had returned the bottle to the table. Then he rose, withdrew a money-wallet from his coat, fumbled inside it, and stepped over to the bar. He threw a five pound note on the counter – more than ten times his bill – and marched out towards reception. The steward's mouth dropped open. He looked at me and I waved for him to keep the money. I slipped my pipe into my pocket, donned my hat, picked up my stick, and left my overcoat behind.

I arrived in the reception hall in time to see the gentleman walk out the main entrance. I went after him. It was nearly ten o'clock and few people had braved the cold, wet night. He had turned left and was now striding along East Terrace towards the cliff. I followed, bending forward against the stiff sea breeze blowing drizzle in my face. The gentleman left the road, passed the footpath leading down to the pier, and continued for the cliff, high above the bathing beach. I am, as my name suggests, unusually tall, so I was able to close the distance between us without exerting any more effort than my quarry.

I was some twenty feet away when he slowed down to a halt a short distance from the cliff-edge.

I picked up my pace.

He reached inside his right trouser pocket.

I had not committed an act of violence in over

nineteen years, but the movements came easily, without conscious thought.

His hand emerged clutching a Derringer. He raised it to his right temple. He drew the hammer back.

I hacked at the pistol with my Penang-lawyer, knocking the weapon into the air and over the cliff.

He turned around, dazed and uncertain, seeing me for the first time. He swayed slightly, unsteady on his feet.

"Who... who are you?"

"My name is Roderick Langham."

He blinked and lost focus again. "I'm Wilfrid Fletcher. I'm... I *was* the Chief Magistrate of the Pitcairn Islands. I have seen terrible things... monsters."

"So have I," I replied.

He nodded slowly.

"I think you had better come along with me. I live just a little way down this road."

II

I ensconced Fletcher in my study at No.10 Flowergate rather than the larger room below that served as my sitting-room, dining-room, and library. My reasons were twofold: I did not want Mrs Knaggs disturbing us, which she would if she saw the lights on downstairs, and I was worried Fletcher would disappear if he was too close to the front door. My kitchen is, inexplicably, on the first floor of the house, and I was able to keep an eye on him while I prepared refreshment for us. I decided that we had both had too much stimulation for one evening, so I brewed a pot of tea and toasted the last of the day's bread. I needn't have fretted for Fletcher. He followed me meekly and, after making use of the water-closet, collapsed in the armchair. I lit the fire while the tea leaves were drawing and the toast cooking. When I returned with a tray, he had not stirred. I placed a cup of tea and two rounds of buttered toast on the side-table next to him, set the tray on my desk, and drew the dining chair closer.

"I noticed there were only three chairs at the table downstairs," said Fletcher, as I took my first drink of tea.

"Yes, I spend long hours at my desk and find the support eases my back pain."

"You are a writer?"

"Of a sort, yes. I have been a soldier, a detective, and an invalid. Now I write mystery and adventure stories for magazines." His attention seemed to drift away. "Perhaps you would be kind enough to tell me of the circumstances that have brought you to this pass?" He nodded. "May I ask you to be entirely frank? You said you have seen monsters. I saw one long ago in a place called Assam, near the Himalayas. I saw another, more recently and much closer, for this, also, has been one of the dark places of the earth. You need not fear my disdain or derision."

"Perhaps I should fortify myself first." I waited while Fletcher ate a slice of toast. When he was finished, he had a long drink of tea, sighed, and began. "My people are the Fletchers of Yeadon, near Leeds, and we are a cursed race. I am grateful that the curse runs only in the male line of the family. I have had six brothers and five sisters. All of my sisters are married with issue of their own. The dilution of their blood with that of their husbands seems to have lifted the curse, for between them they have fourteen offspring, seven boys and seven girls. Neither I nor my brothers have offspring. Two of us have reached thirty, but personal and professional success remained elusive. My eldest brother, Edward, served the 5th Northumberland

Fusiliers with distinction in the Black Mountain Expedition, but had only reached the rank of major when he was killed in action in South Africa. I am thirty-one years of age, have been a colonial administrator ever since leaving school, but never rose beyond the rank of assistant commissioner. I spent the last four years in the Pitcairn Islands. I doubt you have even heard of them."

I was dismayed to learn that Fletcher was in fact more than twenty years my junior. "I believe they are in the very middle of the great Pacific Ocean."

"Indeed. There are four islands, but only one is inhabited and that with less than one hundred souls. The nearest land is over one hundred leagues away and barely less remote. They are quite literally the backwater of the British Empire, populated almost entirely by blood relations, and plagued by the biological and social problems that accompany hyperbolic homogeneity. I have been Chief Magistrate since the annexation, with little prospect of promotion to commissioner or lieutenant governor. I am now the only one of my brothers living and were it not for your gracious intervention, would have completed the curse's work on my own." He paused to take more tea.

"That seems remarkable. May I ask how the others died?"

"Lancelot was my parent's third child and died shortly after his birth. Our family was free from tragedy for twenty-six years, but then I lost three brothers in less than twelve months. Harold was listed as missing in action during the Matabele War, Arthur was a victim of death by misadventure in the Pyrenees, and Herbert died in strange circumstances not too far from here, near Kingston upon Hull. Edward's death left only myself and my youngest brother, Henry. He went into the priesthood, but was – like the rest of us – unsuccessful in his vocation. He was twenty-nine before he assumed the responsibilities of a vicar and then in a parish so remote to have been equivalent to my lowly dominion. Are you familiar with Great Billington?"

"No, I am not."

"It is a tiny hamlet on the moors, a few miles from Goathland." I knew the moors very well and had visited Goathland several times so I was surprised by this intelligence. "Henry took up residence at the vicarage in the summer and it was with great sadness but not great surprise that I was informed of his death last month. I resigned my office immediately and begged passage on the naval vessel that brought me the news. I returned post-haste, ahead of my luggage, arriving in Whitby last Thursday."

"May I ask a question?"

"Certainly." Fletcher made use of the opportunity to take the second slice of toast.

"I applaud your filial love, but that seems a drastic step to take. Would your superiors in the colonial service not have afforded you a leave of absence?"

Fletcher wiped his mouth with his handkerchief. "I was about to throw in the towel anyway, but I'll come back to that later if you like. On Friday, I met with Reverend Perkins, Henry's superior in the church, and Doctor Abbott, who had performed the post-mortem examination. Henry had been laid to rest in the Church of Saint Mary by Perkins in the interim. Curiously, he had registered my name alone as his next of kin. Indeed, now that I think on it, I believe my sisters are unaware that they are down to their last brother. Abbott informed me that Henry had died from a lightning strike. I was told the poor chap's exterior was covered in what doctors call 'feathering', a fern-pattern made by broken blood vessels; his interior was far worse, with his intestines burned beyond recognition and both eardrums burst. Abbott said he would have died instantly, but I am not sure if I believe him.

"Now you might think that given the curse to which I believe the male Fletchers are subject, a lighting strike is precisely the sort of nemesis I or my brother should expect. You would no doubt be correct, but there were two points that piqued my curiosity. First, in the only letter from Henry that reached me prior to news of his death, he mentioned several pagan practices in the village. He said that although the population ostensibly venerated Saint Cuthbert, they actually belonged to a religious cult known as the Old Faith and worshipped a pre-Christian deity of unknown origin. Second, I thought it strange that a hamlet boasted a vicar. I'm no expert in church hierarchy, but Great Billington has a population of forty-odd souls and should have been allocated a deacon rather than a priest. It seemed somewhat like giving the Pitcairn Islands its own governor. I mentioned this to Perkins, but he said that the village had been bigger in medieval times and that the post was traditional, in much the way that Whitby retains its own bishop. After visiting Henry's grave, I didn't have anything with which to occupy my time, so I found the Literary and Philosophical Society and asked to look at the local records. I couldn't find any mention of Great Billington, which made me think Perkins' story a fabrication."

"I have a County Series map of the North Riding. Would you mind if I fetched it? Thank you. Do polish off the rest of the toast if you're hungry."

When I returned Fletcher was doing just that. I located Goathland on the map. With Fletcher's assistance, I found Great Billington in a natural depression between Danby High Moor and Wheeldale Moor, under Pike Hill Moss. I resumed my seat as Fletcher resumed his tale.

"I went back to Perkins, told him I was going to visit Great Billington, and asked if I might stay in the vicarage, assuming that the hamlet had no hostelry. He did everything in his power to stop me bar refusing to give me the key, but I did not relent. I took the train to Goathland on Saturday morning. The inn-keeper there also attempted to dissuade me from going to Great Billington. It was only when I told him that I would walk if he did not provide me with transport that he hired me a horse and cart at an extortionate price. He also pressed a curious little star-shaped stone on me, which he said I should keep upon my person at all times. I reached the village quickly and found the vicarage without any trouble. Within the hour, I received an invitation to luncheon with the squiress at Billington Manor, an elderly widow by the name of Potter. She too was full of the superstitions of the area and told me how the isolation of the community had contributed to the continuation of certain ancient traditions. I must admit that I had already seen disturbing signs of the insularity with which I was familiar from my colonial experience." Fletcher shuddered. "Mrs Potter practically begged me to stay at the manor and, when I wouldn't, warned me to remain indoors if there was a storm.

"The next day was Sunday and I wondered if there would be a service in the absence of any official representative of the church. And this is where things really become strange. Individually or in pairs, every single person in the village except Mrs Potter performed a small ceremony in the churchyard, laying some offering before a little statue. The ritual was perfectly coordinated such that no person, couple, or family met any other. I watched the whole thing from the vicarage window. I returned to Billington Manor to ask Mrs Potter about it and she told me of the Old Faith and showed me an old book that catalogued the practice. Despite the fact that she'd been harping on about pagans and druids, the title concerned New England, not old England, so I confess I didn't pay much attention."

"Was it *Of Evill Sorceries done in New-England of Daemons in no Humane Shape*?" I asked.

"Yes, I think that was it. Why?"

"Remarkable, quite remarkable. I shall let you finish."

"I was intending to return to Goathland the following day, none the wiser and disappointed that my brother's last months had been spent in such a wretched place, but the barometer fell rapidly on Monday morning. I decided to stay and see the phenomenon that had put paid to poor Henry. At midday, with the clouds brooding overhead and the atmosphere tense, the villagers began to gather in the churchyard. They started chanting in an alien tongue and were swaying in unison as if under hypnosis by the time I arrived. I tried to engage several of them in conversation, but none took any notice. When I reached the front of the crowd, I was astonished to find Mrs Potter. I tried to talk to her, but she took no notice either so I picked up the statuette." Fletcher shuddered again, more violently this time. "Suddenly, the chanting stopped and the squiress pointed at me, letting forth an awful high-pitched screech. Something like *he has violated Cath-arta*. Then... my God... then the entire village – about forty men, women, and children – tried to tear me limb from limb."

"How did you escape?"

"When they threw me to the ground, the stone the inn-keeper had given me fell out and they backed away as if it was an incendiary device. I fled the churchyard for Billington Manor, stole a horse, and rode back to Goathland. I am not a great rider, but had some small practice in the Pitcairn Islands. My arrival in Goathland was contemporaneous with the train – on which I leaped without ceremony. I'm afraid that I spent the rest of Monday and most of Tuesday drinking. I won the Derringer off a Moldavian sailor in a game of Old Maid last night and decided to use it this evening. I've not thanked you for saving my life yet, but the thing is, I'm not sure if I wouldn't be better off dead. I hope you understand."

"Your life is your own; you may do with it what you wish. I do hope, however, that you will at least postpone a final decision until you have had a good night's rest." He nodded. "It is such a pity that you lost the stone in the struggle; I should like to have seen it."

"I didn't. I picked it up before I shot off. I thought it might be useful if I was caught."

"You have displayed a remarkable presence of mind, Mr Fletcher, and I suspect there is nothing wrong with your nerves that a few weeks' rest won't cure. May I?"

He dropped a small, green rock in the palm of my hand. The material was soapstone and it had been carved with very little skill, producing a warped five-pointed star. There was an engraving in the centre, which also evinced poor workmanship and vaguely resembled a flaming eye. I had read several descriptions of the star-stone before, though I had not thought that I would ever see one. I realised why the device in the centre had been described as both a flaming eye and a flaming pillar, but assuming that I was holding the genuine article, it was a flaming eye.

"Do you know what it is?" asked Fletcher.

"Yes, it is called an Elder Sign and I think you had better occupy my guest bedroom tonight."

III

I rose earlier than usual on Thursday morning, roused Mrs Knaggs, and proceeded to visit first the Royal Hotel, then the bathing beach, and finally the police station. I woke Fletcher at nine o'clock and broke my habit of having a light breakfast to join him for a hearty – and meaty – offering from Mrs Knaggs. The clock had just struck ten when we left the table for the comfort of the armchairs in front of the fire. I prepared my after-breakfast pipe to accompany my coffee and offered Fletcher a cigar, but he declined, claiming that he had consumed too much alcohol and tobacco in the last three days.

"I have a proposal to put to you, Mr Fletcher, if I may. Allow me to begin by recounting my movements this morning. I went back to the hotel first-thing and asked who you were and if anyone had seen you depart last night. When the attendant said not, I mentioned that I had seen you at the cliff edge when I left and that I was concerned for your safety – I shall explain in a moment. At dawn, I began searching the beach for your Derringer. I was able to make a relatively accurate prediction as to where it landed given the angle and force of my blow and the trajectory of the firearm's descent. I am so glad that your hand is less swollen, by the way. After an hour I was convinced that the pistol had been swept out to sea by the tide. I then visited the police station, where I told the constable a version of the evening's events. I said that I was concerned for your safety and felt responsible for not having approached you when I saw you atop the cliff. I made no suggestion of suicide, only that you may have been unsteady on your feet due to the amount of alcohol you had consumed. It is far too early for the police to investigate, but the constable made a note in the occurrence book."

I lit my pipe before continuing. "I have long suspected that North-East Yorkshire is as much, if not more, of a centre for the worship of the Old Ones as the notorious Miskatonic Valley in New England. This is, I believe, the Old Faith to which your brother referred and is quite simply the cult of elemental evil. There are four Old Ones – demons, devils, or elementals – one each for the elements that the ancients believed constituted the basic building blocks of the universe. Thus far, I have discovered three sites, at which all signs of worship have been destroyed. The earth temple is at Towton, the scene of the bloodiest battle ever to have been fought on Britain's soil. The air temple is at a place called Faxfleet, at the confluence of the Humber and the Trent, and used to be a Templar Preceptory. The water temple is in Scarborough, underneath the castle. From various cross-references I was able to make, I guessed that the fire temple was somewhere on the North York Moors. It seems you have found it for me and that, unlike the others, the cult of *Cthuga* is alive and well."

Fletcher nodded, but the strain on his face was terrible to see. "That was the name Mrs Potter screamed."

"The book she showed you is a history of both the elementals themselves and their respective cults and contains all the details of the rites required for the revival of the Old Faith. It is known as the *New Dunnich Manuscript* and was written by an anonymous high priest of the cult, believed to have emigrated to the New World in the seventeenth or eighteenth century. The manuscript seems either to have either made its way back to here or to have been copied prior to the high priest's departure. Now, do you not think it extraordinary that you just happened to find yourself a hotel frequented by the only man in England with this knowledge?"

"I must confess, Mr Langham, that nothing would surprise me at this juncture."

I removed the Elder Sign from my pocket. "This is a symbol of the Elder Gods, a quartet who are said to struggle with the elementals for the soul of mankind. The gods are known by the names of the races that settled on the east coast – the Celts, Romans, Saxons, and Vikings – as Nodens, Mercury, Donar, and Tir. Over the last two millennia, their worshippers, forming a kind of counter-cult, have destroyed three of the four temples of the Old Ones. The earth temple at Towton and the air temple at Faxfleet were both razed above and below ground. A grove of trees was planted on the site at Towton and is now a small wood, although it is the only wood I have ever known devoid of all fauna. The Templars built their preceptory on the ashes of the air temple. Now, not even the foundations of the preceptory are visible to the casual visitor. The water temple at Scarborough was sealed by worshippers of Nodens, but not destroyed. It now lies directly under the chapel in Scarborough Castle. I suspect that your unfortunate brother's church has either been built on the site of the fire temple or is a disguised fire temple. It is not unknown for the worshippers of elemental evil to conceal their cult under the trappings of Christianity in much the same way as the cult of the Elder Gods. I think you should keep this." I handed Fletcher the Elder Sign. "It has been given to you for a purpose and it is not mine to take."

He shrugged and accepted the stone. "Do you believe all this – in the Elder Gods and the Old Ones?"

I puffed on my pipe. "I believe that cult and counter-cult have battled each other in secrecy over the centuries. I believe that the counter-cult is extinct, as are the earth, air, and water cults. I had hoped that the fire cult had also been consigned to history, but your tale indicates otherwise. I do not know if there is anything behind the cults. Though I am sceptical by nature and scientific by training, I have seen evidence of more than my education and experience can explain. The status of the water temple as sealed rather than destroyed may, for example, explain the profusion of giant sea creatures whose skeletons have been found on these shores. The hypothesis that the rock is particularly well-suited to preserving fossils accounts for the fact that the vast majority of the remains are prehistoric. The hypothesis that the priests of Dagon summoned his servants accounts for the fact that a small minority of the remains are more recent. I do not know which is correct – perhaps they are both true."

The blood drained from Fletcher's face. "I have seen such a creature. In July. I used to join the crayfishermen when they set their nets and rigged their moorings in Bounty Bay. On this day, a shark surfaced alongside. One of the men sounded the alarm; luckily none were in the water. I made some study of sharks during my time in the Pacific and I am able to calculate their length with precision, using the distance between their dorsal and caudal fins. This shark was as long as the pier itself."

"And how long was that?"

"One hundred and fifteen feet."

I put my proposal to him.

IV

Telegram from Roderick Langham Esq. of No.10 Flowergate, Whitby to Mrs W.H. Potter, Billington Manor, Great Billington:

Whitby GPO, 11.16 am, December 13, 1906:
WOULD LIKE TO DISCUSS ACCESS TO NEW
ENGLAND MANUSCRIPT IN YOUR
POSSESSION IN EXCHANGE FOR ACCESS TO
LETTERS OF REVEREND DYER IN MINE STOP
WILL CALL AT MIDDAY ON SATURDAY STOP
LANGHAM

Agony Column, *Dailygraph*, Thursday December 13th
1906:

*Missing – Mr Wilfrid Fletcher, formerly of
Yeadon, Leeds and Adamstwon, Pitcairn Islands
and presently a guest at the Royal Hotel. Last
seen on East Terrace at approximately 10pm last
night. Mr Roderick Langham, of No.10
Flowergate, fears that some harm may have come
to him, and will pay three guineas to anyone who
can provide information as to his whereabouts.*

V

I set off for Great Billington in my wagonette at a few
minutes before nine on Saturday morning. I left an
anxious Fletcher smoking one Black Russian after the
next in our shared sitting-room at Mallyan Spout
Hotel. As a precaution, I had employed a skill I had
not had cause to use for many years and disguised him
by dying his hair and beard and applying greasepaint
to his skin. The devices narrowed the gap between us
completely with the result that Fletcher was not out of
place among the other elderly ladies and gentlemen
who had come to Goathland to take the waters. As a
further precaution, he had adopted the alias of
Williams and retired immediately to our suite, where
he had remained ever since. The morning was cold
with an icy breeze blowing from the west, where dark

clouds brooded in a bruised sky. Although Great
Billington was less than four miles hence, I was
concerned about losing my way, for the hamlet was
accessible only by a series of the faintest of trails, made
by the infrequent wheels of the grocer's wagon. There
was no postal delivery to Great Billington and what
little post arrived waited at Goathland General Post
Office until the grocer sent his delivery or one of Mrs
Potter's servants made a rare appearance.

I left the village by the Egton Road, with Scar Wood
and the River Esk on my right, and gently rolling
moorland all around. When the road turned north, I
continued west along a stony track which cut through
the wood, crossed the river on a rickety old bridge, and
passed the entrance to a prosperous-looking farm
before curving south. It was a relief to turn out of the
wind, but I kept my scarf wrapped around my face and
my hat pulled low on my ears. I could see a small grove
of trees a few hundred yards ahead, which I was
expecting from committing my map to memory. I was
progressing as planned.

Fletcher and I had arrived in Goathland the
previous day. While he kept out of sight, I continued
to pursue the inquiries initiated on Thursday. From
the inn-keeper at The Lancaster Arms, a man by the
name of Talbot whom I had met on a previous visit, I
had discovered that the Elder Sign he had pressed
upon Fletcher was the property of an American
gentleman by the name of Keane. Two years ago, he
had set out on precisely the same journey as Fletcher
and failed to return. The stone had fallen out of his
pocket when he had mounted his cart, but Talbot had
only discovered it after his departure. Keane had never
been seen again, nor had Talbot's cart, which was why
he had charged Fletcher an extortionate price, and
required me to buy both wagonette and horse
(although he did offer to buy them back at a slightly

reduced price in the unlikely event that I returned). When I asked him what the danger was in Great Billington, he said "witches" and refused to elaborate. Following Keane's disappearance, the police had made inquiries in the hamlet to no avail and Talbot had sent a letter to his address in Arkham, Massachusetts which was returned to sender. I was the first person to ask about him – albeit indirectly – and he was the first person to have visited Great Billington since Talbot had acquired ownership of the inn at the turn of the century.

The track turned west again and the land began to sink. The green fields of the farms gave way to patches of purple heather that meandered under barren brown hills. Egton High Moor rose steeply to the north and Wheeldale Moor more gently to the south, both white with snow. After a couple of hundred yards, I fell in alongside Wheeldale Gill, passing Scar End Wood at the foot of Wheeldale Moor. As I descended, the wind speed dropped and the first snowflakes began to fall, dusting the landscape.

My second inquiry had been at the post office, where the postmaster confirmed that one of his employees had delivered the telegram to Mrs Potter's butler, a Mr Whateley, in person. There had been no reply, from which I assumed that Mrs Potter was desirous of our meeting – either lured by my mention of *The Letters of Reverend Dyer* or concerned about Fletcher revealing her conspiracy to authorities religious or civil. I had met with both Dr Abbott and Reverend Perkins on Thursday. I knew Dr Abbott quite well, for he was my own physician, and he had confirmed Reverend Fletcher's death by lightning. I had then visited Reverend Perkins on the pretext of concern about Fletcher, whom I had already reported to the police as missing. Perkins confirmed that Fletcher had come to see him, but did not give the impression that there was anything sinister about Great Billington and did not try to dissuade me when I mentioned I was going to look for Fletcher there.

The track curled around Pike Hill, the only high ground in the hollow I had entered. Ahead, I could see the white slopes of Rosedale Moor. Great Billington was somewhere off to my left, through the trees of Pike Hill Moss. I spotted a small stone bridge between the boughs, the only evidence of human habitation beyond. On the other side, gravel had been strewn in imitation of a track. The wood or "moss" was narrow and the gravel became firmer as I emerged onto a particularly barren stretch of low moor. It did not take much imagination to call Shakespeare's blasted heath – with all its connotations – to mind and the coincidence of a heavier snowfall was not reassuring. The path descended again, winding off to the right. As I rounded the bend, I saw two small cottages, one on either side of the path, a few dozen yards apart. The path curved left, falling off further, and I shortly arrived at the hub of the hamlet, half a dozen cottages dotted around a junction shaped like a "T". There were no people or even animals to be seen. The only sign of life was smoke from two of the chimneys. Fletcher had provided me with a detailed description of Great Billington so I knew that Billington Manor was to the left, out of sight behind a screen of pine trees, and the church and vicarage off to the right, barely visible behind the snowflakes being blown in my face. I had made good time – it was a little after ten – so I turned right.

The church and vicarage sat opposite each other about a hundred yards up the path. There was one other house on this side of the settlement and it looked just as empty as the vicarage. The vicarage was a Tudor cottage in better repair than any of the houses I had seen thus far. The church was much older and may even have been Norman if the arched top and heavy oaken door of the vestibule were original features. I brought the wagonette to a halt, dismounted, and threw a blanket over the horse. I opened the gate and entered the churchyard. It was filled with tombstones, most of which were broken or cracked, and some of which bore inscriptions that were still legible – at least in part. *Jabez Jonathan Dunlock and Elizabeth ... Gone to The Lord, AD 1687 ... Eleanor Anne Allen ... Passed Away AD 1701 ... Robert Francis Whateley, Who died ... aged 44 years*. There were a large number of Dunlocks and Whateleys and Allens laid to rest, but no Potters. I wondered if the late squire had his own mausoleum and saw a small but substantially-built structure at the side of the church. I walked over, my shoes crunching through the settling snow. The stonework was indeed a tomb, with two bones carved at right angles and surmounted by a skull in lieu of the usual cross over the door. A macabre conceit typical of the sixteenth and seventeenth centuries. The emblem was weathered and difficult to discern courtesy of defacing by means of a chisel or similar instrument. There was no family name on the mausoleum. I left the resting place of the Potters – if that's what it was – and continued through the graveyard, finding more Dunlocks and Whateleys, as well as a few Perkinses, before reaching a lych-gate. I opened the gate and entered the portico.

The small stone carving Fletcher had described was resting on a ledge where it was only visible from outside the graveyard. It was about nine inches in diameter, roughly circular in shape, and made of an unfamiliar brown granite. What looked like spikes protruded from all sides of the globe, which balanced on four particularly sturdy specimens. On closer inspection, the spikes resembled tentacles or flames. Given what I already knew, I guessed that the idol was a very crude representation of a ball of fire. If my researches had been accurate, Cthuga was served by ball lightning in the same way that Dagon was served by sea monsters past and present. Famously, a ball of lightning had entered the Church of St Hilda in Whitby during the consecration ceremony in 1867. Several people were injured and one killed, which had prompted much speculation on the wrath of God and the desirability of having a Catholic church in the town. I speculated as to how Fletcher had picked the idol up. It must be heavy and there were no spaces large enough for a firm grip between the flames. I leaned my stick against the gate and rubbed my gloved hands together while I considered where to place them.

As I reached for the idol, I heard the crunch of footsteps in the graveyard. I quickly retrieved my stick and turned to the gate in time to see a small, solid figure emerge through the falling snow. The man stopped behind the gate and stared at me. He was about five and a quarter feet in height, thickly-set, and of an indeterminate age between twenty-five and fifty. The face under the bowler hat was hideously ugly. The man had a large, bulbous nose, a protruding lower lip, and his eyes – which were set very close together – were not quite symmetrical. His skin was an unnatural colour, with a very light purplish tint, and he appeared to have failed to shave the left side of his face as closely as the right. Never before had I seen so many signs of consanguineous breeding in a single individual. I doubted whether Fletcher had seen worse on the Pitcairn Islands. The man opened the gate.

"Good day," I said.

"Mr Langham?" he asked. "My name is Whateley. I'm the butler at Billington Manor. Mrs Potter will see you now."

I took out my watch. It was not yet eleven. "Our appointment is for midday."

"I will drive you there in your cart."

I waited a few seconds, but saw no reason to prolong the standoff. I walked through the gate, towering over Whateley as I passed, and retraced my steps. Thick clouds eclipsed the sun as swathes of snow descended to earth.

VI

I saw very little of the hamlet or the manor during the short journey. Though the wind was at our backs, visibility was reduced to twenty yards or so. The manor was protected from prying eyes by a line of pine trees. Once we had penetrated these, I could only see a lawn on either side – now a flat white blanket – and then what appeared to be a modest stone mansion of two storeys, with a turret above the vehicular entrance. We drove past this to the main entrance, which faced south. The walls of the manor were already white, the snow clinging to the ubiquitous ivy. Whateley stopped the wagonette and I dismounted. The moment my left foot touched the ground, the snowfall stopped. It was quite disconcerting and I glanced up, but the heavy black clouds had not moved. The front door opened before I reached it. I could not suppress a start when I saw who stood behind it. She could have been Whateley's twin and I couldn't help wonder whether she was his sister, mother, daughter, wife, or some combination of these. Fletcher must have found himself right back in his worst Pacific nightmare. *This, also, is one of the dark places of the earth*. The female Whateley took my hat, stick, scarf, and overcoat without a word. The reception area was a room rather than a hall. It was appointed in a practical manner little given to decoration, with cocoanut matting on the floor and stairs and light-coloured oak panelling on the walls. There were no paintings or mirrors.

"Mrs Potter will see you in the library."

My diminutive companion led me through a similarly plain parlour into a long, narrow room with bookshelves covering three of the four walls. The remaining wall boasted four sash windows, with a settee and roll-top writing desk positioned so as to benefit from the natural light – though there was not much of it at present. Scattered around the rest of the room were a tall gas lamp, a large globe, and a lectern supporting a medieval illustrated manuscript. Above the back panel of the desk, a white bonnet bobbed up and down. My escort grunted, a face appeared beneath the cap, and Mrs Potter stopped her writing. She dismissed her servant and rose.

I was relieved to see that she bore no resemblance whatsoever to the Whateleys. She was, in fact, remarkably tall for a woman and in remarkably vigorous health for a sexagenarian. She stood straight-backed and steady, her movements were clean and brisk. She had an aristocratic, aquiline profile and a skin tanned by the sun but without excessive wrinkling. I imagined her leading an active, outdoor lifestyle, and could only conjecture as to what kept her in this godforsaken place. When Mrs Potter stood before me, I realised she was in mourning. The white bonnet was a widow's cap and she was clothed in the bombasine and crepe of the recently-bereaved. Our late queen had made prolonged mourning fashionable, however, so there was no way of telling when Mr Potter had died.

"Mr Langham, I am Mrs Potter." I heard the sound of thunder in the distance.

"How do you do?"

She did not answer, but indicated the settee and

resumed her chair, adjusting it so that she was facing me instead of her letters.

"Allow me to thank you for receiving me on such short notice, madam. I— "

"May I come directly to the point, Mr Langham?"

"Of course."

"I have consented to this intrusion because I should like to know how the contents of my library have become the subject of gossip in Whitby. I can only imagine that it is the doing of Mr Fletcher, the brother of our late vicar. Is that correct?"

"Yes." I did not volunteer any further information.

"Mr Fletcher arrived last week, obviously in a state of distress. I received him for luncheon that day and tea for the next. He spent the interval asking the villagers pointless and accusatory questions, as if they had been responsible for calling down the lightning that killed the vicar. My impression on his second visit was that he was mentally unhinged. This was confirmed when he burst into the church and disrupted my service."

"You were leading a church service?" I asked.

Thunder rumbled in the distance, nearer than before. "Yes. In the absence of a clergyman, the locals look to me for spiritual leadership and I have taken on the responsibilities of a sort of lay-deacon from time to time. Great Billington is not popular with vicars, who tend to move on to less remote parishes as soon as decency permits. My late husband and I valued this very remoteness above all else and chose to remain in the place of his ancestors in order to pursue our collection of hermetic and arcane manuscripts in private. You will notice a large number of antiquarian tomes on these shelves, many are rare and some unique. What I am least desirous of is for the contents of my library to become public knowledge. It would bring no end of... *visitors*." Her expression made it clear that I was the first of these undesirables. "Do you disagree that I have the right to privacy, Mr Langham?"

"No madam, I do not, but I hope that you have included a provision for the collection in your legacy."

She ignored my comment and continued. "Thank you. I beg you to ask Mr Fletcher to respect my privacy."

"I'm afraid I am unable to do that. Mr Fletcher has disappeared and I fear that he may have come to some harm. I was, as far as I know, the last to see him. He was very maudlin and heavily under the influence of alcohol. When we parted, I saw him walk towards the West Cliff. He has not been seen since and I confess I feel responsible for leaving him."

"There has been a body?" she asked.

"No, but often no body is found. The tide."

"I see. What did he tell you of the book from New England?"

"He mentioned a garbled title and I asked him if he was referring to *Of Evill Sorceries done in New-England of Daemons in no Humane Shape*. He said yes and that he had seen the manuscript in your library."

"To whom have you communicated this information?"

A muffled explosion rent the sky. "No one. If you are in possession of the *New Dunnich Manuscript* I should very much like to see it for myself. I have a small official capacity in the Literary and Philosophical Society and I can offer *The Letters of Reverend Dyer* in exchange."

"I am not interested in the letters of a lunatic."

"But I have collected all five, as well as the letter from Reverend Conybeare."

Mrs Potter reached her left hand behind the desk panel and rang a bell. "Good day, Mr Langham, Whateley will see you out."

I stared at her without moving.

She broke the silence. "There is a storm coming. I suggest you make haste."

The female Whateley arrived. I rose from the settee and followed her out.

VII

The thunder brought a translucent white haze with it rather than snow or rain and visibility was once again reduced. There was undoubtedly a tension in the air, but my aged joints made no protest. The wagonette was waiting for me, having been turned to face the exit, and the horse was nervous and skittish. I saw the male Whateley shambling off into the mist. As I mounted, the first flash of lightning illuminated the sky, several miles to the south. I unhooked the reins, cracked the whip, and set off. I had no desire to drive all the way back to Goathland in the storm. I was not particularly concerned about the lightning, but the snow would surely resume its descent shortly and even if it didn't, the haze was damp and would leave me soaked through long before I reached the hotel. Fletcher had given me the key to the vicarage, which I had been unable to use due to the male Whateley's interruption of my investigations. I would proceed there now, find an outbuilding to shelter the horse, and take refuge from the storm. While I was there, I could also keep an eye on the church, although I had no intention of disrupting any ceremonies that unfolded.

Once I was through the trees, I felt the wind and wrapped my scarf around my face again. There was another muffled explosion behind me – followed by a moment of brightness – as if the storm was descending on Billington Manor. I arrived at the junction: right through the hamlet to civilization, straight ahead to the vicarage. I flicked my whip, but the sound was drowned by a deafening discharge of lightning. The horse took fright, reared up, and a gust of wind dispersed the mist. Fifty yards ahead, I saw a line of two dozen-odd men, women, and children. They were swaying in perfect unison and uttering a low, rhythmic chant.

The half-light of the dark day disappeared in a brilliant flash of energy as a bolt struck the earth off to my left. In the moment of illumination, I saw that every villager was holding a weapon, mostly agricultural implements or household tools. The horse lurched forward. I dropped the whip, slammed on the brake, and grabbed the reins in both hands. There was no way I'd be able to turn the wagonette around with the animal in a frenzy. It reared up again, kicking the air in a gesture both futile and frantic.

Thunder boomed directly overhead, there was another brilliant flash, and an explosion flung me from my seat.

I was knocked over the backrest into the wagonette, the smell of burned flesh and melting metal filling my nostrils. When I lifted myself up, I saw the horse had been struck by lightning. Its flesh smouldered and sizzled as the metal bit melted into its jaw. The animal had died instantly. I retrieved my stick and jumped down from the wagon as quickly as I could, which – for a man in his fifties who has not enjoyed robust health – was not very fast at all. A lightning bolt burst in the air, this one above the vicarage. Without looking back at the villagers, I staggered off into the haze.

I reached the junction, turned left, and made haste. Thunder rolled, roared, and rumbled. In the heavens, Donar – Thor to the Vikings – beat hammer against anvil. The sky bellowed, the earth shook, fiery sparks flew, and I cowered beneath the clouds as I pushed on.

After a minute, I glanced back. I couldn't see anyone behind me. Two minutes later I was through the tiny cluster of houses and approaching the first bend in the path. The slope seemed steeper than on my arrival and the snow underfoot made the going more difficult. I was breathing heavily by the time I approached the last two houses in the hamlet. The thunder was continuous, but I had left the lightning behind. One more slope to ascend, one final turn to the right, then Pike Hill Moss would be in sight. I increased my pace, pushing hard on my stick.

I rounded the bend and met the rest of the villagers.

Another two dozen men, women, and children, carrying flails, rakes, crooks, sickles, billhooks, knives, hammers, and pans. They were less than twenty yards away through the haze, swaying and chanting.

"*Eh-ya-ya-ya-yahaah, e'yayayayaaa!*"

I halted.

"*Cthuga!*"

I turned around.

"*Ngh'aaaaa, ngh'aaa, ngh'aa!*"

I could see no one behind me, but I knew the others were coming.

"*Cthuga!*"

I turned back to the line and felt nauseous as I realised that every one of them shared the Whateleys' blood. Fathers and daughters, mothers and sons, brothers and sisters... generation after generation, generation into generation... the result stretched out before me.

"*H'yuh, h'yuh, h'yuh...*"

There was a flash of light from above the line of villagers.

"*...Cthuga!*"

A ball of flame with the circumference of a wagon wheel streaked through the sky towards me. I saw two hollow eyes and a gaping mouth in the fire, but it may just have been fancy. I let go of my Penang-lawyer, the fireball struck the stick and metal and wood exploded, throwing me into the air once again. I landed in the snow at the side of the path, breathless and stunned. A second later, I realised my right glove and sleeve were on fire and rolled on top of them, rubbing them into the icy powder. I lay prone, gasping for breath, the smell of smoke thick in my nostrils.

"*Eh-ya-ya-ya-yahaah, e'yayayayaaa!*"

Slowly, the crowd of villagers shambled forward. I did not have the strength to rise.

"*Cthuga!*"

Another flash of light from above them.

I closed my eyes and awaited the impact.

"*Ngh'aaaaa, ngh'aaa –* "

I heard shouts, the neighing of a horse, a gunshot.

Definitely a gunshot, definitely not thunder or lightning.

I opened my eyes and saw that the bright light wasn't another ball of lightning, but the sun breaking through the clouds. A horseman surged through the line, scattering villagers before him. He fired in the air a second time and even the most resolute cast their weapons away and fled. It was Fletcher, mounted on a black steed, reins between his teeth, a revolver in one hand and the Elder Sign in the other.

I scrambled to my feet.

As he closed on me, the sun was eclipsed, the heavens opened, and there was an almighty crack. A flickering fork of electricity struck him. I threw up my arms for protection, but there was no explosion. The blue fire simply disappeared into Fletcher's left hand. I saw a fistful of dust spray the air as he rode past. Fletcher fired over his head once more, tucked his revolver into his belt, and turned his horse. He broke into a trot, reached down to heave me up behind him, and kicked his heels into the horse's flanks. As we approached the moss, the thunder began to fade. By the time we had rattled over the bridge, it could barely be heard in the distance. When we reached the road to Goathland, snowflakes began to fall again.

VIII

I had taken possession of Fletcher's trunk on Thursday, when it had finally arrived from the Pacific. Had I known that it contained his New Army and Navy Colt revolver, I would have demanded that he relinquish the firearm and things might not have gone so well for us in Great Billington, Elder Sign or not. Fletcher could never explain why he had stolen a horse and followed me, only that he heard the thunder and had a premonition of death, which is hardly surprising given his brother's fate. As soon as we reached Goathland, I sent a telegram to the Commissioner of the Metropolitan Police, hoping the use of my former rank would produce a rapid response. That same evening, a squad of heavily-armed policemen arrived with a troop of Yorkshire Hussars and a tall, corpulent old gentleman from London. They set off into the night and rounded up all but eight of the villagers after a brief skirmish. A battalion of Green Howards arrived at dawn on Sunday and spent the next three days hunting the fugitives down. Seven were killed while resisting arrest. The charred remains of the eighth, believed to be Mrs Potter, were found near Russell's Wood. The official verdict was self-immolation, but other rumours persisted. By Christmas, Great Billington had been razed to the ground and erased from official maps. Little Billington and Billington remain, both in the county of Bedfordshire, but there is no more Great Billington. There is only a barren lowland the locals call Devil's Hollow.

Rafe McGregor is the author of The Value of Literature, The Architect of Murder, six collections of short fiction, and one hundred and fifty magazine articles, journal papers, and review essays. He lectures at the University of York and can be found online at @rafemcgregor.

New Year's Day: midsummer in Australia. In Perth, twin brothers Aaron and Matt have graduated high school and are enjoying their last few months of summer holidays before adulthood while on the other side of the country, something has fallen from the sky, heralding the dawn of a new age.

As a terrifying plague spreads across Australia and the world, Aaron and Matt find themselves scrambling to survive, fleeing the city, refugees in their own country. Tormented by strange dreams and beset by violence, they must struggle to find the remnants of their family and survive the Rise of the Undead.

Give You a Game?

Michael Wyndham Thomas

It was the scarf. They said the desk had been cleared but a bit of dirty-looking tartan still poked out under the lid. The desk had been moved to the side of the classroom but with its back to the wall, so you could still sneak a glance at the scarf. During the last day of term, he found it harder and harder not to.

"Away with the fairies again, Paul?" Mrs Watton's voice wasn't unkind, hadn't been at any time throughout the year. Without resentment, Paul turned back to his book. But he still saw the scarf like a pattern behind the words he read, and his heart was still on fire.

The kids scattered at the summons for tea. Once it was issued, front windows were slammed all along the street. Two brothers wrestled at their gate-post to see who'd be first to shoulder the back door off its hinges and forget to wash his hands. One boy, as usual, had to be called three times.

Only Paul was left, looking down at his shoes and the small ridges in the concrete road, wondering if the press of his feet had made the road go like that. From an open window somewhere came the song everyone was singing or sending up. Someone saw someone else's love yesterday and she told them what to say. Say-ee-yay. It seemed to Paul that the flock of *Yeah, yeah, yeahs* made the day very different, like strange birds on the roof-tiles. I could fly away with them, he thought.

A horn sounded and he turned to see Mr Phillips's Ford Anglia, light-green, nipped little angles. Smiling, Mr Phillips gestured that Paul might like to step aside. The car crept past and Mr Phillips gave him the kind of wave that Mrs Watton had given him earlier that day, at the end of the school year. He'd seen his mum doing something not dissimilar, when they were seeing off some relatives at the station. Vaguely he supposed that it was one of the many things he'd be doing sometime. Adult things. A special energy would flow into his hand when he reached an age he couldn't imagine, and before he knew it he'd be waving with assurance in clothes he'd chosen himself. But he couldn't see himself getting to that.

What next? He had no idea. There'd be tea, yes, but his mum wasn't long back. The kids had had to make way for her car just before play broke up; it'd be a bit longer before she called him. But after tea? He'd never felt like this before: simply moved without thought in the unslipping hula-hoop of friends, school, records, evening play, holiday exultation. Hadn't he just been shouting and tackling with the best of them? But in the middle of it he'd sort of gone elsewhere. He'd gone on charging about with the others but he sensed that, at any moment, their arms and legs would cut right through him as if he were just a bit of afternoon heat their efforts had troubled.

His mum was pretty brisk. Presently he'd hear his name, once: she wasn't really a street-shouter, preferring to add "It's stone-cold" in the kitchen if he was late. Still, best walk towards that single call. But he couldn't move – no, he could but was scared of what might happen. I put out one foot, he thought, then the other, then the first. But what then? Where do I go? He pictured the house-front to which his efforts should take him. Somehow he didn't trust that they would and for a second he wondered if the house existed. "My house," he murmured. It sounded as unlikely as the bit of French his uncle had tried to teach him. Je touche le tableau noir. I touch the blackboard. Bonkers. Why make strange noises when you said you were going to touch and the blackboard was what you'd be touching? But "My house" sounded strange, too. All that business of making air and twisting your mouth round it. If someone was in front of him right now and he said it, would they understand?

All the others. He envied how they'd made their bee-lines when tea was called. Natural sprints and swerves, no need for thought. He'd done the same before today. But now he was thoughtful, though not in the way people meant it (stupid words again, twisting about when they should make steady sense). Thoughts were all over his mind like butterflies trapped in a room. Inviting him – daring him? – to cup them in his hands, even one, and get a good look. Some of them trailed something, vapour, a shadow, like the start of a clue, a way in. Like a scarf hanging from a desk-lid.

"All right, Paul?" Mr Phillips, now out in his front garden, waved. "Thought you'd test my brakes back there?"

Paul waved back. The butterflies surged as a single arrow. He gave his feet a go, one foot, other foot... it worked but he wouldn't have done it if he hadn't had an audience, a grown-up at that, with a grown-up's assumption that kids liked stillness about as much as bathtime. One thought came clear through the butterflies and probably kept his feet going. After tea – yes, the game again. They'd all be back, he could run right into it in a single move, his bee-line, table to street. The old jumping and diving, new ideas played out along railing and privet, by walls so high they pushed the sky away. That got him to the curve of the road, within sight of his home. But he stalled again. Je touche le tableau noir. The picture he'd conjured now seemed as mystifying as that. The butterflies were a snow-storm.

Just one more thing he had to try, though it felt worse than moving his feet. "All right, Paul?" Mr Phillips had said. How strange his name had sounded, sudden on the air. Like nothing he'd heard before. So now, how about...? Drawing a deep breath, he whispered it to himself, briskly, then stretching it like the gum Mrs Watton was always confiscating from John Muldoon. It didn't sound any friendlier.

A familiar trickling began in the pit of his stomach, ice water, such as he felt at the moment when a difficult sum started to get away from him in class. *If it takes three men five hours to dig a trench two yards wide by... I buy A for one-and-thruppence, B for sevenpence-ha'penny, C for six...* Now he envied the trench-diggers, the talkative shopper. How safe to live in a world where you only have to stick spades in the ground or walk – no, run – about the shops with money spilling from your fingers. He'd go and live with them, dig away and pause only to stock up on chocolate.

"Paul!" His mum. The butterflies parted long enough to him to bend all this strangeness his own way. He was a pilgrim in fog, he imagined, a space buccaneer just landed on a planet whose shapes and colours he didn't recognise. That got him past the curve to the start of the rise.

The nudges came first and then the sniggers. Much elbowing, pointing. You just knew the dirty tartan scarf was on its way, along the railings that joined the school playground to Whitmore Park. You just knew the dirtier coat was trailing after, and the ciggy and, more than once, the slippers. Or the donkey-jacket, the plimsolls, the greasy muffler, a ciggy again. Other parents came streaming down Wellington Road or Fraser Street with their children, past the tidy houses with the burnished front steps and razored privet. The scarf, the dirty coat, the donkey jacket issued from the darkness beyond the park, where starlings thronged the black roof of Newbold Brakes and machines belched behind the gates of Wilkinson Packings.

Halfway along Fraser Street, Susan Reilly timed it to perfection, bouncing out of her house, joining the throng but somehow looking as though she were walking in lone elegance. Her mother, head cleaner, was already in the school, loudly supervising a last bit of spit and polish before assembly.

"My mum said she wouldn't use that scarf to wipe our toilet." More sniggers as countless eyes skewered the tartan. The bright sparks got their usual cries ready, timing them as Susan Reilly timed her launch upon the world.

Parents presented their children at the gates like little gifts whose shiny footwear would shortly renew tarmac and parquet. Only sometimes was the moment robbed of its lustre by the revving of the cars from which a small group of white-collar heirs emerged. Even Susan Reilly at her stateliest was pushed to match that.

"Hey, Sean!" And the moment had come. At a certain point towards the Fraser Street end of the railings, the dirty coat or donkey jacket turned and retreated, leaving the scarf to slope along on its own.

"Seany! Want me to show you what water looks like?"

"Cooked more sausages for us, Seany?" – this a

reference to the scarf-wearer spending a whole lunchtime in the toilet and forgetting to flush.

"How are your pets, Sean Riordan?" yelled Christobel Foulkes, a match for any boy in scrapes and malice. "Look, I can see them jumping off his head."

Laughter and at least one face turning to check if a certain car had been and gone – and, if it had, "You need to get your mum in here, Paul, with her bag of tricks."

Now Christobel bent double in a mime of furious scratching: "One of them's on me already... hey, get off", as a bright spark's hand joined in but went unsmacked.

"Get yer mum, Paul, or we'll itch to death."

"We'll get measles again."

"We'll get that spinal biff."

Paul a little apart, putting on a smile as his serious eyes watched Sean Riordan come through the gates, repelling the last parents like a force-field.

"I could live in there."

Paul's hand traced the bark of the tree by the front wall of Mrs. Middleton's bungalow. It was a strange tree, having no kin among the birches or laburnums elsewhere in the road. Its leaves were bluey-lilac, sort of, small and close, like weird snow that had stopped in mid-fall.

"Jacaranda, that," said his uncle, who'd knocked about a bit. "Possibly. Or something damn like. Shelter, they need, a spot on the sunny south coast. How it's surviving up here..." A slow shake of the head, such as his uncle delighted in. "Magic."

Jacaranda... the kind of name a space buccaneer would give a new planet. He could fold up his ship, stow it in the trunk, shin up the branches and make camp, send signals back to Earth behind the leaves, nice and safe, unspottable. By the time he'd given HQ his readings so the fleet could follow, it would be night and he could slip out, snoop around, send more information. At first light, he'd sort his ship out and return to his forward base, Planet Banyan, a tree whose roots dropped down, said his uncle, like pillars in a church. Prop roots, apparently. He might tell HQ that Jacaranda would be his forward base from now on, that he'd meet the fleet there. Of course he'd have to make dead sure of the Jacaranda terrain so there'd be no nasty—

"Stare at it all you want. It's when the footballs fly into it that I get livid."

Paul jerked back.

"Hey, don't fall in the road." Mrs Middleton was smiling. "I heard your mum, lad, better cut along." Waving, she disappeared behind her frost-glass porch.

Paul got out of sight of the bungalow, just, but his feet stalled again.

"All right Da-vid, we saw you qui-ver, kis-sing Margie Fa-llon – down by the ri-ver."

Squeals.

"How many kisses did you give her altogether... one... two... three... four..."

The rope arcing, two feet hopping in, up-down, four feet, up-down, six feet, a caught ankle, the rope dropped, more squeals. Half a playground away, David Monkton, face burning, cuffing off friends: "Her fancies you, that Margie."

"What time is it Mr Wolf?" John Muldoon hunched against the wall, back to his prey, growling. Christobel Foulkes daintying up in front of the rest, quick glance back, prepared lisp, "What time is it Mr Wolf?", a giggle mid-question. John swinging about, arms stretched, prey scattering, Christobel languidly petrified, John grabbing her, "Harr-arrrrrrrr!"

Spitfires and Stukas, British pilots with American twangs, enemies who can manage nothing more than "Aaaaieeeee."

At lunchtime on the last Tuesday of term, Paul was just stepping out of his plane after bombing Foe-land to smithereens. Damn and blast, he'd nearly overshot the runway, which was why he was by the playground wall, far from the rest of the squadron. Clambering gingerly from cock-pit to wing to ground, he found Sean Riordan in front of him.

"Ok, Pauly?" Even the act of speaking seemed to stir the smells in his clothes.

Everyone knew the drill. If you were ambushed by the tartan scarf at playtime, you'd make God's own noise to get the herd's attention and then absorb yourself into its safety. All the cat-calling was reserved for the morning arrival, when Sean was put in his same old place for the day. There was no need to waste further words. Once or twice, maybe, someone would cry "Gyppo!" from the herd's bowels, or John Muldoon would yell something about his big brother and Sean's mum.

But Paul said "Hey Sean" now. Sean's eyes widened and immediately he rooted in a pocket.

"Got these." Two round objects lay in his palm, woody-looking, serrated like duffel buttons. "My dad got them. Conkers."

"Conkers? In summer?"

"Magic conkers. Give you a game?" Sean draped two lengths of string over the conkers, ready-knotted.

"I'm in there twice a day," said Paul's mother in his head, overheard talking to dad one time when Paul was just off for a street-game. "Insulin. Poor old lady. The filth of that room. Romancing all the time. Princess Margaret coming to call if you believe her.

Says she has a nephew in Paul's class. My-eye. Shouldn't think any Riordan's been inside a school."

Paul had of course never let on about this, but you don't always need words to say stuff. Sean had threaded the first conker.

And all across the playground, something started: a hum with hisses mixed in, the sound of townsfolk when, after biding his time, the mysterious stranger starts the brainwashing. The threaded conker in his hand, Paul turned to see walls of dead blank faces, bodies serving the hiss-hum – louder, louder.

"Get away from him, Paul" – John Muldoon, terror-struck scientist.

"His mom'll have yer" – Christobel Foulkes, never one to miss a chance to be ten years older – "Prozzer!"

And now John Muldoon was inching forward, reaching a hand as though Paul had turned to stone and the ground was breaking up beneath him.

"For pity's sake, man," he cried, Quatermass-brisk.

The hiss-hum stopped. A knot of bodies parted. John Muldoon was left leaning forward, arm out, a snake-belted, pocket Eros.

"What have you all been told? What have you all been told and told?" In the silence, Mrs Watton walked up behind John Muldoon, reached round and lowered his arm. Sean Riordan kept close to the wall as he ran away. Paul watched him go, expecting him to melt through it, aware of the magic conker still in his hand.

An outstretched arm, a hand flapping. Up the rise, Paul saw the diminutive figure: his younger sister, dispatched in lieu of another reluctant yell from his mum, dumb-showing him to get his skates on. Skates would have been the thing right now – rocket-powered, of course. But he'd left them on Planet

Jacaranda. His sister vanished and he got himself up to a couple of yards an hour, for a couple of yards.

"And the gentleman was very angry."

On the last Wednesday morning of term, the Headmistress paced up and down the assembly hall.

"Think about your own houses. Can you see your own houses?"

Nods here and there, a scatter of "Yes, Miss."

"What do you do in your own houses?"

Something from the middle of the crowd, foolishly clear.

"All right, John Muldoon, see me after. Now what do you do?"

Eat, Miss. Play, watch tv. Sleep, Miss.

"And you're all safe, yes? You're all safe in your houses."

Yesses, mostly.

"And if you fell out of the windows, would you be safe then?"

A Woodbine-sounding chuckle.

"Bernard Page, with John Muldoon after. Well, would you be safe?"

"No, Miss."

"No, Christobel, you would not be safe. Just like you won't be safe if you go through that gap. I've had" – her fingers got counting – "two telephone calls and then the gentleman came to see me. From" – chilly and slow – "the Council. Now it's not just this school. But they have seen children getting over the boards and through that gap. We have told you. Told you and told you. If your parents are not – not! – meeting you at four o'clock, you stay in your groups and you keep to the roads."

Stepping back, she looked everyone over, row by row.

"Can you all swim?"

Silence.

"Can you? Who cannot swim yet?"

Hands up, about half the hall.

"Exactly. And even if you can, you-stay-in-your-groups-and-you-keep-to-the-roads."

Paul dragged on, and now the street was frosty and cold. It was last January again and they were getting into dad's car for Manchester. A second cousin or great aunt or some outlier had... well, mum was telling dad that the black was showing up all his dust but then she pulled off her hat and plonked it on her lap, muttered about flipping veils.

For the afternoon, Paul and his two sisters were parked with someone while the adults vanished. There were colouring books and comics, cakes and chat about favourite tv programmes. Paul had brought his own stuff and sat apart, studiously creating a moon colony, thin spiky buildings and monorails overhead. He hadn't a clue what the adults were up to. It sounded like there'd be a lot of them wherever it was, murmuring in that not-for-children subtone they could turn on and off, all in black (barring that ridge of dust on his dad's shoulders). The cousin or great aunt would be there too but not quite in the same way. Moving among them? Not likely. What had happened to her slowed you down, he surmised. But moving nonetheless, perhaps, as if on the other side of a window to the rest. On view (his parents had used that phrase) but separate – as you'd be separate from the road, say, if you pushed down those boards and squeezed through.

He blinked. His gate swam up five houses away, and that funny trellis entrance his dad was always about to sort out. Like a lych-gate, his uncle said. They'd said

those words on the way home, mum and dad. And
sombre, at which his older sister had cried "Sombrero!"
and been shushed. "Abide with me," his mom had
sighed. He knew what that meant and for a moment
had wondered if this cousin or whoever was with
them, in the boot.

On Wednesday night, it had turned shivery cold and
rained hard. Thursday morning was all fog – crazy for
July, but then all the factories and engine yards around
didn't need much encouragement to smother
everything. Paul's mum had an early call-out – filthy
old Granny Riordan maybe – and had offered to drop
him and his sisters off at a friend's near the school.
Yes, cried the girls, but Paul had seen the adventure in
the situation and said he'd catch up with David
Monkton and the other knot of boys from round King
Street.

Which he didn't try to. This was weird and
wonderful, Jacaranda weather, and who knew what he
might encounter squawking or tendrilling out of the
mists – aside from blokes in peaked caps and mufflers,
with snap-tins and Bernard Page's Woodbine cough.

At the top of Loxdale Street, he just made out David
Monkton's lanky frame up ahead. Oh, well... he
accelerated, only to see that David and another boy
were trying to drag each other down a pathway
between two houses—

"This is your final hour, Dan Dare!"

"Noooo! Noooo!"

—till a woman appeared from one house and told
them to scarper, that there'd been enough trouble.
Paul stopped dead. Now here was adventure, better
than mucking about with David Monkton, who was
rubbish at remembering Dan Dare stories. He waited
while the fog swallowed up the boys' hoots and

footsteps and the woman went inside. Assassin-like, he kept close to the fences till the pathway opened up on his left. The fog had sliced the top off the town's noise. Up the path he tiptoed, eased aside the flimsy boards and squeezed through.

It was colder, foggier than on the pathway and the street. Before his eyes things hardly moved at all. Newspaper, was that? A piece of tarpaulin from one of the barges? He stood transfixed by this seeing and not seeing, his mind folding into itself. The fog was unhappy because it had been called down in midsummer. Or the water was, because it couldn't drag along. Hence the sobbing. Rubbing his eyes, Paul stared through the chalky air. The sobbing was somewhere to his right and, as he moved, the fog seemed to pull itself aside as if it, too, couldn't bear the smell. The figure, small, looking down, far from the starlings of Newbold Brakes, the roar of Wilkinson Packings. No scarf, Paul saw: perhaps it was stuffed into his pockets with his gloves and balaclava, a whole new bunch of conkers, the kitchen sink. How else to explain how they looked?

Ok, Pauly? The small shoulders heaved. Magic. The arms wrapped tight as if pleading for heat from this unforgiving day. Give you a game? John Muldoon would not forgive, or Christobel Foulkes. The new school year would not forgive, nor the mind-bending stretches of time ever after.

"Sometimes ya gotta do bad to do good." The voice of Gabe Tomorrow the Horizon King rang through Paul's head as it had a few nights ago in the living-room. His mother had paused in her hunt for thread and wrinkled her nose: "Ya gotta. Can't they speak properly? And what sort of talk is that? Do bad to do good. If I tried it, Health Office'd have me out on my ear."

Paul didn't know what Gabe meant and his words

got no clearer as he moved forward, reached out a hand. The fog tightened again. Sounds warped out of true. "Must've been someone's clunky old flush somewhere," the woman in the house might have said after, if she'd heard. "The council keep promising to come round to fix them but... phuh, talk to yourself."

Lych-gate. Paul stroked the trellis's twining leaves, willing the feel of Mrs. Middleton's magic tree back into his fingers. At the back of the classroom, the desk up against the wall. Under the lid, the scarf. Sometimes ya gotta. Good out of bad. By doing? Letting? Which, Gabe? Did I copy you right? But the credits had rolled and mum had said, "Right you lot, pyjama time."

And now his mother stood at the other end of the trellis tunnel and his sisters' heads poked out from behind her. She spoke, he read her lips. What time do you call this? Well? She shifted her weight. Maybe a change of tone. Paul. Paul?

Between him and her a window. So thick, so close that, as he opened his mouth, the pane fogged.

Michael Wyndham Thomas's novels include The Mercury Annual and Pilgrims at the White Horizon, and his poetry collections include Port Winston Mulberry, Batman's Hill, South Staffs, Come to Pass and The Stations of the Day. His work has appeared in The Antioch Review, Critical Survey, The London Magazine, Magazine Six, Stand Magazine and the TLS. His novella "Esp" was shortlisted for the UK Novella Award. He is currently working on Nowherian, the fictionalised memoir of a Grenadian traveller. Twitter: @thomasmichaelw. Blog: swansreport.blogspot.co.uk. Website: www.michaelwthomas.co.uk.

The Baby Downstairs

Jessy Randall

The baby downstairs in 6G would not freaking shut up. Desperation had set in in 7G. Mark and Sally, newly married, were each privately considering dastardly acts. It had been almost two months since they'd rented their apartment, but nothing had gone as planned. This time together was supposed to be a continuation of the honeymoon – round-the-clock sex, candlelit dinners, surprise presents for each other. Instead, they'd spent eight weeks in mutual hatred of the baby downstairs. Now Christmas was almost here, and they each had secret hopes and plans for their ordeal to come to an end.

"Made a lotta love on that couch," intoned Mark as he pushed the old sofa into place. He was speaking in the voice of a pharmacy school friend famous for announcing, with just that phrase, the extent of his conquests. Sally gave Mark a wry look, since they had, in fact, made a lot of love on that couch, and would, in the future, make a lot more, probably. They were covered in paint by this point, and tired and sweaty, even though it was a chilly fall day outside.

They had almost broken the piano moving into their new apartment, but soon everything was arranged. Cleaning and painting and unpacking took the whole weekend. They were combining two places' worth of furniture and books – Sally, a college librarian, owned six bookshelves and the books to fill them; she lugged box after box from the elevator to their door. Plus, there were all the wedding gifts.

A notice in the elevator of the building beginning "Howdy Neighbors!" reminded all tenants not to use the garbage chute between the hours of 11 p.m. and 8 a.m. and welcomed the new tenants in 7G. "That's so nice – they would never do that in my old building," said Sally. She repeated this sentiment when they walked into the empty apartment and found a fruit basket from the building owners and an invitation to the weekly wine and cheese event in the lobby.

By Sunday afternoon, they were finished unpacking; they lolled around on the hardwood floors of their new home, reading the paper. Both Mark and Sally had been living in dinky studios; now they had two bedrooms and other rooms besides, even their own washer and dryer!

As the light in the apartment began fading, Mark got up to take a shower. Through the sound of rushing water Sally could hear him singing his usual song: "I've got a mule, her name is Sal / fifteen miles on the Erie Canal / she's a good old worker and a good old pal / fifteen miles on the Erie Canal." She pounded on the open bathroom door and began stripping off her clothes. "You quit singing that insulting song right now or you're going to get it!" As soon as she was naked she jumped into the shower and swatted Mark on the rear.

"Hey, it's not insulting – the song says you're a good old pal," said Mark. "Isn't this water pressure the greatest?"

"So far, being married to you is working out fairly well," she said, scrubbing his back with their recently-unpacked shower scrubby. They dried off on their new wedding towels, fluffy and lush. Sally got down the plastic container of birth control pills from the medicine cabinet and took today's pill with only a small hesitation. (Mark got free pills for her every month – a not-quite-legal perk of working as a pharmacist.) They were in no hurry to start a family. There was plenty of time. She should at least finish out this container.

They went to bed on Sunday night in their own bed in their own bedroom. They were full of hope and confidence.

At 3.30 a.m., the baby in 6G started crying. Sally and Mark woke up simultaneously and stared at each other. It wasn't really crying, it was more like screaming. Or not screaming: yelling, on purpose. The baby was yelling its head off, *waaaaaaaaaaaah,* as if the entire world was collapsing. The baby's cry grated like a teenager's whine. It was awful. It was so loud it was as if the baby was right in the room with them. Right in the bed with them! Their alarms were set for 7.30. They rolled their eyes at each other, snuggled back into the covers, and tried to ignore the crying, but they couldn't get back to sleep.

The next morning was the same. And the next, and the next. Sometime before four the baby began its infernal racket. Sally kissed Mark on the mouth and said, sleepily, "It's called colic." She'd looked it up.

"What's colic?"

"Something babies get. It makes them cry. Nobody really knows what it is. It's a mystery, like crib death, Sudden Infant Death Syndrome."

"Can colic kill a baby?"

Sally laughed. "I wish! No, they just outgrow it eventually."

"Eventually? How long is eventually? A week? I can't stand this for another week. I drank five cups of coffee yesterday and I still felt like crap all day. Maybe we should cross our fingers for crib death."

They laughed. "Well, I suppose we could put a note on their door or something," said Sally.

"And say what? 'Tenants of 6G: Make your baby stop crying in the middle of the night'?"

"Maybe they don't realise how thin the floor is. Maybe we could convince them to put wall-to-wall carpet all over their ceiling, to sound-proof it."

"I'll sound-proof *you*," said Mark, closing one hand playfully over Sally's mouth as he wiggled his other hand under her nightgown. "Make me wake up in the dark, will it? I'll show that baby," he said.

By the tenth morning, though, it really wasn't funny anymore. The baby seemed to have the lung capacity of a long-distance runner. It never ran out of breath. It yelled from before four in the morning until almost six. Most mornings, the parents just let it cry. Sometimes the mother or the father came in and murmured soothing words, which Mark and Sally could not quite make out; the soothing words did not charm them or the baby.

On the weekend, they learned the baby's name. The wailing started at around 3.00 a.m., and stopped abruptly, replaced by the mother's voice: "*Wheeeeeeee! Wheeeeeeee!* Millicent's going *wheeeeeeeee!*"

"Millicent, huh," said Mark, who was beginning to think he didn't want children, ever.

Sally was thinking the same thing. She'd never been all that into the idea of motherhood, anyway. "I guess the mother is throwing the baby up in the air and catching her, to make her stop crying," she said.

"We could pound on the floor. Or run the vacuum. Or we could go down there, and ask them to be quiet, or leave a note in their mailbox."

"They might just get mad at us, though. They might think we were being rude," said Sally, who lived in constant fear of being accused of rudeness. "I don't feel like getting up, anyway," she continued, grumpily. "I feel like being asleep."

As soon as the mother stopped saying *whee*, Millicent started crying again. Mark thumped his foot on the floor, rhythmically. This did no good at all, so he got up and started playing Iggy Pop's "Lust for Life" at full volume to drown out the sound of the screaming.

A few minutes later, the tenants in 8G above them began pounding on their floor, which was Mark and Sally's ceiling.

When Sally got home from work on Tuesday, Mark was in the shower singing his mule song. She walked straight into the bathroom without knocking and said, "Please don't sing that song anymore. You know I find it irritating." She stalked out again.

Mark stopped singing for a moment, and then started again, louder. "I've got a mule, her name is Sally / fifteen miles on the Erie Canally / she's a good ol' worker and a good ol pally..."

"You think I'm kidding around?" said his wife, from the other room. "I am *not kidding*." She was getting a little weepy. "I have had a hard day, you know."

"Well maybe I had a hard day too, did you ever think of that? You know Tuesday is the day all the pharmacy shipments come in. I've been typing labels all damn day."

"Just stop singing that song."

"You can't tell me what to do," said Mark. He turned off the water and continued humming the tune. Sally went into the bedroom and slammed the door.

"What the hell is wrong with you?" Mark yelled from the bathroom.

Sally opened the door an inch and peeked out, saying "I'm sorry, I didn't mean to slam it," in a calm voice. She then closed the door quietly but firmly, and locked it. Mark could sleep on the couch.

"Waaaaaaaaaaaaah! Waaaaaaaaaaaaah!"

　　"Wheeeeeeeeeeeeeee! Wheeeeeeeeeeeeee!"

After several weeks of being woken before four a.m. every morning by the baby downstairs, Mark and Sally were seriously considering moving out. Their future appeared bleak before them. To pack everything back up seemed an impossible task. They had gleefully thrown away the styrofoam pieces and special boxes that protected their new computer and television and food processor; all their packing materials were in the landfill. Besides, they couldn't afford another move. They had put down the first and last month's rents on this place, invested time and affection. To leave would be giving up on their marriage, on *them*.

"I checked some sources on baby health at the library," said Sally from under the covers. "They all say that the crying stage doesn't last forever."

"Well, I don't have extra time at *my* job to be goofing off trying to fix my personal problems. Hey, maybe we could put a hex on little Millicent. Can you look that up? Do you have any sources on witchcraft?"

"Very funny," said Sally. "Ha ha ha." Although, actually, it occurred to her, the rare book department owned three or four ancient books of spells, and her set of keys included one to the locked case. She turned away from Mark in the bed, thinking. No one had requested any of those books in all the years she'd worked there. Maybe they weren't even catalogued. And the building-wide "Secular Secret Santa" exchange was about to start, a perfect time for anonymous gift-giving.

She and Mark were no longer a team. Instead they were competing for the position of most-bothered-by-the-baby-downstairs. Sally claimed her nerves were frazzled and she couldn't concentrate during the day; Mark said he was beginning to hate the entire human race. They tried going to bed earlier. They tried wearing earplugs to sleep. They tried getting up with the baby and playing "Ace of Spades" or dance music at top volume. Some nights they banged out duets on the piano until the upstairs neighbours complained. The bawling of the baby downstairs cut through all their efforts.

Husband and wife made errors at work: Sally at the reference desk, Mark at the pharmacy. Sally spoke sharply to a young man who didn't know how to do a simple keyword search. Mark accidentally switched two prescriptions, catching his mistake just before a woman walked out the door with the wrong medicine. Mark and Sally used the baby downstairs as an excuse for their mistakes, but worse, they used the baby as an excuse for being mean to each other.

When Mark got home from work, he didn't say hello, just sat on the couch and turned on the TV. He had bags under his eyes. He had been very secretive lately, and strange; staying late at work and muttering to himself. He told Sally he was experimenting with something, but didn't give any details. He'd hidden a small plastic vial behind the spice rack in the kitchen.

Sally was in no better shape. "I have to read something for work," she said, "do you mind turning the volume down on the TV? You know the people in 8G are probably about to call the cops on us as it is."

Mark sighed and turned the volume down one

notch, but as soon as Sally looked away he turned it up again three notches. The baby downstairs wailed – lately it cried all the time, not just in the middle of the night.

"Are you going to do those dishes?" asked Mark. The colander was soaking in dirty tomato-sauce water, and used dishes were spilling out of the sink onto the counter.

"Are *you* going to do them?" asked Sally, not looking up from the old, leather-bound book in her hands. She and Mark deserved better than this. She knew they could be happy if they could just get this one problem fixed.

She could not seem to get rid of the herbal smell on her fingertips. She hoped it would not be long now before she got the recipe just right.

"I have an idea," said Mark, a glint in his eye. "Let's give 6G a Secular Secret Santa, even though they're not the people we were assigned."

"That's just what I was thinking," said Sally. "Something edible, you think? Something a baby might enjoy?"

"That was exactly my plan!" said Mark. "Great minds think alike!" He had bought a dozen apples at the grocery and was already mashing them at the kitchen counter.

"Those apples smell funny," said Sally. "Like medicine."

"They're just apples," said Mark. He washed his hands and went to the other room for wrapping paper. He was gone for about five minutes. When he came back, Sally was standing exactly where she had been, though a bit out of breath. "You're right," he said, "Now that I think of it, they do smell funny. Like tea, or some kind of potpourri. Did you put something in the bowl?"

"I don't notice any potpourri smell," said Sally. "Let's wrap up the jar and leave the package outside their door, with a nice note. Right away, before the potency fades. The potency of the flavour, I mean."

"I'll deliver it right now," said Mark. "I'll put it in front of their door, and they'll assume it's their Secret Santa present." He'd seen enough romantic comedies to know that a man had to fight for his marriage, for his happiness. Sally was worth it, worth the risk.

The next evening, Sally and Mark arrived home at the same time and got in the elevator together. Sally pressed the button for the 7th floor. On the wall of the elevator was a new notice: "We are sorry to announce that the family in apartment 6G has experienced a terrible loss. Millicent Phillips, age sixteen months, has passed away. The exact cause of death has not been determined. A memorial service will be held in her honour..."

Sally took Mark's hand. They smiled quietly to themselves, not looking at each other. When the elevator stopped at their floor, they practically skipped down the hall to their apartment. They each had a secret now, a secret they could never, ever tell each other. A secret that would bind them together for the rest of their lives, though they wouldn't know it, and would never have a chance to discuss it. It could have been Sally's potion or Mark's tranquilizer that killed poor Millicent, or a combination of the two. It didn't really matter, in the end.

As if to reward them, a gift sat on their doorstep, a big white bakery box. "Our Secret Santa!" said Sally. "*Secular* Secret Santa," said Mark. Inside the box sat a luscious-looking chocolate cake with two plastic forks.

Mark and Sally took several bites before noticing how weird the cake smelled. By then it was too late, and the poison from the tenants in 8G had already taken hold.

Jessy Randall's science fiction stories and poems have appeared in Asimov's, Lady Churchill's Rosebud Wristlet, Strange Horizons, and Theaker's ("The Night of Red Butterflies", December 2013). Her most recent book is Suicide Hotline Hold Music, a collection of poems and comics. She is a librarian at Colorado College and her website is http://bit.ly/JessyRandall.

The Constant Providers

Charles Wilkinson

A year ago their vans appeared in our lanes: overcast late October after an Indian summer. I'd no worries then about my daughter or what the winter would bring.

It was Dai Roberts who noticed them first, and asked me if I seen them down by the entrance to Wegg Farm and outside the gates of the church. I hadn't, but a day later there were two parked up on the lay-by and a third half way up the track leading to the woods. The vans were milky blue, as if they came by special appointment to dismantle the bright weather, clear away the last of the fine days: all our shining hours, the gold on the leaf, the sharpest shadows.

About that time, farmers started to complain of long narrow trenches dug in the fields. There was even one in the churchyard. Owen Parry said it was something to do with the electric, definitely. But no one could point to a single cable that had been laid or even to men in yellow jackets with spades. The sides of the vans were plain blue, no name or even a company logo. Sam Evans, who worked at the garage, said he couldn't even be certain what make of vehicle they might be.

My wife walked out over Christmas. Now it's just Bethan and me. I work from home with my dictionaries, translating the grief of foreigners. We live in the small red brick cottage you pass on your way to the incinerator. When my daughter was young, I'd say I coped well enough as a father. But a week after the vans arrived, during the winter of the money spiders, I felt disquiet stirring beneath the flat surface of our uneventful lives.

One evening Bethan was late home from school. The days were shortening. As she walked up the path, I was leaning on the gate. The sun sank behind the mountains, lending the light a tint of Welsh red gold. Conifers darkened, fletching the foothills with black arrows. A cold wind from the west trembled in the laurel bush.

"What you doing out here out here, Da?"

"Waiting for you, girl. Teacher kept you in, did she?"

"No, nothing like that."

She'd just turned sixteen: whey-faced, her eyes green, hair blonde all that summer but a shade darker in the hard months.

"So where were you?" I asked, opening the gate.

"Just walking. Not a crime yet, is it?"

Her slight build added vulnerability. Though the worst weather was to yet come, she was shivering as she walked beside me on the path, her arms crossed, holding her coat tightly. Perhaps she'd been with some boy. I couldn't believe it was serious, not yet.

Over supper, she said, with no reference whatever to anything else: "They're filling them in."

"What you mean by that?"

"Those ditches, channels... they've been filling them in. With earth. They look like the graves of thin people. That's what Bryn says."

I had his name now, without even asking. No need to press her. To my knowledge, there were two Bryns in her year. I'd find out which one had taken a fancy to her later. Looking back, I couldn't have imagined how irrelevant that was to prove.

The next day I went out before breakfast. The sun had yet to sear through the morning mist. In the churchyard, the yew tree's darker smudge lowered over grave stones dissolving in the high grey-green grass. The visibility was just good enough for me to see that the trench nearest to the gate had been repaired, smoothed over with slick red clay. For a moment, I had a vision of men working at night, aided by occult electrical equipment, adjusting the dead to some strange new dispensation: bones rewired, the dreams of ghosts collected from the skulls and preserved in the cloud, to be accessed if the old tales were needed.

When I returned from my walk, Bethan was sitting struck mute at the kitchen table. I didn't understand this at once. A bowl of cereal was in front of her; the radio was on: a sober voice describing the weather, the front moving from the west with a black burden of rain, the best of the brightness to be weak sunlight an hour before dark. It was not until I'd put the kettle on to boil that I turned back to her. She was staring straight ahead at the far end of the table.

"Bethan?" I said.

No reply. Her mouth was very slightly open. There was no light of expression in her unblinking gaze; only the barely perceptible movement of her chest was proof she still breathed.

"Bethan? What's the matter?" I shook her shoulder, gently at first and then with greater vigour. She rocked back and forth – less pliable than a manikin. I took her wrist in my hands. Her skin was not quite cold. A faint pulse.

Then I noticed a blue object at the other end of the table. Its smooth curves gave it the look of having been worked by man. But was it metal, mineral or a new substance conjured up in a laboratory? At moments it had a matt finish; but when picked up, it shone until its lustre seemed more than surface deep. Taller than it was wide and of no obvious utility, I was tempted to find some human or animal symbolism in it, yet its shape defied easy categorization. A protuberance that resembled a head was clearly nothing of the sort when viewed from a different angle. I could only assume it was an abstract sculpture, an artwork from a school I had yet to come across. I picked it up, using both hands, which proved unnecessary as it was less heavy than I had imagined. When I glanced back at Bethan, I saw the angle of her head had shifted, so that her eyes were fixed on the blue object.

"What is this, Bethan? It's not something I bought." I hid the object behind my back, half-expecting her head to drop forward, but she remained in the same position. I transferred it from one hand to another. It felt too light to be made from a material found in nature; even coral would have been heavier. I put it back on the table. After I phoned the school and the surgery, I carried her up to her room. The ancient stuffed bears on the shelves, the dolls with glassy black eyes – all were less disconcerting than what was on the kitchen table. As I laid her on the bed, her eyelids closed.

When I went back downstairs, I examined the blue object again. There was something about it I disliked, without being able to express why. It was neither beautiful nor ugly; only the glow it emitted when held hinted at its attraction. Although I was convinced it must be man-made, at least in part, I could not imagine the mind that created it. Was I upset because I believed the object to be meaningless? Or did I suspect it had a meaning – or perhaps a use, one which I lacked the capacity to grasp? But wherever it belonged, it had no business being on the kitchen table. I removed it to a window sill in the living-room.

An hour later, the doctor arrived. A squat little man with wiry hair and black framed glasses too large for his thin face, he seemed angry at having to make a home visit.

"I'm sorry," I said, over my shoulders, as we walked upstairs. "I didn't want to move her far. Not while she's unconscious."

I opened the door of the room, half expecting to see the sheets turned back, my daughter vanished. Perhaps the dolls on the shelf had changed places with the bears, such had been the day's strangeness, its disorder. But everything was as I had left it. Even the position of Bethan's head on the pillow was unaltered.

"Umm," said the doctor, having examined her at some length. "Catatonia, that's all I can say. But why should she be in this condition? Has anything like this ever happened to her before?"

"No, nothing remotely like it."

"Well, she isn't in any immediate danger, as far as I can tell, but if she stays like this she'll have to go in. If there's any change in her condition, you're to get on to the surgery at once."

I decided to go to the front door by way of the living room. "You don't think that all of this could be anything to do with that blue... over there?" I said, gesturing towards the object on the window sill.

The doctor took a few steps towards it before swinging back to me with a snort. "Good lord no! What makes you think that?"

"It's just that I've no idea what it is."

"Surely it's just some sort of arty rubbish. A what do you call it? A mobile. Part of some installation, perhaps. Not my bag at all, but the wife seems to understand it. Makes it out of tin foil and other gunk and then sticks it in the garden."

"That's reassuring. Of course, that's what it is."

"Why, what on earth were you imagining?" he said. "Voodoo? Here, in Wales?"

Once he had left, I went outside and stood on the front porch. I could see half way down the drive. The distant mountains and foothills had been erased by the morning mist. A grey squirrel sat cloudy and motionless on the lawn. I watched the slow descent of a tiny spider, its silk line invisible, so when it stopped for a moment, it seemed to be suspended there without support. There are connections we cannot see. As I stepped back inside the house, I thought of the complex of buildings made out of steel, glass and cables on a ridge above the village.

To us, he was Hirsmann: an American who'd bought a byre on a hill in Wales and knocked it down. We didn't know he owned a TV station, flew a private jet and was soon to install a helipad where old Eli Morgan had once milked cows. Of course, we were aware of the name of his company – New Empyrean; there was a sign half way up the steep road. But not one person in the parish, not even Roger Ward-Griffiths, who held a degree in Political Geography, had heard mention of New Empyrean's worldwide empire.

Hirsmann was not much around the village, although there were reports he had been spotted three of four times collecting parcels in the Post Office. Casually dressed in black denim, scuffed trainers and T-shirts emblazoned with a company logo or the names of west coast colleges, nothing about him spoke of money, except his shiny car parked outside. Later, when we found out more about him, we thought he was too young to have amassed a fortune and own a business with branches in twenty-seven countries.

Before the day the doctor examined Bethan, I'd only glimpsed Hirsmann once, a gangling man with the stoop that comes from long hours crouched over a keyboard. Our eyes met for an instant. He had down on his upper lip, not stubble. There was no mistaking the penetrating intelligence in the gaze behind the steel-rimmed glasses.

The morning after being struck mute Bethan came down to breakfast unaware of what had occurred.

"And so you're saying I was completely out of it yesterday. Have I got that right?"

"The doctor has no idea what caused it. None at all."

She was unconvinced at first, although little persuasion was needed for her to agree to a day off school.

When I came down from my office, three quarters of an hour before lunch, Bethan was sitting on the sofa in the living-room, the blue object on a side table in front of her.

"Is that thing yours?" I said, hearing the reproach in my voice too late.

"Yes. What of it?"

"What indeed! Perhaps you'd like to explain its presence in our home because it's certainly not clear to me. I'm not... angry," I added tetchily, blundering from sentence to sentence.

"It was free. What are you so worried about? I mean it's not as if I've spent actual money on it, is it?"

"Bethan, listen. I'm only asking for some explanation of its function. You must know what it's for. And oh, I'd be interested to know how you came by it."

She stood up and grabbed it. "So you're saying I can't keep it. Is that it?" she cried, cradling it in both arms.

"No, that's not what I'm saying."

"Oh, I see. You *only* want to know everything about all of my possessions and what I do with every second of my life. And I can't accept anything from anybody unless you know all about it."

Holding the blue object as tightly as if it had just been born, she swept off towards the staircase. Minutes later I heard her footsteps on the landing upstairs. I waited until the sounds stopped before going into the kitchen. Just as I began to search for the biscuit tin, I saw the blue van parked outside our gate. For the first time, I acknowledged what I was no doubt already subconsciously aware of: the sign on the road to New Empyrean, Bethan's object, and the vehicle outside were the same blue. But this van had an addition to its roof – not unlike a damaged satellite dish. As I watched, it revolved very slowly. It was white and in shape close to a flower with the petals welded together. I opened the window. There was a driver in the front seat, his face blurred by what looked like frosted glass. Although the dish made no sound as it turned, there was a perfume in the air that overpowered the scent of damp leaves and earth – how tempting to dip into the cup and dream of the sweetness kept in there.

The next day, in spite of her protestations, I took Bethan to the surgery. Nothing was found to be wrong with her. Her answers to the doctor were terse. I decided against mentioning the blue object or the van outside our home. Acquiring a reputation as a madman would not have advanced my cause. She returned to school the same afternoon.

Even now I am not sure what instinct impelled me to visit Dai Roberts' small holding. I told myself I was going to buy fresh eggs, but I knew Dai's daughter was about the same age as Bethan – and wasn't he the first person to notice the blue vans in our lanes?

I parked in the muddy yard and got out. It was raw on the open mountainside, the chasing clouds switching light for shadow and back again; sheep huddled together on the ridges of a hill fort; a dwarfish bare tree contorted in continuous winds. Dai was often out chopping wood in the yard, but there was no sign of him. A blunt foursquare building covered in dark grey stucco, his house lacked even the consolation of a good brick porch. Three old Fords were rusting away on a patch of grass. As I walked towards the front door, I glanced up at the windows on the second storey. In one of them was a row of books, against which was propped a blue object. From where I stood, it looked similar, if not identical, to my daughter's. I pushed the bell and when there was no response knocked loudly. A faint squelching was succeeded by Dai in wellingtons emerging from the far side of the farmhouse.

"Afternoon, Dai," I said walking towards him, skirting the worst of the mud-puddles on my way. "I've come to buy half a dozen of the finest and freshest eggs laid by the most free-ranging hens in all of Wales."

He was a short, thickset man with tousled grey-ginger hair. As soon as he saw me, his freckled face broke into a smile.

"Your Bethan all right now? Not been well at all, my missus was after telling me."

"She's on the mend, thank you. I hope you won't think I'm prying, but I couldn't help but notice there's one of those blue... I'm not quite sure what you call them... sculptures, may be..."

"Oh that would be our Aronwy's. And very taken with it, she is."

"Yes, but what is it?"

"Don't ask me. Lots of the youngsters have one nowadays. And as long as it makes her happy, that's all that matters."

I followed Dai as he walked towards the coop. Behind the smiles he'd always been cagey, or so I thought. Perhaps there was something about the blue objects that was capable of suspending the perennial suspicions of country people.

"Who else has them?"

"The Jones boy up at Bwlch, the Ward-Griffiths twins and Olwyn Pugh, to my knowledge – but there are others. That's a fact."

"Have any of them experienced any ill effects."

"Well, some take to them better than others. So I've heard. Aronwy was a bit tired when she first started using it. Overslept for a couple of days, but now she's adjusted she's fine."

"But where are they getting them from and what are they for?"

"Oh, it's none of my business," said Dai, handing me the eggs. "All I know is Aronwy absolutely loves it, she does. *Da, it's got everything I need...* is what she told me. Well, you can't argue with that."

As I drove back to the village, I passed one of the vans going in the direction of Dai's smallholding. The flower-dish on top was not only revolving but moving up and down on a long metal stem. Though the idea was absurd, I couldn't help thinking it was tracking every fear and desire for miles around, sucking them down though the bowl into depths of the van to await transmutation into that which is not only asked for but provided.

In November, it was dark by seven o'clock. Bethan kept to her room while I sat on the sofa watching the television: pin men playing football in a white and black snowstorm, the voices of the commentators distant, barely comprehensible through the static, as if they were broadcasting in discomfort from the South Pole. The reception had worsened after Bethan came home with the blue object, although it was hard to be sure the events were connected.

At ten o'clock I made hot chocolate and called up the stairs to her. No answer. I checked her room. The blue object had vanished from her bedside table and her raincoat was not on its peg. I hurried outside. At the bottom of the road was a wavering blue shape, visible intermittently. As I ran towards it, the glow steadied, becoming more like a lambent flame, a pilot light in a dark cellar. I had never seen the object at night, but I was unsurprised by its luminous properties. Yet although I knew what I was pursuing, I had no way of understanding what powers it possessed. The echoes of my racing footsteps rattled and sang about me as my shoes slapped the pavement. No matter how fast I ran, I did not seem to be closing the gap. Once, I lost sight of the blue light and was tempted to call out for Bethan, though the black night's cerements hid her from me.

My paced slowed, first to a lope and then, as I reached the hill on the far side of the village, to a hobble. As the blue light rose higher and higher above me, I realised I was heading in the direction of New Empyrean. At least I could be sure where she was going. If I could just reach the ridge ahead of me, I would be able to see the company's campus quite clearly – provided it was illuminated at night. I took a deep breath and forced my leaden legs into a jog. A minute later, I was standing on flat ground that must once have been cut into the side of the hill, although whether it had been used for agricultural or defensive purposes I could not say. I had expected the building to be floodlit, but dark inside, apart from the wing

Hirsmann was reputed to use as his private apartment. In fact, every window blazed with a furious white radiance that seemed in part to be driven by hundreds of people, men and women, dressed in blue. They merged for a moment, only to separate and then come once more together. In spite of the distance between us, something about their posture, their movements, suggested intensity, a continuous act of concentration, where many minds were joined together to achieve a common purpose. Smaller lights were enclosed in narrow glass tunnels, which radiated like flattened legs from the building's abdomen. There was no sign of Bethan.

Once I had collected myself, I made my way across the wet grass. How odd there was no pathway for the workers; perhaps they seldom left the building. The main entrance was small and it was some time before I was able to distinguish it from the surrounding plate glass. Before I could push the handle, the door slid open soundlessly. A woman equipped with a corporate smile and dressed in a blue uniform walked towards me.

"Your daughter told us to expect you. If you're looking for her, she won't be long. Another three days at the most."

"I'd be grateful if you'd take me to her now."

"I'm afraid that's not possible. She's already gone through," said the woman. She had a very faint American accent.

"Then I should like to see Mr Hirsmann. Immediately."

"He is unavailable at this time."

I glanced around the lobby. The walls were made of polished steel that reflected nothing but their own twisting blades of light, a shifting dance of grey, black and silver. There were no doors apart from the front entrance.

"This nonsense... it wouldn't be any chance be connected to that blue contraption... whatever it is... the one she came home with? I mean what is it... exactly... that you do up here?"

"We make provision for those who ask for it?"

"Really? Well, Bethan has become a very strange girl since she's had your... device. I assume she got it from here. Hides in her room the whole time. Gone right into herself, she has."

"It's through being apart that we come together."

"Really? Well that's one I'm going to have to think about!"

"It's connecting to the blue that's the constant above the clouds – all the information... and more."

"I've no idea what you're talking about. Tomorrow I'll be back here to see my daughter... If she's not delivered to me, I'll call the police."

"Sure. That'll be fine," the woman said. "Have a nice night."

As soon as I was outside, I decided to search for another entrance; in such an enormous complex, there had to be more than one. I walked round the side. The squares of light cast down from the windows grew fainter. Somewhere in the unfathomable darkness around me were faint disturbances, perhaps shifting hooves, the sound of animals breathing. I thought of the ghosts of Eli Morgan's herd, grazing in midnight pastures. I glanced up. It was odd how little I could see, even with the moon almost full. The mariners' map was bright with galaxies, as if the stars had been bored deep into the radiance beyond. I had never been able to make the connections, draw the invisible lines that revealed the plough or the bear.

I had almost reached the back of the building; the windows above were black and inscrutable. Then as I turned the corner I saw it, covering the entrance: a web, glowing with incomparable blue brilliance, as if

its guide threads were directing me down to the
world's fine days held within.

The village is quiet now. There are fewer people in the
streets and the traffic, never heavy, is scarcely more
than a trickle; apart, of course, from the ever present
blue vans and lorries. In spite of the lack of logos, we
know who owns them. Sometimes they are parked
outside our houses and work places; often, we glimpse
them through cloud, coming up and down the hill
where Hirsmann has his business, the domain where
he adjusts the temperature of the hours.

Bethan has left school. She says that like me she will
work from home, although not in the old way, of
course. My hopes of seeing more of her are vain. Her
world is in her room. I think she has forgotten the
meaning of a sparrow.

Few of us use the Post Office and there are rumours
it will close. Certainly the time when Hirsmann was to
be seen in there is over. I have heard New Empyrean
has its own delivery service. It was a surprise then,
when I went in to post a parcel yesterday, to find it
busy. Roger Ward-Griffiths was in front of me in the
queue. As ever, he had the haggard look of one worn
out by the burden of being an elderly father.

"How are the twins?" I asked.

"Less trouble nowadays. Thank goodness. It's helped
that they've left school."

"But I thought they'd only just started at the
secondary."

"It wasn't working. We took them away. With New
Empyrean, you don't have to do anything yourself;
there's certainly no need to employ a tutor. The
settings have to be changed every now and again;
that's about it."

"But aren't they lonely? Surely it would be good for them to have a friend come through the front door?"

"Why ever would you think that? They have themselves – and contacts all over the globe."

"So it's as simple as that. Send them to their room and shut the door."

"More or less. We still have to feed them, of course. At least, until New Empyrean Catering is up and running, which should be any day now. I've been really impressed by them, as service providers: they're constantly available; the slightest glitch and your child goes straight in or they send someone round. As soon as the adult package for my age group is available, I'll sign up right away."

Once there were fine Octobers: clear, calm skies corralled in high pressure; now most days we have low clouds, wisps of milky vapours; mists that used to last a morning become the froth on nightfall. It is claimed that this is good for receptivity. Whenever it is fine, the sheet weavers are up with the dew. This year their cobwebs are denser, closer to becoming silky shrouds. *We add a little luxury to the new style of death that we weave,* say the spiders; *and now it is cold we are coming to every house. Look how we build in all the corners of your life.*

At night I dream of New Empyrean. Perhaps because I could not bring myself to break the blue net, I accepted their assurances: your daughter will be returned to you, changed for the better. In the silver threads, the web being woven right across the world, sits Hirsmann – all the luck his, the money spiders spinning, their electricity incessant in his hair.

I still go for walks. Sometimes I believe I alone keep the flowers in existence, recollect their fragrance and bright petals, though there are still a few of us in far-flung hamlets and farmsteads, or with one clean room free from the spider-webs. We have not yet betrayed the old words; and we remember the birdsong, the branches where the nests were held, the speckles on the eggs. Yesterday I discovered that Bethan has forgotten blackbird, foxglove, brook, willow, dog-rose, dandelion, a boy with the name of Bryn. This is no kind of nominal aphasia, merely one language replacing another. Soon I will no longer understand what she says. Perhaps somewhere, in the remotest valley, is the girl who will live to be the last woman to name a tree from its leaf.

Charles Wilkinson's publications include The Pain Tree and Other Stories (London Magazine Editions), Ag & Au (a pamphlet of poems from Flarestack), and his collection of strange tales and weird fiction, A Twist in the Eye, now out from Egaeus Press. His stories have appeared in Best Short Stories 1990 (Heinemann), Best English Short Stories 2 (W.W. Norton), Unthology (Unthank Books), Best British Short Stories 2015 (Salt) and Best Weird Fiction 2015 (Undertow Books), as well as in genre magazines/anthologies such as Black Static, Supernatural Tales, Horror Without Victims, The Dark Lane Anthology, Theaker's Quarterly Fiction, Phantom Drift, Bourbon Penn, Shadows & Tall Trees, and Nightscript. He lives in Powys, Wales.

Man + Van

David Penn

As long as I'd known Peter he had always been a man for country pubs, wine bars and civilised beer gardens, and the Lamb and Flag off Chingford High Street was the direct opposite of those sorts of establishment. So why on earth had he invited me to meet him there, especially on that hot May day? As I approached it I saw three white vans parked outside – no surprise in itself, but what you could see of the hostelry between them didn't exactly make the heart sing. Charcoal- and cream-coloured paint was flaking off its Edwardian exterior, tattered and faded red curtains hung crumpled in smeared windows, and the interior had obviously never been repainted since the days when you were allowed to fill a pub with tobacco smoke. There was a dartboard in one corner and a battered pool table in another, overseen by one of those tacky, ermined portraits of the King. About half the clientele were men between the ages of eighteen and fifty, most of them wearing baseball caps. The other half were pensioners. I couldn't see a female, except for the one behind the bar.

I looked around but didn't notice Peter at first, and assumed he was late. Then I took a second look at a figure hunched on his own over a small round table. He was wearing a black baseball cap and a white T-shirt that was far too big for him. He caught me looking at him and lifted his hand in salute, nodding towards me. Could that be Peter? He raised his head, and the peak of his cap with it.

It was him, but dressed as I'd never seen him before. The last time we'd met, only a couple of months previously, he had been wearing his customary red jeans and denim jacket. He was an artist, and had never been afraid of the stereotype. Was this some effect of Annie leaving him? That had happened only a few weeks ago, according to his brief email. Or were his normal clothes all in the wash? I knew about domestic routines going to pieces.

I walked over. "Peter?"

"Yeah. Watcher mate. What can I getyer?"

The "cockney" accent was, to say the least, a surprise. The Peter I knew had affected aristocratic tones, if anything – *Withnail and I* rather than *The Long Good Friday*.

"Oh..." I stuttered. "I'll have an oran... pint of lager please." As I'd begun the words "orange juice", he'd stared at me, and I mean stared, without question giving me to know that such a drink, here, was not an option.

"Right you are."

When he stood up – and I hope he didn't see my scowl of incredulity – he hunched his shoulders inside his shirt, as if to make it look as if he had bulk in there, which he certainly didn't. Peter was so scrawny he found draughts hard to stand up in. His wife used to tease him about it but he'd tell her a genius didn't need muscles. Now he was holding his arms out by his sides in a bar-room waddle, as if he was beefed like the Hulk. Was he drunk perhaps? A month-long post-separation bender? I sat down chuckling.

He came back holding two pints, even though the one he'd left on the table was only half finished. But he didn't seem drunk.

"Howyer been mate?"

I struggled to keep a straight face.

"You know: as well as could be expected. Look, Peter: What is going on? Why are you dressed like this? Why are we meeting here? Why are you *talking* like this? Are you in some sort of disguise? Hiding from someone?"

"I come here quite a lot these days, mate." He raised his eyebrows, as if daring me to criticise his favourite establishment. "And it's Pete, the moniker."

"'Pete'? Oh-*kay...* Pete." I laughed again, to show I was in on the joke, though I wasn't at all sure I was.

"Things have changed James. You'll see. Anyway, cheers."

We chinked glasses. He sat over the table in that mirage-muscled hunch. "And by the way it was *you* who asked to see *me*, wasn't it?"

"Yes, but not *here*. You did insist, though." I stared at him, waiting for him to crack, let me in on the gag, but it didn't happen. "Still, the reason I wanted to see you is that I find myself in rather the same boat as you, old chap."

"Same boat?"

"Yes. Sam left me. A fortnight ago. Walked out. It had been building up. I think she always saw me as pretty hopeless, but when I lost my job – she wouldn't have said so, but I think that was a bit of a trigger, the last straw. And of course, she's always had this thing about me being eccentric..."

"You *are* eccentric, James."

I looked him up and down, from the absurd cap to the bottom of his unironed chinos and oversized trainers, and smiled.

"So anyway," he said, "you can't sit on your arse any more in that antiquarian place, your girlfriend's left you, and it's all come crashing down round your ears."

"No need to gloat."

"I'm not gloating, mate. Sympathising. It's the same

for me – plans in ruins. But I tell you, I've found a better way of life, mate. I really have."

I was beginning to get seriously worried about him now, but I let that pass. "Well, it's something in that area I wanted to see you about. Look, I know you haven't been getting much work lately, and as for me I'll never get another job in the book trade now. I can't afford to keep up my flat, not and live in it. And I thought, well... I could *let* my place, you see, and more or less live on the rent, for a bit anyway... if I had somewhere cheap enough to hang out... I thought: 'Well, Peter – Pete will have a spare room.' I wouldn't get in the way of your art work. Maybe just for six months, even, until I get back on my feet. We could re-live our student days, eh? A couple of old hell-raisers."

Peter and I had known each other for twenty-five years. And our student days – at St Martin's – were legendary.

He gazed pensively at the ceiling, as if he'd blown a smoke ring up there. "I kind of thought you might have something like this in mind... yeah... Well, I suppose I *might* like the income; that would be great... as a sort of a supplement." He stared up a bit more.

"Your place is ideal for parties, isn't it?" I said encouragingly. "That through lounge." I thought back to my frequent visits, before Annie's departure. Peter's place was pretty substantial for a terraced house. A long but narrow affair with a kitchen at the back. Surely it must be feeling like too much space for him on his own.

A small smile crossed his face and I saw something again of the old libertarian.

"Well, it's an idea. Hmmm... But the first thing is, you'd better come and look at the house," he said. "I made some changes after Annie moved out."

I couldn't think what could be so radically different

it would put me off, but I went along with it. Perhaps I'd find out there what on earth was going on with Peter/"Pete".

The first change I noticed was in the street itself. Just like mine in Herne Hill, it was filling up with white vans. It seemed to be a sign of the times, the way the economy was: more people turning to self-employment in various forms. Outside Pete's house itself was a large Transit – and a skip. Thinking I recognised one or two items of furniture poking out of it, I went up to investigate – and stared back at Pete in horror.

"That beautiful coffee table, and your rattan chairs... This *is* your stuff, isn't it? You really are going through something, aren't you? The male menopause? Or were you really that angry with Annie?"

Pete laughed. "No, I'm not angry at all, mate. And there's nothing wrong with me, I can tell you. There's never been anything less wrong with me. That stuff – it's not worth much."

"*Worth* much?" My mouth must have widened like a sink hole at that point. I don't think I had ever heard Peter use the word "worth" – in the context of money – in all the years I'd known him. Even though he had been forced, as he would have put it, to turn to illustration for a living, it had always been art that had meant everything to him, *art,* whether it turned out to be "worth" anything to Mammon or not. Now he was skipping furniture that he himself had lovingly restored, a 1960s coffee table, the South-East Asian pieces he and Annie had so proudly collected, and goodness knows what else. I delved further into the skip. Under the furniture and a soaked carpet I found a layer of Peter's own paintings, all damaged by rain, some of them slashed into meaningless strips.

"*Peter!* I mean, Pete!"

"Things change mate, things change. Life moves on. Pictures: I don't touch that crap any more. What good does it do anyone? Honest – I've found a better way of life these days. You'll see what I mean. That's the second skip I've filled, mate. They took the first one last week."

I stared at him. He unlocked his front door, and only now did I notice – aghast – that he had tarmacked his front garden. Even though he didn't have a vehicle small enough to park in it. I looked around the street. *Most* of the houses had tarmacked front gardens – or shingled ones.

"Less bother," he said, over his shoulder. I felt my flesh drain of blood.

If possible, the inside of the house was even worse.

"Done a lot of work on this," Pete said proudly. Gone were the varnished pine floorboards that he and Annie had spent weeks putting in place, smothered over now by beige carpet tiles. A leather sofa dominated one side of the front room, facing a stone fireplace. Above the fireplace was a flat screen TV as big as the pool table I'd seen in the pub. Pete went to the back of the house and opened the door into the garden. I heard a deep bark and a bulldog leapt halfway up Pete's chest, rocking him back so that he had to steady himself on the doorpost. "Good boy, Elvis," he shouted.

I dropped into a tubular steel chair in the new dining area – which was dominated by a steel-finished sound system – and put my head in my hands. Had Peter actually undergone some sort of personality crisis after Annie left? This couldn't be an act, could it? No one would take an act this far. Was it a psychiatric condition? Would it be possible to talk to him about it without sending him into a paranoid rage? Just as importantly, could I really move in to *this*, this set-up, at all? The thing was, I had no plan B. I couldn't afford to live in my own flat any more. If I went for housing benefit they'd ask me to downsize – drastically. There were no jobs in my line of work and I had no intention of hawking my CV around call centres. What could I do?

"Move in when you like, James," Pete said optimistically, as if he had read my thoughts. "As long as you still want to." By this time the dog was trying to lick the nails off my fingers. The thing actually seemed to like me, for some unknown reason.

I just hadn't considered the possibility that Peter could have changed – that anyone could have changed – so much in a couple of months. The old Peter and I would have got along famously in the same house, just as we had at art college. I had simply assumed that my moving in would be fine, so not only had I not conceived of a back-up plan, I'd already packed my stuff and agreed a moving date with tenants – despite any impression I'd given Peter. I hadn't left myself any other option.

"In a couple of weeks?" I said. I persuaded myself that maybe I could help "Pete" find his old self again. I don't think I did manage to keep the despair out of my voice. But I'm not sure that this new Pete even noticed. "I just need to get a tenant for my place," I lied, "but I guess I'll have no trouble finding someone. Then there's getting my stuff moved. But that shouldn't be a problem either." I pulled out a handful of cards from my pocket, all saying "Man with van" in one form or another. I'd picked them up in the lobby of my apartment building over the last two weeks, instead of automatically recycling them as I'd usually done. At least twenty had come through the letter box even in that time.

"Oh, don't worry about that, mate," Pete said. "That's what I do. Van man. I can pick your stuff up for you."

"Oh, Christ," I murmured before I could stop myself.

When Pete came to my place – with his van – he wasn't nearly as polite as I'd been on my visit to his.

I guessed he'd arrived before he even touched the bell. I heard a vehicle draw up outside and the door slide open and slam shut, then there was a strange "oi-oi" or "ay-ay" call echoing around the neighbourhood for a few minutes. It was like listening to the cries of some exotic bird species. I twitched my curtains and there was Pete opening up the back of his van, and making that call over his shoulder to other baseball-capped men in the street, many of whom were also opening up the backs of white vans.

"Phew!" he said as soon as he walked in. "What kind of tenants are you hoping to attract with that *decor*? A bunch of hippies? That's incense I can smell, isn't it?"

I admit to being completely baffled. Peter and Annie had visited Sam and me many a time, and seen every last piece of "decor" I had – just as he had smelled most of my incense – and never talked about any of it in these terms, though even then it hadn't all been to his taste. His "hippies" comment for example seemed to be in reference to the – very floral, I admit – *trompe l'oeil* of a Roman garden, which a mutual friend had painted for me some years ago in the living room. Peter had sat dining in front of it scores of times in the noughties. But, really, I was beginning to think that Peter/Pete had descended into some very serious kind of personality disorder.

I decided it probably was worth trying to talk to him on a serious level about what on earth was going on with him, when I could. If he carried on like this though, how long would I be able to stand it?

I still thought I'd persevere with plan A for the meantime, but leave most of my stuff unpacked at his house. I'd see how things went. If living with this new Pete proved to be unbearable, I'd just have to think of some other way of responding to my new financial circumstances. That's if I couldn't talk Pete round somehow.

All the way from Herne Hill to Chingford he had his window down with his elbow hanging out of it, tooting other white van drivers – of which there seemed to be hordes – and dipping his cap at them or holding his hand up palm open in that macho sort of a way, as if to say "this hand, which has such power, I hold open to you in peace". He and I hardly spoke because he had a football match on the radio at ear-splitting volume the whole journey: Leyton Orient versus Brentford, I think. The Peter I had known had held football in contempt.

In his street I could have sworn there were more white vans parked even than on my last visit, many of them with little flags of St George planted on the dash or in the windscreen. As Pete drew up outside his house, a neighbour was getting out of *his* white van – in the inevitable white T-shirt, jeans and baseball cap, red in his case. Pete said "'aright mate?" and the neighbour barked exactly the same back, neither of them so much as glancing at the other, the peaks of the caps steering straight ahead like rhino horns.

Pete and I hefted my boxes and things out of the van and placed them in my assigned bedroom and a shed at the bottom of his garden. I noticed that, somehow, it was the vast majority of my books and my Samuel Palmer prints that ended up in the shed.

When we had finished, Pete said "Here, siddown" and pointed to the sofa. He came back from the kitchen with two cans of lager and plonked one in front of me.

"Cheers," he said.

"Cheers," I said.

Elvis, who had run at our heels since my first box entered the house, sat on his master's feet, lolling his tongue on the carpet and panting at me.

I let silence reign for a moment as we drank but I knew I had to speak soon – before Pete switched on a soap show or some kind of brain-shattering music.

"Pete, I can't help noticing: you've changed. I mean, dramatically. I thought it was a joke at first but it clearly isn't... is it? No. Even you couldn't keep this up for so long without laughing. What is it? What's got into you? Is it some way of rejecting Annie, your old life? Does it have to be so extreme?"

He stared at me under his cap for a few seconds, as if I was some slightly irritating guest on a TV chat show.

"People change, don't they James? I got fed up with trying to make a living out of drawing stuff, that's all. A mug's game. I met some people..."

"Met some people?"

"Yeah, down the pub. They made a few suggestions. Got myself a van. Now I do odd jobs, bit of decorating, building work, moving people... And I work for myself, that's the point. Don't pay no bloody taxes to no fucking government. All the profits go to the boss: me."

"But you always *did* work for yourself, as an illustrator..."

"Nah, not really. Contracts and whatnot, deadlines, editors... nah. *This* is the life, mate. Free and easy. I never sign nothing." He swept his hand in front of him, a slow chop as if calming a sea. "Cash in hand. I'm doing all right mate, I can tell you..."

I could sort of see what he was saying, but it didn't really make any sense. His insistence that he was more his own boss now sounded odd. It sounded like a script. Picked up, I conjectured, from the "people" he had met in the pub. I'd never thought of Pete as suggestible.

"Who are these people you met?"

He looked uncomfortable for a moment.

"Just people. Down the pub – the Lamb and Flag. I'll introduce you to them one day."

"But I can't see it, Pete. The life you're living is no better than your old one, financially or otherwise. It's narrower, more limited. Why would you give up what you had, everything you had, give up a skilled, creative life, for... for being a handyman."

He started to roll about in his chair as if he was looking for something to throw at me, or as if overcome by some frenetic motor nerve disorder. I felt quite alarmed but carried on.

"Even if what you say made some kind of economic sense, why are you *talking* like this? Why are you dressed like this? Surely none of that is necessary?"

"Look... 'Handyman'?" he exploded. "'Handyman'? Watch it, mate." He shook his head, gritting his teeth as if to hold back friendship-ending words, and stroked Elvis as if preparing a weapon to fire. "I ain't no fucking handyman," he said slowly.

I rocked against the back of the sofa. This was *not* Peter.

He sighed and shook his head again – there was no getting through to me. "You probably *wouldn't* understand. Times have changed. We're not fucking hippies any more, you and me. There's no room for fucking art-loving hippies these days I can tell you. You've got to go with the flow, mate. See what's happening and move with it. Not fall behind the curve." He tapped the side of his head. "You've got to think, see the way things are, adapt... Just got to fit in to survive. You've never realised that, have you? Always been off in your own head. You've never tried to fit in. You never *saw* what there was you needed to fit in with. If anything you've done your best *not* to fit in. But that's kids' stuff, mate. And that's because you're eccentric, mate. Eccentric."

Of course, he pronounced it "essentric". He lifted the beer can to his mouth with an air of finality, of having made a conclusive diagnosis. Then his shoulders dropped. He had said his piece and felt more relaxed.

"Look, for both of our sakes," he said. "We'll give it three months. If it's not working out, this, in three months – the summer, basically – I'm going to pull the plug on it. That's enough time. If we see the warning signs, that'll give you time to evict your tenants and move back in. No harm done. But three months, that's it."

Unfortunately not even that conversation, with Pete's warning at the end, put me off our arrangement, not for the time being. At least we'd been able to *have* a conversation, I reasoned. I wanted it to work because I still liked Pete, I still needed somewhere to live or at least bide my time and, strangely enough, I had seen in that conversation some flashes of the old Peter: refreshingly direct, authentic; an honest communicator who hid nothing from you.

I unpacked a little. I went to the shed to retrieve some of my prints and books. (Decently, Pete had given me a key to the padlock.) I thought perhaps having spoken to him on the subject once, I could do it again – and gradually, maybe, find out what was really happening, why this extraordinary change, help him.

Meanwhile, I engaged with my project of having a loosened-up summer, of letting my hair down, experimenting, shrugging off the blues, kicking out the jams, unbridled by ordinary domestic life.

I went to concerts, nightclubs, hung out in trendy

cafes and tracked down the "alternative scene", as I understood it, wherever it might manifest. I hadn't thought I'd feel out of place in any of those situations, a man in his forties, not with the liberal-minded young people of this day and age – but I did. There seemed far fewer forty-year-olds about in such environments than I remembered from my pre-Sam days (she had been more of an art gallery and opera type). There were fewer thirty-year-olds, come to that. And even the twenty-year-olds looked somewhat wary. Then one night I found out at least one reason why. I went to a gig in Hammersmith, just a run of the mill hippy-anarchist band, and it was gate-crashed by a whole mob of men in T-shirts and baseball caps. They stood in rows challenging the kids to a mass fight, chanting in time with jabbing fingers something they evidently thought was morally improving. The kids weren't up for a challenge. They ran. No security guards or police came anywhere near the incident.

I told Pete about it but he just glanced wearily at me and said "Better stay away from places like that, mate" and went back to his football match. It was chilling, frankly. I felt like a teenager admonished by his older brother.

I lay on my bed like a teenager too that night and thought about giving up on the whole idea.

But then something rather marvellous happened.

Kind of out of spite towards Pete I bought a Volkswagen camper van and painted it electric green and pink. I planned to use it one day to drive around Europe, but meanwhile I drove to all my "freak hangouts" as Pete began to call them. One of these was a little yoga studio I'd discovered, right there in Chingford. It was a tiny ex-pentecostal church hidden away down a side road, about a mile from Pete's house.

These days it had attracted enlighteningly critical graffiti such as FUCK OFF HIPPES, PREVETS and FAGGUTS but the people who ran it soldiered cheerfully on, and there was a hard-core of about twenty regulars who said the graffittists' karma would get them one day. I'd go there once or twice a week, early in the morning if I got up in time, or in the evening, to a beginners' class. The bearded and pony-tailed beginners' teacher was merciless in his pursuit of perfect *asanas*, barking orders as if on a parade ground, but I always came out of the sessions feeling fuller of the joys of life.

One thing that helped greatly in this respect was the presence of a pretty young woman called Natasha. She had a goofy smile, a mop of uncontrollable hair and a nose ring. I tried steadfastly not to look at the tantalising offers of belly and cleavage that appeared through her loose clothing during the class's contortions. But after only two weeks I did manage to get her out for a coffee. It seemed I still had the old charm – or at least something she didn't object to. Subtle questioning revealed that she didn't have a boyfriend, lived on her own and was into Dostoyevsky. She was a hygienist at a private dental practice and was bored.

She approved enthusiastically of my project of finding a new post-serious-relationship life for myself – "dropping out" as she excitedly called it. She said she wouldn't mind accompanying me to a concert or two, as long as I went with her to poetry readings. I volunteered to do that with her first, and for a reward I got her into bed.

That was at her place, a bathroom-sized "affordable" bedsit in Walthamstow. She was hospitable enough, handing me a goats' milk coffee and a yoghurt in the morning, as I uncramped my body and slowly recalled where I was. But I felt it was only fair to invite her back to mine, or Pete's, as well.

She knew all about my situation, so she wasn't surprised at the juvenile fun we had as I tried to smuggle her in late at night. I thought I'd succeeded, but there was a rather pointed, unnecessarily loud cough from Pete's room as we crept across the landing. Of course we'd been unable to suppress our giggling.

The night was utterly sublime.

But the morning was appalling.

I took her down to breakfast to meet Pete. In hindsight this was a very foolish idea indeed, especially as Pete was probably looking for a flashpoint between him and me, a *casus belli,* to help him get a few things off his chest. But I had thought that this, having a girl over, of all things was something he would understand, take in his stride. Surely he hadn't changed *that* much since our St Martin's days. And if a white van man can whistle at short-skirted "birds" out of his white van window, can't his lodger bring one home?

Apparently not. Unless Pete simply took a dislike to Natasha. True, she was dressed pretty informally: bra-less, as she usually was, in a rather loose, low-slung T-shirt, cut off above her gold-ringed belly button, and some shorts. But nothing in her appearance would have fazed the old Peter – except to elicit some rather too frank compliments.

She looked at me with touching uncertainty outside the door of the living room, but I guided her in, whispering that it would be all right. Pete was in his trainer bottoms, bare-chested – such as his chest was – with *The New News of the World* spread out on the dining table in front of him, open at a double-page spread of Cheryl Cole on a beach. An egg-smeared plate with two crusts and a used tea-bag sat at the centre of the table. Elvis grumbled from below, then stood and barked.

"Oh," was all Pete said to either of us, and stared directly at Natasha, from top down.

She tipped her head at him and smiled in painful friendliness. "Hello," she jingled. I gripped her hand. Pete frowned, got up and took his mug of tea and paper through to the lounge end of the room. I smiled desperately at Natasha but she simply raised her eyebrows and sat down.

"Got any coffee?" she asked.

Relieved she was taking it so well I picked up Pete's used plate and bolted into the kitchen. "Yes, definitely. But no goat's milk, I'm afraid."

I had forgotten myself in my elation. Pete chortled – loudly – without looking up from his paper. Of course, every fragment of my conversation with Natasha from then on received a running commentary in a range of vocalisations from the sofa, subtle or unsubtle.

"Apple juice?"

"*Christ!*"

"...run out of brown bread. White?"

(Laughter.)

"...nice day. What about going over Wanstead Flats?"

("*One way of putting it...*")

After fifteen minutes, I couldn't stand it any longer. I apologized to Natasha, just loud enough for Pete to hear, and suggested we went back upstairs. She put on her jacket and we went out for the day.

"I really am sorry," I said as we walked. "I had no idea he would be like that."

"It's all right," she said, wobbling her head. "I've met worse." She smiled and kissed me, then ruffled her own hair as if freeing it from some restraint. She didn't mention the subject again, and – with the merest atom of suggestion – I was given to understand that I shouldn't either. I knew exactly what that conversational black-out meant. It meant I could never invite her back again. I would have to rely on her bringing me to her place, when she said so.

That night Pete and I had a tremendous row.

When I walked in he was watching television. He didn't look up or say anything. I crashed about in the kitchen as I made myself a drink, to try and get a reaction. Nothing. So I wasted no more time.

"What the fuck was that all about, this morning?"

For a second I thought he wouldn't answer me. An American football game blared on.

"Fucking good touchdown," he said. "Look, I don't want to ruin your fun, but if you're going to bring a floozy back, the least you can do is ask me..."

"A 'floozy'?" I shook my head. "I really don't know what's got into you Pete. You knew this was going to happen."

"If you want to hang out with a bit of brass it's up to you." He still wasn't looking at me. "But you *ask* me if you want to bring her back here. And I would have said 'No'. This is not a cathouse. And I don't want no fucking hippies coming in here." He picked up his *New News of the World,* crunched it up and threw it in the bin. "What are the neighbours gunna think?"

I felt sick.

The next few times I saw Natasha, I thought I was starting to lose her altogether. Associating me now with the shock of meeting Pete, I assumed, she started to withdraw. I could feel it. I was less welcome to lie in, the mornings-after. I needed something to win her back, something to please her, freshen up my image.

I got two tickets to Glastonbury from a grifter in a local pub – not the Lamb and Flag; someone I'd heard about through my hippy/dropout contacts. They cost me two thousand pounds, cutting a fair swathe into my emergency savings. But I thought it might be worth it. Look, I was forty-five. You only live once.

One thing was certain: Natasha still liked my camper van. She revelled in its flowery day-glo glory as we cruised down the M3, triggering honks and inarticulate yells from capped men in vans, suited men in Mondeos and entire families in four-wheel drives. When we got to the festival itself, though, things were not quite so jolly.

It was full to overflowing. As always, many more tickets had been sold than officially existed, and a lot of people had gate-crashed, finding their way around, through or under the fencing, but this year, whereas the festival's capacity was about 150,000, 300,000 had turned up, or so a radio news report estimated. There seemed to be an even stronger will than usual among the country's youth to be there. Crowds of face-painted, tattooed, barefoot and bejewelled kids wandered the Somerset lanes or squatted outside the perimeter fence. But we noticed they weren't the only ones. Strings of white vans pulled up at the gates; their drivers presented tickets and were waived through. At one point a whole coachload of men in caps – you could see the peaks yawing and tipping through the windows – drove in. Was there some kind of van man rock band playing this year?

We were told we could walk into the festival on a daily basis, but there was nowhere for us to camp. We had to find one of the satellite camping grounds and pay the extortionate price. At least it was relatively peaceful, with only one other camper van and a few tents. We parked in a corner between a hedge and a small tipi. We had a clear but very distant view of the Pyramid Stage. We didn't even try to get into the festival itself that first night. We drank some Pimms I'd brought instead.

We woke in the morning to the smell of frying. Natasha got up and I heard her draw back a window.

"Hi," she said to someone.

"Hi," a young male voice called back.

"Nice morning."

"Yeah. Want some breakfast?"

"What are you cooking?"

"A prince's breakfast of fried bananas and quinoa."

"There are two of us.

"The more the merrier."

She gave me a shove and told me to get up and come out. I affected to be asleep to make her talk to me and explain what was going on. Then I said I'd join them when I was ready and rolled back onto my side.

When I did finally stagger out, Natasha was squatting with a scrawny lad in his early twenties, so I guessed – her age – with a heap of mud-set hair and a nose ring. They were deep in conversation, but both looked up as I opened the van door.

"This is Rama. He lives in a commune outside Frome."

"We prefer to call it a colony?" said Rama. "'Commune' has violent associations we don't want?"

"He's a Hindu. He practises transcendental meditation and yoga." Natasha smiled at him as she said it. He smiled back.

"Great," I said, accepting a plate of fried mulch and a fork. I wasn't sure about the food, but my dawning morning consciousness suspected it was in my interests not to let Rama have Natasha's exclusive attention.

However, after that first meeting it seemed somehow unquestionable that Rama would accompany us wherever we went. I sensed I was not to object and be "possessive" so I didn't mention it, tried not to let my irritation show and strove to be friendly to Natasha's newly attached waif. That first morning the three of us toured the main festival sites, Rama acting as guide. He and Natasha pored over the line-ups on her mobile and decided which bands were worth seeing. For lunch, he took us to the most eco-friendly stall. He introduced us to meditation in the afternoon in the Blue Buddha tent.

I might have been more jealous if it hadn't been for another preoccupation: all day, everywhere we looked, gangs of baseball-capped, white-shirted, beer-swilling men were roaming the fields, and not looking as friendly as everyone else. They seemed to expect the more normal festival goers – usually much younger – to get out of their way as they wandered freely – and the kids always did.

"I don't like this," said Rama. "Very bad vibes. I keep thinking Altamont."

As the afternoon wore on and the capped men's faces reddened, the atmosphere grew worse. There seemed to be a zone surrounding a big white tent, within which any normal Glastonbury punter was made to feel extremely unwelcome, deflected like ants around a bonfire. Rama was growing visibly more concerned, and to my horror led us towards it.

"There shouldn't be no-go areas?" he said. Natasha's eyes met his in that straight-as-an-arrow earnestness the young have. He touched her arm. "I think I want to see what's going on."

Gangs of capped men roamed the zone, more or less overtly guarding their patch. They didn't physically try to stop us moving through, but the glares and comments got more menacing the nearer we approached the central tent.

Natasha coolly ignored the whistles and "Arightdarlin"s but flung back a righteous "Fuck off" when they inevitably insulted Rama, or even me.

"What you doin' with that poofter, Darlin'? You wanna be with someone who can gerrit up." This in reference to Rama.

"Brung your granddad with yer 'ave yer?" This in reference to me.

With some disgruntlement, I noticed that there was more heat in her reaction when it was Rama who was ritually abused than when I was. But I could hardly complain when she was the little Boudicca ensuring we didn't receive even worse treatment.

Despite all this, and increasingly close passes by the gangs, Rama led us on towards the tent itself. At the entrance, he turned and faced us dramatically.

"You can wait here if you want? Or go back? I want to see inside. Something isn't right here."

Natasha made a defiant upwards nod, indicating the tent with her chin. I was frankly terrified, but of course I had no choice. I couldn't let the two of them carry on alone. As it was, I was beginning to feel like the baggage-handler on Rama's missionary expedition.

But I have to say the mission to the tent was worth it. We walked in to the sight of a vast plasma TV showing Formula 1, and a crowd of perhaps three hundred can-carrying men standing in front of it. At the back of the tent was a replica pub bar. There were three pool tables dotted around, and five or six dartboards set up on pillars. Just about everywhere possible, there were St George flags – flanking and behind the bar, on either side of the TV screen, hanging from the sides of the tent, and on much of the clientele's T-shirts and caps. The music of Madness blared from a sound system.

Rama led us round like Christ inspecting the Temple, under a hail of stares and muttered invective. Twice a capped man stuck out a foot to try to trip him up. Each time he stumbled but Natasha launched impressively fluent abuse at his attacker and Rama carried on bravely. I trailed after them, managing nothing but a weak smile, beginning to wonder with a cold spinal tingle whether I might bump into Pete.

When we finally left I felt weak with relief. I insisted on finding somewhere we could get a decent drink, and briefly it was my turn to lead – to a marijuana-filled tent set out like a tropical bar where I ordered gin; the other two drank coconut juice.

Rama looked grim and kept shaking his head.

"Bad vibes, man. *Really* bad vibes. It's not like anyone should be banned from coming here? But there are certain expectations? If you come, you try to get on with everyone? They're muscling in, these guys, somehow. And they're what a lot of folk have come here to get away from. There are some worrying trends in the mainstream..."

He said he felt he ought to go and alert someone about the growing tension he had picked up throughout the grounds. He was worried. He told us to wait where we were and disappeared.

After half an hour, during which Natasha frowned distractedly and kept gazing across the site, he came back looking no happier.

"Spoke to a couple of stewards," he said. "Tried to warn them. Funny thing was, they didn't look bothered at all."

Natasha took his hand under our table.

"But I put the word around with some other people. I told them we'd better be ready for some ugliness sooner or later. They didn't think I was wrong. But the best way to respond to it is not to respond? Stay cool. That's what they want, these people. They want a reaction."

He wasn't at all wrong.

That night everyone surged around the Pyramid stage. I had not taken much notice of the actual festival line-up, assuming I wouldn't have heard of any of the performers anyway, but Natasha had told me that the Upstarts were billed to appear, having reformed especially complete with Chrissy Hartman. Now that was a band I did know, from my student days, when they were huge. I was surprised that

Chrissy Hartman was still alive, never mind performing. There had been a lot of speculation about whether she would actually make it onto the stage, considering how ill she was, but they said she was determined to fulfil her booking. It was touch and go right to the last minute. The rest of the band – mostly not, in fact, original members – slumped on and tuned up, but then there was a long pause. It was like waiting for an appearance by the Queen in her latter days. But finally Chrissy was escorted on by a couple of muscular assistants to wild whoops and applause. Lighters and mobile phones sparkled among the crowd.

When everyone had quietened down, Chrissy bent over the microphone and said, in almost a whisper: "Never give up. Never surrender" and the kids went wild again. I didn't know what was behind the advice, quite, but it seemed to mean a lot to her audience. Natasha and Rama were practically in tears. Then Chrissy launched raspily into "Light in the Tunnel", to sustained cheering, many singing along in congregation-like delirium.

But almost immediately there was heavy jostling all around us. Waves of human pressure came towards us from the back, and we turned to see the crowd parting like water around oil. Three or four hundred can-waving, baseball-capped, T-shirted heavies were forcing their way to the front, jumping and twirling as if they were born Irish jiggers, singing something I couldn't at first make out. As they pushed their way further in though I realised what it was: a version of a football terrace song: "Chrissy Hartman walks on water, ah-la-lalala, la-la-la-*la*". I gathered it was meant to be ironic.

At first nobody tried to stop them. A few ineffective stewards made attempts to reason with them. Chrissy swore at them and tried to sing a little louder. But at last the patience of the crowd snapped, and the capped men got what they wanted: a surging, swirling battle. Bottles and cans hurled, punches thrown, small groups and pairs of men in strange waltzes of violence, whirlpools and tidal waves of fight. Rama, shaking his head, took Natasha's hand and led us in a weaving retreat to the thinner edges of the audience. The Upstarts were escorted off the stage. Someone came to the microphone to try to establish order. Other rock stars preached. Floodlights were switched on. Within a few minutes most of the crowd had pulled well back to leave a crazily whirling centre. A helicopter dropped out of nowhere, drenching the scene with its searchlight. After half an hour a surprisingly massive police force arrived and broke up the fight.

And Glastonbury was cancelled.

We drove Rama back to his community, or "colony", in Frome. The lucky colonists lived in a huge Georgian house with gardens that amounted to a park. There were wood carvings and metal sculptures on the lawns and dream-catchers over the doors.

Rama gave us lunch and herbal tea and walked around the gardens with us. Natasha and he spent some time somewhere alone together while I was entertained by a bearded elder in the lounge. His brain had obviously been randomised by LSD but he was friendly. In between indecipherable stories, accompanied by baffling but elaborate hand-gestures, which seemed intended to convey mystic import, he gazed at me with watery eyes as if he was about to cry for me. They told us to come back whenever we liked. Why didn't we come and join them, or some other community out this way? It was rotten everywhere else. Anyone with any sense was moving West. Natasha and Rama kissed at the gate and we drove off.

I said nothing to Natasha that might indicate jealousy.

All along the A-roads and motorways to London we

were hooted and roared at from vans, packed holiday-making family cars and even coaches. There was something triumphal in the blaring horns this time, as if we were captives in a victory parade.

By the time I got back to Pete's house, having dropped Natasha off at her place – she said goodbye with a peck – I was exhausted. I felt literally ill and about twenty years older. For some reason it felt natural to tell Pete the whole story of the trip, Rama, the battle, everything, spill it out, confide, as in the old days, as if he would be a sympathetic listener.

He nodded in front of *Homes Under the Hammer* as I spoke, saying nothing until I'd finished, then turned to me with an oddly empathic frown and said "I told you not to get involved with those people". He meant Natasha's type, the "freaks" as he continued to call them. Then he went and got me a lager from the fridge. I was very grateful for it.

I only saw Natasha a couple of times over the next two weeks. Without anything being said, it suddenly seemed out of the question that I would sleep with her ever again. Then – it didn't surprise me – she announced that she had quit her job and was moving out West to live with Rama. They had been Skyping ever since we'd got back, it seemed, and had decided that they ought to be together. All the astrology said so. The *I-Ching* and a version of the Mayan calendar said so, and that was the direction their karma was taking. Why didn't she just tell me she fancied him, I wondered. But it was pointless arguing.

"So what are you going to do now?" Pete asked me during our fourth pint in front of the snooker that night. He didn't even try to hide a smirk.

"Dunno," I said.

"Seems to me there's only one thing for it." He

disappeared up to his room for a couple of minutes, then came back with a dark blue New York Yankees cap and fitted it quite gently over my head.

"And from now on you'd better be Jim. Drop this 'James' stuff," he said, "Oh, *James*," affecting the King's accent.

I didn't resist. Any will to do that seemed to have drained out of me. The very next night Pete took me to the Lamb and Flag. Whereas most of the clientele had been wearing baseball caps and T-shirts on my last visit, now all of them were, including the landlord and his bar staff, not excepting the sole female among them. St George crosses and badges had proliferated as well, I noticed; and one or two of the burlier men were sporting something I had never seen before: St George arm bands.

As we walked through, Pete made something of a show of me. He stopped with me in the middle of the saloon bar and addressed the crowd:

"Oi-oi guys. This is Jim," he said, and patted me heavily on the back. "New boy. You'll be nice to him, won't you?"

From the paused darts- and pool-players, from behind half-lifted pints, there was a chorus: "Arightmate." "Hiyermate." "Oi-oi." As I walked through, a few guys even raised their glasses and called "Cheers", "Goodonyermate".

Pete took me to the bar.

"Those two blokes at the end?" he whispered. "I'll go up and talk to them. You follow after a minute and offer us all a drink, casual-like, like you can afford it no bother. And how are you at darts these days?"

I saw from the twinkle in his eye that he was remembering our skills as students.

"Funnily enough, I still enjoy a game every now and then."

"Good stuff."

He sidled up to the two heavy-set men at the end of the bar, and a minute later I joined them, waving a sheaf of notes and asking them all what they were drinking. "Rightmate." "Cheersmate." Lagers all round. When I'd handed out the drinks, I hung about behind Pete. The conversation wandered between the merits of a few goalkeepers, gloating invective against the poor remains of the EU and "The-Mrs-is-glued-to-the-X-Factor".

"Game-a-darts?" Pete suggested after a while. The four of us went to the board. Two guys who had been playing stopped, nodded at Pete's friends and walked away. We were to play pairs, Pete and I against the other two.

As we picked our sets of darts from the shelf under the board, Pete whispered to me: "We're going to lose, of course, but not too badly. Do a few trick shots, you know – trebles, a bull's eye or two – enough to show them you can play. But we ain't gonna win, aright?"

I don't know why he assumed I was still capable of too many "trick shots", but I did summon the necessary reflexes for one or two. And apparently they had whatever effect Pete was hoping for.

We lost – just, with one last cliff-hanger round, making our whole performance perfect, Pete told me later – drank six pints each, played pool and lost again – including losing a bet this time – then went for a vindaloo. I remember nothing after staggering into Khan's, but apparently I made some comments about the German national football team, French women and Scottish independence (of the "best thing that ever happened to England" type) that went down well.

The next morning Pete woke me up with a coffee.

"You passed," he said.

"Passed what?" I was rubbing my forehead to get at the chap throwing bricks around in there.

"You're one of us now, mate. Well, you do need a van. But we'll fix that up quick enough."

I also needed a little training, it seemed. Although, as Pete was at pains to point out, white van men avoided working in pairs, if possible, he took me out on the road with him for a couple of days to show me "the basics".

"You don't wanna be doing something wussy or stupid – it'll get back to the wrong people."

In the interests of this training, we went out dropping Pete's business-touting leaflets. Pete would park in a likely-looking residential area, give me a pile of them and we'd take a street each.

"Just stuff them through the letterboxes." If I saw any other van men I was to tip my cap, give a mock salute, say "oi-oi" or "arightmate" or any combination of the above.

It turned out there were scores of other men doing exactly the same rounds, all with, from what I could see, practically identical leaflets: "Man + Van, Anything Moved, Painting & Decorating, Odd Jobs". Some letterboxes were actually crammed with leaflets and it was hard to fit ours in. I had to push so that the whole wedge of paper fell in, then poke my leaflet after it. There were so many men and leaflets that I began to wonder who we van men were trying to sell our services to – each other?

"Don't you worry mate. With unemployment what it is, there'll be plenty of people moving – repossessions. Or wanting bits of work done if they stay put. They can't afford real removal men, can they?"

"But don't all the unemployed become van men – or women?"

Pete screwed his face up as if he'd never considered this, as if being a van man was so obviously to belong to an elite club that my point was self-evidently absurd.

"Nah. There's call centres, aren't there? Supermarkets. Door-to-door selling. Parcel delivery. Plenty of jobs. Or just the dole. That's what most of them end up doing, innit, taking the dole. Lazy bastards."

Still, watching the traffic of white vans up and down the street, the other capped men going from door to door, and the overstuffed letterboxes, I couldn't help feeling there was some poor logic behind the whole situation.

Another classic means of van man advertising was to stick posters onto bus shelters, the windows of abandoned shops and particular walls that for no obvious reason had begun to attract posters. We did this together because one of us apparently had to keep an eye out, as this particular activity was nominally illegal.

One bus shelter in Loughton was so covered in Man + Van posters that I couldn't find a place to stick ours. I started to strip one off to clear a space.

"Oi! Don't do that," said Pete, pulling my hand away. "Nah. We don't do that. That's not on."

"But there's no room."

"Well, then there's no room. We go somewhere else. Competition mate, free market. We believe in that. But fair play too. Just imagine if we all did that to each other, sabotaged each other's posters? There'd be chaos, mate. Chaos. Very ugly."

There was a recreational aspect to these publicity runs too, which mainly involved shouting abuse. Of course, I had experience of this from the receiving end, but it was no less alarming – or distasteful – from the inside.

If as we drove we passed anyone who looked remotely different – say, men with long hair or beards or wearing anything colourful – Pete would shout "Poof" or "Fucking hippy" or "Wanker". Anyone who looked a bit dishevelled was called a "Scrounger". Beggars he would more or less try to run over. Anyone a shade less than pale was invited to "go home".

Women – except "bag ladies" and "single mothers" (which seemed to mean very young mothers) – were largely spared this, but of course any remotely attractive woman (without a child) would be wolf-whistled or have "Hello-darlin'-give-us-a-smile" chanted at her. Any wearing short skirts or anything else alluring would be bluntly invited into the van. Needless to say, no invitations were accepted, but that didn't seem to be the point.

Another pastime was making perfectly innocent pedestrians or other drivers think they had done something wrong. Pete would occasionally – it seemed at random – toot and shake his fist at people crossing the road, even behind him, as if they'd been jay-walking and almost caused him to crash. He turned out to be brilliant at acting furiously indignant – I think he even convinced himself he was. A man in a blue suit checking his watch on the pavement received a blare of the horn, "wanker" and a fist shaken in the wing mirror. When he looked up astonished, Pete mimicked his expression as if to say "Don't give me that – don't pretend you don't know what the problem was", then erupted into laughter when we were out of sight.

Very entertaining.

I couldn't help feeling glad, after an induction like this, that white van men didn't work in pairs. On my own I could practise a milder version of these sorts of behaviours, if at all. And maybe *not* listen to Five Live all day at speaker-wrecking volume.

On the subject of having my own van, my first suggestion was that I simply got my VW sprayed white. Somehow – I don't know, for sentimental reasons – I wanted to hang on to it. But Pete said emphatically that a VW camper was *not* an appropriate vehicle. I'd have to sell it and get another make – he would provide a list of approved ones.

So I put the old girl, as I thought of her, on eBay. Pictures from all angles. Me leaning against the snub bonnet and smiling. Shots of the inside to show her roominess. A list of all her marvellous specs. What was on the clock. I wondered if the advert might attract some last, mad, hopelessly romantic traveller.

I couldn't have been more wrong. What it attracted was savage vandalism. My drawing attention to my multi-coloured van like that seemed to have driven at least one person into a frenzy, because one night I came back after a van run with Pete to see it coated with lava-like layers of white paint, from roof to wheel arch. The windows were covered. Dribbling waves still oozed down from the roof, where whole cans had been upended – one or two big pots were still there. Across the sides and windscreen, in black, were daubed: "FUCK OF HIPPEY", a "peace sign" with a penis in the middle and all the usual things.

I sat down on the kerb. I was surprised at the shock I felt, like a blow to the stomach.

Pete patted me on the shoulder. "Ah well, you were trying to get rid of it anyway. I think this puts it beyond question."

I thought that was a little insensitive, although he wasn't to know what the horrible mess meant to me. I had only just realised it myself. It was the kicking away of a ladder, one I hadn't even known I had left in place, the final extinction of a dream.

On inspection the camper van was still mechanically fine, and would be saleable after some – pretty extensive – cosmetic work. I scraped the windscreen and drove it to a garage.

Every vehicle in the garage was white. The mechanic who was sent to look at my wreck did so with distaste, but not because of the slogans and senseless destruction: his revulsion was for the bits of pink and day-glo that had escaped the vandalism.

"Simplest thing would be to spray it all white, since someone's done half the job for you," he sneered.

"Yes. White is what I had in mind," I said, realising at the same time that – strangely – I was lying. I knew as I spoke that deep down, I *hadn't* decided that I wanted the van painted white, not wholeheartedly. But I left the vehicle in the mechanic's capable hands, though I lingered at the workshop gate staring at it long enough to elicit another raised lip.

Pete bought a couple of six packs to commiserate with me, but also to mark my passage, it seemed to me, into a sunny new phase.

He kept cheerily toasting me, my new life – and my new van, which would surely come. There was something else on his mind too, though. Something he wanted to tell me, wasn't quite able to say right out, but was clearly excited about. It eventually came out anyway in dribs and drabs.

"Ah well. At least painting it white will make it easier to sell," he said. "Then you're set up, aren't you? Get yourself a decent van and Bob's your uncle. Working for yourself."

"And you can put the rent up."

"Yeah. Well, we'll have to think our living arrangements over."

He switched the TV on and watched *X-Factor Europe* distractedly. The uniformly English judges laughing at the continental auditioners' accents and wardrobes was no more than background static for either of us.

"Yeah. Your own van and your own business," he mumbled. "You'll be fully fledged. Ready, I reckon."

I waited. "Ready? To run my own business?"

"Yeah. Ready for that." He laughed, bit his lip and sank more beer. "And something else."

"What?"

"Ah... never mind." But he turned and gave me a wild grin. He was like a child who knew a new game.

"What, Pete?"

"Something pretty big, mate."

"Pete! Come *on.*"

He laughed. "I'm not sure I'm supposed to tell you. It's *big.* It's still at the planning stage."

I stared at him.

"Oh, all right." He stabbed the red button on the remote. "But fucking keep it to yourself for now. We're going *West* mate."

"West?"

"Yeah. The big push. You know all these hippies have congregated out there, right? I mean, some of them never came back after the last Glastonbury – you'll know all about that. We heard that more went West after the Isle of Wight too. They're all out there trying to set up some 'alternative lifestyle' bollocks. They're more or less all in one place.

"Well? Don't you get it? They've made themselves a sitting target. It's irresistible." He was grinning, the beer shining his lips. "This is going to be the Big One. We're *all* going down there. To sort them out, once and for all. Fuck them and their alternative. We can clear the land of hippies and perverts forever."

I stared straight at him. I tried not to show the shock I really felt. Not only at the fact that, somewhere, this was Peter Soames saying this, my old art school buddy, the old arch-liberal, but at *what* he was saying, what he was actually, earnestly saying. The horror, the barminess of it. And yet from all my experience over the last weeks, how could I not have seen this coming, that it would one day get this serious?

"We've had skirmishes already," he said delightedly. "Some blokes have been going down there all summer and setting things straight. Keeping them on their toes. Keep the enemy stretched, gradually weakened, not knowing what to expect. Classic tactics. Rommel used them. Now we're ready for the Big One. I reckon you're up for that, aren't you?"

I didn't answer. My mind turned to Natasha, and even poor naive Rama.

We continued to watch the judges ritually humiliating foreigners on behalf of the British public, and I didn't make any reference to what Pete had said, or ask any questions. He might have thought that strange, or might have thought I was being wisely circumspect. I didn't really care. After a decent interval I went up to my room and emailed Natasha – I'd kept her address – to warn her about what Pete had told me. For good measure I texted her too.

A few days later I got a call from the garage telling me my van was ready. I went to pick it up. They'd done a good job. Not a single square inch of the bodywork was anything other than white, except for the chrome.

I paid them and drove her away. Back outside Pete's place I took more photos of her, went in and uploaded them and new text onto eBay to replace my old advert. I was about type the words "*white* VW van" when I stopped, my fingers curling over the keyboard.

I cancelled the advert. I walked, or maybe even ran, to the nearest Halfords, searched the store and eventually found the tiny section they had reserved for non-white car paint, and stuffed about thirty cans, of every available colour, into a basket. The checkout woman looked so alarmed I thought she would call the manager – but after staring a second she carried on beeping my stuff through. I guess a purchase was still a purchase. I left with three bulky plastic bags full of spray paint.

Outside Pete's place I set to work. I covered every square millimetre of that van with the most lurid, ridiculous, showy, loud, clashing colours I could pour on. I painted spirals, stars, peace signs, rainbows, ringed planets, fucking elves, and gnomes on mushrooms. People stared of course. Curtains wafted. Passing men in white vans slowed down and gave me a very serious look-over. Some yabbered into mobile phones.

I didn't care. I'd never felt better in my life.

I went inside the house and packed every bag I had with as many of my possessions as I could fit in, loaded up the van, left the rest and headed for the M25. I got up Shostakovich's Eighth Symphony on the iPod, *The Rite of Spring,* Miles Davis, *Soft Machine 3,* the New York Dolls, Yes's ridiculous *Tales from Topographic Oceans,* and the poor old Upstarts. I sang along to it all, howling like an idiot. I hurled my baseball cap out of the window. I smiled and waved at everyone I passed. I slowed down for crossing pedestrians. I gave buses a friendly toot. I shouted "You're very welcome here" at anyone I thought looked vaguely foreign.

I'd hardly got out of Chingford before the first white van started following. It was soon joined by another. By the time I was on the M25 there were three tailing me. One got up alongside and the capped passenger took a photo of me. On a relatively uncrowded stretch of the M3 they tried to force me onto the hard shoulder. But a police car started shadowing us and they pulled back.

Past Farnborough, a small flotilla got on my tail. The motorway at that point was packed, so there wasn't much they could do except try to keep up. The slip roads from Basingstoke onto the M3 disgorged a dozen or more vans. Again, all they did was follow me, talking – no doubt to each other and to more distant van men – into their mobiles as they watched me.

By the time I got onto the A-roads to Frome I was being followed by a whole fleet of white vans, at least twenty, chunking out a whole section of tarmac in my wake. I expected some sort of attack – heading me off, barging into me, as in the movies – at some point, but nothing happened. They simply kept following.

I texted Natasha to tell her I was coming, and why: I wanted to join Rama's colony; I claimed sanctuary in it; I didn't want our relationship back; I was desperate. I told her I was already close by and that unfortunately a whole attack squadron of white vans was tailing me, and the colony should get ready for them. Hopefully my email and text of a few days ago had put them on guard anyway. If I was leading these maniacs to the colony, they would have found it sometime in any case, and this way at least the colony couldn't suffer a surprise attack. Not that I knew what peaceful hippies would do faced with a barbarian invasion. But the bottom line was: I was desperate; I wanted to be on *their* side, Natasha's and Rama's, the right side, wanted to be *that* James, not the Pete-created "Jim" I had come so near to becoming.

I found the narrow lane that led to the colony and swung along it as fast as I dared. The white vans were now a tail whipping in my wake, one I couldn't possibly lose. Twilight was settling in and their headlights flicked on, dazzling me in my mirror.

I almost despaired of finding the drive to the house itself, which I remembered led at right angles from the lane, after a gate. But all at once looming out of the dusk was a huge painted sign saying "Ksantiloka", the name the colonists had given their community, across a background of rainbows, lotuses and blue krishnas. There had been a scrappily painted sign there on my first visit; this one, luckily, was an unmissable upgrade.

I raced along the drive and curved round towards the house itself, my heart lifting in hope. The trail of white vans was still whirling after me. I texted Natasha, to say I was here – but so were our enemies.

"Just come to the door," she texted back. A little uncommunicative, but then she probably knew it was no time for nice chatter.

When the house itself loomed into view, what I saw – even in my headlights – gave me a shock. The whole front of the house was draped in a huge mural, painted onto stitched-together sheets, with a massive central tree, cavorting Pagan gods, the Mother Goddess, planets, moons, rainbows, whales and spiralling psychedelic patterns. The statues in the garden seemed to have multiplied, with additional Shivas, goddesses, Pans and other figures with horns that, it struck me, were quite menacing.

The front door opened with a tinkle of wind chimes as I ran towards it. Three figures emerged through the lozenge of light – I made out Natasha and the thin figure of Rama, but I didn't recognise the third. I ran up to them. The third figure held out his palm flat towards me in a halting gesture.

He had extremely long hair decorated with gold and silver emblems, and multiple sets of heavy-looking beads draped over a kaftan.

"Just hold it mate," he said.

Both Natasha and Rama smiled but looked quickly away from me.

"You can't come in here," said the man.

"What...?"

Behind me a van whirled into the driveway scattering shingle. Pete got out, shot me a brief contemptuous glance and went and stood in front of his vehicle. He seemed to be carrying something under his arm. Then, it seemed, all the other white vans that had been chasing me slammed into the forecourt.

Capped, white-T-shirted, St George-crossed men climbed out and stood on the shingle in a sort of phalanx.

"You can't come in," said the man again. I stared at Natasha.

"We call him Guru-ji," she said. "He's our leader, now." She still wouldn't look at me for long.

"You come with your van, bringing all these other vans. You can't come in. You're not welcome here. Your kind is not welcome. Your mind is impure. You bring bad karmic effects."

"What..? What are you talking about? I bring what? Bad... *My* kind?" I shouted. "I've come to join you. I'm not any part of that." I waved at the assembled vehicles behind me.

"You're too old, for one thing," said Natasha. "It's a new rule."

"It's pretty much decided, I'm afraid," added Rama, nodding as if at the reasonableness of his own statement, arms crossed. "We told him a bit about you and he weighed up the pros and cons. The line has to be drawn somewhere. We have to be certain who to trust, these days? And we can't run the risk of... infiltrators."

"But how old's your Guru-ji? He doesn't look a day under fifty. And how pure's *his* karma? Come on – let me in." The gang behind me seemed to be getting fidgety. Pete's dog Elvis was out of his van now and advancing, growling.

"He's beyond age," said Natasha. "And his karma is pure, I assure you. His aura says it all. Anyway, there *have* to be rules," she said, with an edge of desperation. "That's the only way we can survive. Guru-ji has taken us from what we were to a new stage, so that we can stand against... against *that*." She nodded at the men and vans ahead of her.

"Natasha... I wanted to join you. I want to be on the

right side. I'm not after anything else. I'm not an 'infiltrator'. Where am I to go, then?" I turned round and now I saw what my old friend Pete had under his arm. It was a flag, and he was unfurling it: a St George cross, red on white, but the four ends of the cross were turned back on themselves to make a swastika.

David Penn's short stories have appeared in the magazines Midnight Street, Whispers of Wickedness and previously in Theaker's Quarterly Fiction, and his poems in Magma, Smith's Knoll and the Poetry School anthology I Am Twenty People (Enitharmon, 2007). He lives in London, where he also works as a librarian.

The Night They Sacked New Rome

Elaine Graham-Leigh

At the end of the passage a line of light shone from the solar, as if the boy had left the VR console on again. That young man was too used to the mansion's steady supply, that was his trouble, too long away from the power cuts. The Governor shook his head and opened the door. The curtains were drawn against the sunset, but none of the lamps were lit. The console was paused on its start screen, casting a blue and green haze onto the huddle of food wrappers around its base. The chair in front of it was empty; so was the sofa, the rug in front of it rucked as if someone had got up in a hurry. On the wallscreen, the new message alert blinked. The air was close, and still, and quiet. There were no sirens here at the back of the mansion, no smoke or shouting, just the hum of the heat extraction system, in and out like breathing. Then the shadows shifted, and clarified, and there were three men there.

Three men, looming in the dimness in the white uniform of the streets; the tunics and tight, half-length trousers glimpsed from a glider window; muscles slick in blue-black arms; raised chins and that challenging, powerful, powerless gaze. Three of them, here where they had no right to be, no reason to be, where their existence was so out of the place he could almost think that they must be VR. But no VR could capture the scent of them, the hint of spice that was the smell of narrow alleys, overlain with cheap body spray and sweat.

He blinked, taking them in. They were an odd embassy, from the riots to the government of New Rome, but perhaps there was no one else to send. He would say that the youth were manipulated by shadowy elders when it suited the speech, but he had never necessarily believed it. Behind them, the boy was leaning against the back wall with his sullen face on, lower lip pouting like a child wanting punishment. He tried to catch his eye, at least look the question of what they were doing here, how they had got in, but the boy kept his gaze on the floor. The three men were silent. Was it a message? An attempt to negotiate? A surrender? They would hardly put themselves in his power for anything else, yet there was the faintest prickle of unease, like sea spray landing on his skin. He looked at them and realised that he would have to think of something to say.

It was not usually a difficulty of his. Born to the lectern, his family used to call him, as thousands of years ago they might have said, to the purple. At school, on the island before the war, he could always win debates, always see the right words stretched out in a glimmering thread between him and his victory. Afterwards, homesick and cold at the Academy in Heidelberg, it was no longer effortless, but with a lost year to make up he was working harder in any case. He had still been one of the handful of stars, the ones who were going places, who would have been the future leaders of the empire if there had been any empire left to lead. In Des Moines once, in his first job in the capital, one of the Three Hundred ruling council praised him, in public, for an excellent speech, and that was before he had aides to write it for him. Of course, there wasn't so much call for speeches in New Rome in these days, now it was no longer the centre of the Terran Empire; now that there were no longer any people here who mattered.

They were standing very close together, grouped as if for defence. The tallest was in the middle, the other two flanked him where bodyguards would have been, if they'd been professional or disciplined. The closest one was very young, the childish roundness of his face accentuated by the puffiness of bad food. The tattoos swirling up his right arm looked new enough for soreness, pink outlining the black on the dark brown of his skin. His soft features were contorted into a ferocious scowl; weakness, trying to look tough. In the dimness he couldn't see the other as clearly, only that he had what he thought of as a North African nose, and that despite the heat he was wearing a woolly hat, pulled down low over his forehead.

The middle one was a little older than his acolytes and bulkier, with the bulkiness of muscle, not fat. The leader, he supposed, although he wasn't sure the rioters even had them. He looked at him, sternly, scornfully, who were they, to think of coming here? He put all of that into his tone and still, when he broke the silence, it felt like a surrender.

"What is this? A deputation?"

He would have expected shuffling and mumbling, the sullen refusal to engage that he got from the boy when he told him off. But the middle one met his gaze, with those wide, black, unknowable eyes. His voice was surprisingly high-pitched, slurring over the rapid street patois that was English mixed with little bits of governmental Latin, but so deformed and confused he could hardly understand it as either.

"Na, na, frat," the middle one said. His hair hung in long ropes over his shoulders. He flicked it back and folded his arms in front of him, gripping his elbows in a gesture that shouldn't have been threatening. "Na, you got it wrong." There was a shade of amusement, incredibly, in his tone, as if he was the equal of the Governor, as if he were winning. "We jus' lookin' around, ent we?"

"Looking around?" He put all the generations of patrician disdain into his voice, sounding the "g" the young man had dropped. "Do you have business here, or are you just trespassing?"

The middle one smiled, and the curtains behind him bellied out in the breeze. Past the terrace, beyond the gardens, the sea muttered against its wall like a distant crowd. If the wind got up it might overtop it tonight, the tide running through the lower garden, sowing the ground with salt. It wouldn't get into the upper garden, or anywhere near the mansion itself, but it was still a reminder, a down payment on the greater storm that was coming. A promise that one day, indeterminate but inevitable, the waves would break over the island for a final time and cover it for good.

It was the battle that did the damage, in the civil war when the officers who would become the Three Hundred overthrew the imperial government and brought the Terran Empire down. He remembered the shelter beneath the big house, the plumes of concrete smoke floating out every time it shook, his aunt clutching him and screaming. Among the noise and the dust, they hadn't known then that one of those blasts destabilised the pilings that fixed the island to the sea bed. Or that unseen, it would start to give way, so slowly that it would be years before they realised that they were slipping into the Med, with repairs beyond their resources the only possible remedy. He didn't know which blast it had been, nor even if it had been one of the strafing runs or the depth charges that had done the damage. His memories of the whole campaign were confused, shattered into fragments of recollection like the flakes of wreckage that still washed up on the beaches after every storm. He remembered Aunt Livia shrieking, the house shaking, and one, calm moment before it started, himself on the dock behind the house, the siren drowning in the drone of the government flyers as they fled away north over his head.

He checked the reports on the levels every day, not because he was hoping that they would tell him a different story, but because it was his responsibility. His ancestors had been among the first to come here to work for the Terran imperial government, two hundred years ago when the island was first built to be the capital of the great Terran Empire, the ancient centre of the Terran power that stretched across the stars. They had come and they had stayed, and even though others had come and gone, even though the Empire had fallen, the colonised planets set free to go their own way and the Terran government reformed in Des Moines, he had come back. He was still at his post, doing the honourable thing; holding the island up.

The rioters, the people of city slums, they didn't have the same connection to the place. How could they? They'd come across from Africa to work and though they'd stayed too, they didn't understand what it stood for. It was like the boy. Tell him about the Terran Empire, about human civilization standing equal to the great races in the galaxy, about Latin ringing out across the light years, and he'd yawn and slope off to the VR console. They filled the alleys with their African music and the smells of their African cooking, clinging to the traditions of places they'd left generations ago, that many of them had never seen. He was sure the boy had never left New Rome in his life, how could he ever have afforded to? They didn't understand what New Rome meant, what it had stood for, what it could mean again. They were just barbarians, vandals, destroying mindlessly, because it was there, because they hated what they didn't understand.

The middle one was smirking at him, slouching. Behind them, the boy was looking away, pretending to be bored, pretending he could be in control of any situation, if only he could be bothered. Such effort he put in, to save his face. He supposed the closer you were to shame, the more you had to fight against it.

"Well," he said, "if you've come here with nothing to say..."

The only way to end that sentence was "I will call security" but he was suddenly aware that he didn't want to, that it felt like weakness, a misstep, like standing on a dock that felt solid but then starting tipping and sliding beneath his feet.

With the riots of the last three days, the city police had had more calls, he was told, than they had ever had before, so much he'd had to order them to stop responding. There were just not enough of them to protect the housing and the remaining commercial districts, and they had to be practical. They had few enough corporates left, the prestige of the New Rome heritage seemed to mean less and less, and if they lost them, what would he have to bargain with? What case could he make for any funding at all, never mind his plans? People had to understand that hard choices had to be made, and he, who did understand, had to make them for them. Yet, he had a swift picture of a sweating householder, yelling "I'll call the police" from an upstairs window at a mob of grinning, rope-haired youths, craning up a dirty street for help that never came.

"Trespassin'!" The youth on the far side pushed up his cap, turning so that the dim light fell across the pimples on his forehead. He giggled. "Yeah, we trespassin'!" His eyes under the woollen brim were wide and unfocused, as if he were high. He bent to the table in front of the sofa, picked up the controller. "You got some good shit here, frat!"

He waved in wild circles in the direction of the screen, fortunately so fast that the sensors couldn't react.

"Put that down!" He didn't mean to say it but he couldn't help it, it seemed so egregious, so ridiculous, that this youth, this yob from the streets should be here, in his mansion, brandishing his tech like it was a weapon. He glanced at the middle one, as if expecting him to control his minion, but he didn't. The one in the hat swung the controller round again, giggling. "Wooooo!"

"I said, put that down!"

He took one angry step towards him and stopped, looking at the middle one's hand flat on his chest.

"Better not, frat," the middle one said.

He was almost exactly his height, standing so close the Governor could feel him breathing. The skin of his throat between the open neck of the white tunic was beaded with sweat, his nose and cheeks shiny with it, but his breath was even and regular, the breath of a young man, in control. He had a scar just above one eyebrow, curving down the line of his eye socket, tightening the skin at the corner of his eye, pulling down the lid like half a wink. He smelt of cloves and of the dark brown reek of the drug they all smoked, seeping from his hair and his skin. The pressure of his fingers against his shirt front was steady, a little damp. The Governor met his gaze and for a moment it was as if he stood outside himself, looking down, wondering that all the choices and all the chances in Des Moines had brought him here, to a windy night on New Rome and a young man's hand on him.

It wasn't very surprising, really. He had worked hard for his positions in Des Moines but it had never been his place, the ideology of the Three Hundred had never been his. Much of what they stood for was right: the primacy of humans on Terra over the colonies, let alone aliens, the importance of stability, respect, order. Democracy only worked after all if you had good enough communications to make sure people voted the right way, and after the chaos of the civil war no one could disagree with the need for strong government. But the way they turned their backs on the Empire, refused to rule the colonies, refused to take up the tradition and responsibility of all that glorious history; that he couldn't accept. It was dishonourable, when it came down to it. He couldn't set aside his love of the Empire so easily. And so he'd watched the promotions, the plum assignments go elsewhere, until the Governor of New Rome had had enough of the island and they needed someone to fill his place. He would, after all, really understand the culture of the place, they said, and there it would matter much less that he didn't have, and was never likely to have, a wife.

At the back of the room, the boy moved, shuffling to one side so that he was half hidden in the doorway, like a creature come in from the sea.

"So," the Governor said to the middle one. "You're trespassing." He kept his voice calm, just tinged with sarcasm, as if he were secure on an Olympian height they would never reach. "What do you expect to get out of it? Is it for bragging, or is this just a robbery?"

The young man stepped back a pace. He held up both hands in surrender, as if acknowledging a mocking hit.

"Hey, we might jus' rob your shit, but na" ...a shrug... "this is about sendin' a message."

The Governor looked around the room, mimed the absence of hidden multitudes. "A message? To whom?"

"To you, frat!"

That had nettled him, he could tell, and he was fleetingly pleased to have got to him, to have scored a point, however unwise it might be. But then, he'd never been much of a believer in conciliation.

"To you, an' your security, an' your cops, an' your ministers, an' everyone else who think they c'n push us around. We ain't takin' that no more. We stand up. We're the ones in charge now, frat, an' you work f'r us. This? This shit here? This is us showin' it."

At that, he was angry as well. How dared they? How dared they? In his mind's eye he saw himself, denouncing them from a great height, as if he'd grown ten feet tall, every word ringing out as clearly as if he had spoken.

Three days of breaking into buildings and burning flyers and you think you run the island? You think you have the skills? The only way, the only way this island stays above the tide is if we convince the government to pay for it, and the only way we do that is if enough corporates are interested in siting here that it might, just might pay them back some day. Do you think you and your little friends here can negotiate that? Do you have a better plan? You demonstrate for better wages, for free doctors, for a new school, precisely because you don't understand that if the corporates think they will have to pay for these things then they won't come, if they think they won't have a compliant workforce, they won't come, and then there will be no wages, no food, no dry land for anybody. You riot because you say security fired on you, but what do you expect? What did you think was going to happen? I have to do what's best for the city, whether you like it or not.

They would slink out, abashed; the riots would be over; he would have saved the city. He felt the pride of it expanding in his chest, pushing out his rib cage like a deep breath, rooting his feet on the floor so that he felt that he was indeed growing taller. He would be powerful, he would have proved it. Everyone would see it, from the government in Des Moines to the boy. And the boy... the boy would come out from the curtain, he would meet his eyes, and give him the awed expression he deserved, but had only ever seen once, on the night they met.

It had been one of the evenings when he'd dismissed his aides and had the driver take him alone into the town. He liked to get the feel of the place, take the temperature of the streets, he said. He had never known what they thought it meant, though the driver knew better than to talk. They'd cruised slowly through the shopping district and turned into the Via Centrale, the long road that had once been the artery of the artistic district but which now bisected the worst of the slums. The boy had been hanging around with a little knot of others on a corner, under a billboard light. He remembered how, while the others had hung back in the shadows, the boy had been balancing on the broken kerb, the light shining beatifically on his white tunic and curled black hair. He'd flung his arms out, gesticulating, laughing at something one of the others said, and as he had turned towards the glider his face had been lit for a moment, as if by a halo, with the fading echo of that smile.

He'd told the driver to stop, opened the window as the boy slouched over. He hadn't been as practiced in his lines as many of the others, his "You lookin' f'r comp'ny" came out more like a challenge than an invitation. He didn't know how long it had been since the boy's first trick, they didn't tend to talk about his past. But when, in the glider on the way back to the mansion, he told him who he was, his "No shit!", that was real. It was more than a year since he'd moved in, he was hardly really a boy any longer, although with his sullenness and his little ways, he still seemed like one. The Governor hoped the boy wasn't too alarmed by the trespassers; he didn't need to be. He would handle it.

He took a breath to begin, chin up, feeling the clarity flowing through him like the start of a good speech. Then he thought that perhaps, after all, he wouldn't lower himself to talk to them; they wouldn't understand, and what was the point in bandying words with rioters? They might argue back, and that would be unfortunate. It was better to be direct.

"I don't care what you think you're doing here," he said. "You have nothing to say. It's time for you to leave."

He unclipped his communicator from his belt and held it up. He was expecting them to leap at that, to try to stop him, to run out. He had his finger curled on the panic button, ensuring he could get his message out regardless of how quickly they moved. He was ready, but they did nothing. The middle one just went on looking at him with that knowing expression, that air of waiting for him to discover something that they already knew. But there was nothing that they knew. He flipped the communicator on and pressed for the head of mansion security.

"Marcus?"

There was a faint hum from the communicator, like the beginning of a connection when the comms system was slow, then nothing. He tried again, trying to keep his face authoritative.

"Marcus, come in."

In the silence, a wave splashed onto the sea wall and fell back, hissing.

"Security? Security, come in."

He found himself looking at the middle one,

ridiculously, as if he had answers, as if he could explain what was happening, even while he was still calling.

"Security? Marcus?"

The middle one reached out and plucked the communicator from his hand.

"They ain't comin', frat," he said. He sounded almost sympathetic, as if he understood how it was to be let down by your subordinates. Perhaps he did. "They ran away. They'll tell you they had to respond to some call or some shit, but they ran away from us. Did you not think how we got in? It only left the surveillance an' the locks."

There was a missing piece there, an element of explanation left still unexplained. Only the surveillance and the locks? It didn't make sense, but more urgent was to impose his authority. They had got one up on him, he had to acknowledge, with the absence of security. He had to get it back.

"Security may be out of reach now, but it's only temporary. They will be back and I will restore order, I promise you that. You'll all be caught and you'll all be punished. If you think this is more than a..." He'd said "temporary" already, but couldn't think of a synonym. "A... a temporary upset, you're kidding yourselves."

The middle one nodded, considering.

"Yeah, that may be. But they ran away fr'm us. They won't forget that, an' neither will we. So maybe we'll win, an' maybe we'll sink, but before we let you turn our home into some outdoor work camp, you've a fight on your hands."

He pushed a rope of hair back over his shoulder.

"Alrigh', let's go. C'm on." He gave the one in the hat a shove towards the door, relieving him of the controller at the same time. "Present fr'm the Governor? I'll hold onto that." Then he looked over the back of the room, where the curtains fluttered in the breeze from the sea. Where the boy was.

"What about you, frat?" he said to the boy. "You c'ming?"

Outside, another wave broke over the sea wall. The boy was still in shadow, his expression invisible. The Governor waited for him to ask what he meant, deny any suggestion that he would leave his home, his comforts, everything he gave him. Him. If he would only look at him, if he could only speak to him, but there was only the sound of the surf, drowning everything else like static.

"Yeah," said the boy.

He walked across the room, past the VR console he'd bought for him, the detritus of the snacks he'd shipped in for him, wearing the trousers and the fitted shirt he'd given him only a week before. He stopped beside the middle one and the middle one clapped him on the shoulder. "D'you wanna do it?" The boy shrugged. He still hadn't met the Governor's eye. There was a pause, then, "Alright. Get goin'," the middle one said. "There's jus' this one las' thin'."

"It's not personal," the middle one explained to the Governor. "It's jus', well, we know this is our island now, we know there ain't nowhere we can't go, but we gotta send that message, ain't we? Everyone's gotta know. It's like, all that imperial shit you like so much, innit? Power of symbolism, an' stuff. You make like you're the Roman empire, and we're like the people that sacked the city. So, it's gotta be done."

He leaned back a little, as if taking a run up without moving his feet. The muscles of his shoulder rippled as he brought his arm back, slow enough that the Governor could admire the curve of his elbow, and the grace of his fist as it drove towards him; slowly, slowly, and then not slowly at all.

The blow landed square on his chin, snapping his

head back, rocking him on his heels so that he lost his balance and fell heavily onto the floor. In the sudden change of perspective, he found himself noticing the dust on the rugs underneath the furniture where the cleaners must have been skimping, a discarded drink bottle, an empty packet. There was also the spare screen controller, solid and heavy. Heavy enough to be a weapon. Carefully, through the throbbing in his face, he started to edge his arm towards it. A sandled foot appeared in his vision, just above his hand. He stopped moving it and turned his head so that he could look upwards. The middle one's face was blurred, little more than a dark shape over him. The voice when it came was clear and far away.

"Don', or we'll really have to hurt you. You stay down, old man."

He lay on the floor for a long time after they'd left. The VR console switched itself off after a while and the room was very dark, with only a line of dimness between the curtains where the wind had blown them apart. Soon security would creep back and pretend they had never deserted him, that it had all been a horrible accident. They would round up some youths that they would call the ringleaders of the riots, and they would punish them, whether they were actually guilty or not. He would go on fighting for corporate support, for government funding, and maybe he would get it. They might repair the pilings, as a cheaper alternative to a new flood of refugees. He would pretend he had forgotten this, that it was unimportant. He might even, once everything had died down, have his driver take him down again to the streets.

It was unimportant, whatever the young man had said. There were no cameras here that they could get at. There were no images, no proof. No one would ever be able to boast of it, that they had sacked New Rome, but they had done so all the same. He knew now that it would never be great again; that he would never be more than the governor of a poor, neglected shanty town that had once, before his time, been a wonder of the world. They would come and get him up, and bandage his head, and fuss around him to make up for their weakness. They would never know that there would be some part of him felled here forever, that even when he was retired to some continental retreat, safe and dry with a view of the mountains and soft-footed, deferential aides, he would still be here. He was always going to be here now, preserved like an ancient relic, fixed as if in amber on the dusty rug, with the bruise on his cheek and defeat breaking over him like waves.

Elaine Graham-Leigh is a writer and campaigner based in London. When not bringing down the system from within, she writes speculative fiction and has had previous stories published in Theaker's Quarterly Fiction, Jupiter SF, Bewildering Stories and The Harrow. Her website: www.redpuffin.co.uk.

Anathema: The Underside

Chris Roper

The settler limped across the cracked earth, following the moon as it rose to mantle the valley in silver. A coarse wind lashed his face and made his eyes water. He leaned into it, worn boot soles flapping as he shuffled forwards, dragging a dirty canvas sack that left a trail of darkness both vivid and terrifying in the moonlight.

After a while he stopped to empty his boots of pebbles and check the wound on his ankle. The rag was caked but dry and this soothed him, made him thankful the flow had slowed. He untied the rag and smelled it and it was rusty and raw and this also soothed him for it meant there was no rot in there.

A great silence fell upon the land and the settler sensed that he was close. From within his tattered jacket he withdrew his mother's pocket watch and scrutinised its markings under the limp light of the moon. Half past one. Another half hour or so and he'd reach the thickened cluster of trees on the horizon and be rid of his burden for good. He replaced the watch in its threadbare enclosure and patted it safely away.

Onwards the settler stumbled, wary and relentless. Near the forest's edge he caught a shadow in the air; it moved slowly, a great wingspan sweeping arcs across the starless sky. It flew under the moon in frightening silhouette – a lammergeyer, come hunting for bones of the lost. It swooped low, curious, then veered away into the darkness. He heard the current of wind in its feathers and it was gone, reabsorbed by the night.

If God were watching he kept awfully quiet in the darkness of the valley floor, and in no shadow or scrap of light could his presence be inferred.

God isn't in this place and never was, the settler thought.

Finally, he arrived at a knot of leafless trees where a noxious burning smell permeated the air. There was no fire or smoke, but his underside knew what burned and the thought chipped at his resolve.

He straightened his back and stretched, examining the boundary he must cross. A mist lay on the forest floor and beyond the first trees he could see nothing of its interior. That he would get lost in there didn't frighten him, for he knew the signs to seek, but his strength was failing. The wound in his leg throbbed and when he loosened the rag, blood coursed into his boot. He unwrapped it, wrung out the excess, and bound it again.

"It won't do no good bleeding in that place."

The settler tensed, shocked at how unprepared he was.

"I said it won't do no good bleeding like that if you mean to cross the mist."

The voice was throaty and heavily accented. The settler twisted left and right, surveying the earth and trees until his eyes rested on a man propped against a tree trunk lying half-in and half-out of the mist.

The man was naked and smeared with the gritty blackness of charcoal. His skin glistened in patches of pale blue, his face lost in a greying beard and the matted unwashed hair of a wild man. In his right hand, he held a wooden semi-spherical cup filled with a milky liquid that glowed in the half-light.

"Who are you?" asked the settler.

The wild man's eyes were white with cataracts, and, had he not pointed, the settler wouldn't have known they surveyed the sack.

"You hurtin' to take that into the forest?" the wild man asked.

The settler wound the sack's leading rope around his left hand. "That's my business," he said.

The wild man shrugged or shivered.

For a while they were both silent, lost in a void that neither would reveal but which made them kin under the gaze of those responsible for it. After some moments, the wild man began again. "You don't want to take blood in there with you, traveller." The viscous liquid in the cup rippled as he spoke.

"My business is blood."

"Not your own it ain't."

The settler noticed for the first time that the wild man's legs were missing. Just above each knee, the skin had healed thick and bulbous around a splintery end of thighbone. The amputation had been awkward: the bones resembled snapped branches.

"I lost them in there," the wild man said, his voice thick with phlegm as if regurgitating something foul from inside him. "But I got out. Got what I came for too." He choked a laugh and swallowed. "You bleed in there, traveller, and you'll be wishing you'd never been born. I escaped, but paid dearly. Now there ain't no way for me to get home. This here draught been my only sustenance, but they can't touch me no more." The white eyes were frozen in their sockets.

The rope in the settler's hands quivered. An awareness of his mother's watch, ticking to the beat of his heart, forced his thoughts from the cripple and back to the task ahead.

"I best be leavin'," the settler said.

"You seem good-intentioned, traveller. Here. Take

the draught." The wild man nodded at the cup. "Drink it quick and don't puke it up. It tastes bad but might just help when you've crossed. I ain't going to need it anymore, anyways."

The wild man crossed his right arm over his chest and held the cup up to the moonlight. His hand trembled with the effort and the settler took it, save it fall to the ground, unsure of its importance but somewhat infected by the gravity with which the wild man treated his tincture.

He inspected the cup, watched the milky sap gurgle around the flaking wood. It seemed too flawless for this place, too pure.

"Where'd you get it?" the settler asked.

The wild man groaned. His chest heaved slowly, expelling puffs of warm breath, each less voluminous than the one before. He seemed to decompose, his cadaverous limbs thinning and sinking as if being reclaimed by the land on which he sat. His lips quivered, and with effort, he sputtered out some final words.

"I found it," he said, "it was where she said it be..."

"What is it?" asked the settler, unwilling and unable to question the man's transformation for this was the way he'd imagined things would be in that place.

The wild man didn't answer but the wind did, abrading the land with an icy dust that scratched bark and flesh alike. It whistled through the trees of the forest like the screams of dying children.

Mesmerised, the settler watched the wild man's skin shrivel to the veiny translucence of a fly's wing, then flake away like old varnish; the hair on his head and of his beard blew away in wisps until all that remained was the brilliance of his skull and the jutting ends of thighbone.

The lammergeyer will eat tonight, the settler thought.

The wind subsided and he relaxed. He peered down at the cup and its contents, unsure of what he would do next. The forest beckoned with its creaking boughs, frozen mist, and myriad shadows that would never rest.

The settler watched the rumpled sack and he couldn't but think it was changing shape, that what was inside was awakening from a sleep so deep that only the richest of temptations would draw it from its slumber.

He placed the cup carefully on the ground and took out his pocket watch. He flipped the gold case open, its underside shimmering like a coin in a sunlit well. Engraved were five words in a script so aberrant in that place as to be like the scrawling of an ancient hand, yet they were his mother's words and the only words he could remember from the old world.

"You are everything to me."

Half past two.

He replaced the pocket watch, picked up the cup, and stood at the border of the forest. Something began nipping at his feet as he shuffled to keep warm and he stooped automatically to remove the affecting stones. But the ground by his feet was wet with blood, *his* blood. It streamed from the bite in his ankle and into the earth, reacting with the aridity of the soil and quenching its crumbling surface.

Ahead of him a funnel of mist as thick as an arm wound out of the forest and probed slowly towards him. The settler looked again at his boots and out of the spreading pool of blood emerged thin bony fingers the colour of ash, with long curving fingernails. They were small and languid, stretching and unfurling, blindly seeking the source of replenishment that spawned them.

The settler recoiled, sloshing some of the cup's contents over the side where it fell upon the fingers raking the topsoil. The ground hissed and the blood dried to a fine white dust; the fingers fossilised and blew apart, disintegrating in the wind until nothing remained but a white smear. The coil of mist retreated as slowly as it had it come.

The settler again took measure of the wild man's gift.

"What place is this that cannot stand a drop of this draught?"

A spot had dribbled down his forefinger and he could feel a strange power within it – an energy as rejuvenating as the forest was oppressive. An antidote to this land? It became all too clear in his mind's eye and he took the cup and settled it on his lips, tipped it back, and drank a tot.

The world opened up in all directions like the tearing of a veil, blinding him. The sap flooded his body, leaving him as charged as the plains under an electrical storm. It surged through his muscles and around the base of his skull where it tightened and tingled his scalp, then pooled in his ankle where it burned and faded away. The settler opened his eyes to the sinewy arms of the forest, feeling stronger than he'd felt in years.

He knelt on one knee and untied the crusty rag, knowing the wound was healed even before his eyes and fingertips attested to it.

Straightening, he stared at the maze of leafless trees with their gnarled roots undulating through the mist, and fancied he saw movement there. Had the sap improved his vision? Ephemera danced under arches of thorn, etched from darkness by such errant moonbeams as dared penetrate the canopy.

A wailing rose above the growl of the wind. Not a howl; although wild, it was not an animal sound. The settler pulled on the sack, tightened the noose and doubled up the knot, careful not to let the bag swing close to his body. He then slung it on the ground and picked up the wild man's cup.

"A man concludes his living when he believes nothing more can be done," the settler said, his black eyes boring into the heart of the forest. "But my purpose is so much more than the sum of my experiences." The trees leaned towards him.

"Suffering is all I know," the settler continued. "Suffering I can do. I'm good at it. Now it's time to give a little back."

He raised the cup in mock toast then put it to his lips and drank until it was empty. Then he licked it clean and tossed it aside, took up the slack of the rope and strode forwards, across the forest boundary, and deep into the mist.

The mysterious vapour carpeting the forest floor was as thick as spider webbing, but it parted from the settler's steps as if repulsed. Inside the forest, the stench of burning was crueller, choking him as he breathed, and the ground was an uneven mess of rocks, roots, and broken branches, making missteps frequent. There was no wind now just an arid cold cleaner and stiller than before.

Only one thought dominated the settler's mind: I must find the pit.

The silence broken by his footfalls was filled with a sense of frozen time, of action interrupted, that led the settler to believe he was being watched. Silhouettes skulked around the trees and would merge with the forest the moment the settler looked their way. Knowing what they wanted, he returned their faceless stares with a grim one of his own.

The animal in him, that rawness of man sprung raging from the land and tamed by reason and God and beauty, guided him unknowingly across the forest floor, and he slid into his blood-hot underside so easily in the darkness of that place that he could feel the atoms vibrating in his matter.

The wild man's sap rode unbridled through his veins, galvanising him. He roved like a beast, unafraid, no longer deterred by the mephitic air but sniffing out the way, his flared nostrils quivering, following the scent of decay to where it lay strongest.

Before long the settler began to feel tugs on the rope trailing the sack. He took this as a sign, and sure enough, he arrived at a clearing that was the beginning of a marsh. The ground beneath his feet lost its rigidity and he could feel clumps of gelatinous soil clinging to the flaps of his boots, the cold of it chilling his feet.

At the edge of the clearing, where moonlight poured in from above, he observed a margin of ancient trees surrounding what appeared to be a black lake, large and flat.

There was no water only a thick fluidity to the soil and a broiling, bubbling surface. Here the smell of the forest was at its most powerful. The settler had no doubt that this was the pit he sought.

The rope pulled on him from behind and he yanked it onto a mound of rotting weeds, pausing a moment to think and bolster his strength.

Gurgling, the surface of the pit rose and fell as if it were the lungs of a giant creature. It occurred to him that he knew not how long the sap would last, nor if it had sustained the wild man for so long given he'd escaped the forest and those that dwelt within it. He'd drunk all that remained, but he couldn't know how long it would defend him from the evils of that place.

The settler surveyed the pit and then the sack. He had to be sure and to be sure he had to open it and throw the contents in. In the pit there was no escape, not even for their kind. The pit was pure, a concentration so undiluted by light or goodness that even the moon was too frightened to illuminate anything below the surface.

The occultist had told him it would be this way. He remembered the exchange as if it had not been him but another taking part in it: the blindfold, the bunker, the smell of urine and faecal matter, the distant scuttling of rats along stone...

"The beings in the forest are attracted to it," she had told him, the weak voice betraying someone old and frail, though he could see nothing through the black cloth over his eyes. "They cannot break that connection. But they fear it. The pit has no bias toward what it spawned and what it did not. It simply is. It craves suffering. It feeds on it. *This* is the essence of evil. Once the suffering ends, it will die. All evil will die." The occultist paused to cough and spit, then she continued.

"It will consume everything it touches, benign or malevolent. The forest-dwellers revere its purity and relish being near it, but even they will not touch it."

"Where do they come from?" he asked.

"It shits them out," she said, her laugh like sandpaper on stone. "Like everything else in the world, what goes in must come out and what comes out is always changed. These forest-dwellers serve the pit by terrorising others – people, animals... And the pain serves to maintain it. Not that it is needed, of course – we cause enough hurt on our own. But these beings have nothing else to do, and as much as they fear the pit that brought them screaming into our world, like any child they seek its approval."

"So the dwellers are a kind of by-product?"

"In a way. Think of them as processed manifestations of suffering. The pit uses what it needs from that going in and regurgitates what it has no use for. The beings are excreta, nothing more. The energy lost from a reaction. They are the lowest form and the least pure. The pit exists to them as a perfect representation, one they aspire to. But they are spiteful, hateful and envious, and very dangerous. If you are not careful, settler, they will keep you in that forest and torture you forever."

"What must I do?"

"Take a keepsake of someone untainted by these things. Someone who loved you. Be sure to look at it regularly. Endure until you reach the pit. And whatever you do, do not throw anything in without watching it sink. You must be able to see it breach the surface, or you will be tricked."

"And what becomes of the thing I throw in – won't that create more?"

"That's the risk. You rid yourself of one, but... Well, whoever said lightning strikes the same place twice, eh?"

The recollection faded and the settler pulled the rope and the sack tumbled from the mound. Something was odd about its shape; it had grown fuller, more solid. The settler stepped back, watching the sack shudder and throb as if something were growing inside. The canvas stretched, and the contents rose in a column to the neck of the bag.

The settler felt eyes on him from every direction. He did not care for his life but wished only that he could end things there and exact some small vengeance on behalf of those he loved and who were now gone. He stole closer to the sack and grasped the rope dangling against it.

Fear did not take him but his hands shook as they slowly undid the knot and allowed the ends to fall. He waited, fists clenched, and his heartbeat ringing in his ears. The neck sagged and the canvas slid down the length of a manifest nightmare he hadn't fully understood until that moment.

His beautiful son, Isaac, pale and bloodied, stood still in the pile of rumpled canvas. His eyes were a bright and piercing blue and tears cleaned shiny trails down his cheeks. There was a look of earnestness on his face, of real, deep love; a yearning for his father so profound the settler choked on the overwhelming sadness that rose from that buried place so fast it nauseated him. It took him back to the farm with his wife cooking rabbit in the kitchen and him outside building the boy a tree house, the boy laughing while carrying the wood to be nailed until he took a splinter in the palm, crying until his father nipped it out and kissed the hand and the boy laughed again...

Before the settler the tiny arms lifted in a desire to be held and at once he mirrored this gesture, desperate for the sweet embrace between father and son. As they closed on one another the sun shone warmly on their smiles then just as quickly the sun vanished, and all was strange, cold, and barren.

The truth bore itself cruelly in the child's disfigurements. A deluge of repulsion swept the settler backwards on his heels as he noted for the first time the child's left arm was not an arm but a crude sewing of a leg, and the right leg a similarly rough graft of the left arm. The child resembled a broken doll awkwardly repaired by something with no knowledge of human anatomy.

All pretence gone, the child's smile twisted and tore at the mouth and hairline. From a mouth too large for its head, crammed with teeth filed to points, came a high-pitched screech that shattered the night and felt like needles driving through the settler's eardrums.

Time stopped. He was as the trees were – a prisoner of the evil in that place, rooted to that foul earth until such time as he would rot into it. He couldn't act, couldn't move.

The boy's limbs, severed by his axe under falling

tears once his son was gone and only the creature remained, were now reattached in spiteful mockery of the human form.

The creature teetered back and forth, one foot and hand gripping the soggy soil, the others clasped toes to fingers as if applauding the horror of its work. The head cocked to one side and blood seeped in red tears from the facial wounds to meet the flow from the sutures.

They might have stood there for an eternity locked in each other's gaze – one trying to recover action, the other wishing to sustain terror for as long as possible. It struck the settler that the sap was still in his system, and with it, a measure of hope, suspecting that the wild man's gift was the reason the creature hadn't attacked.

Even if it meant clutching the body of his son so desecrated and hurling himself into the tarry depths, he resolved to finish what he'd started. His time was at an end and he would have his revenge, and besides, how could he live now the truth of the sack had been torn open? It had been locked away like a bad memory and he'd been so absorbed in his task he'd forgotten to do the one thing that would prevent him failing: *remember*.

I remember.

The settler hurled himself at the horror and it fled, darting from his grasp and scuttling behind him, its screams drowning the crack of wood that broke his fall. A root had punctured his side, but the pain refreshed him and he did not care if it was mortal, so long as he could entice the creature from wherever it now hid before he bled his life away. The forest was a patchwork of shadows and moonlight slanting through the trees, but it would come for him again. They all would.

An almost inaudible screech in the distance was

answered by those of others much closer, invisible, but all around him.

The settler detached himself from the splintered root and pressed his hand to the warm hole in his side. Drops fell silently through his fingers and were absorbed by the earth. He knew the sap had lost its potency as it did nothing for the pain, nor did it accelerate his healing. Dread mounted inside him as the ground began to deform in subtle, covert movements.

The settler crawled away from the edge of the pit as the soil beneath him became stickier. The earth heaved and soil burst into the air, sprouting saplings of things so abhorrent they hurt to look at; they grew and contorted, snapping and hissing as they bore down upon him.

They held his ankles and wrists with saw-toothed claws that cut his flesh as he struggled. The darkness veiled their true forms and the settler was glad of it, fearful the sight of them would render him mad.

He knew what was to come next and would abide no part in the charade. As Isaac's savaged carcass began crawling up his body and breathed its hot meaty stench over him, he said, "Send me to hell if you want, creature, you're already in yours."

A fleshy hand and the rough sole of a foot pressed against the settler's cheeks. A glimmer of something benign and innocent flitted across the creature's black eyes, and the world collapsed...

...In a meadow wet with morning dew the settler lay. A child's laughter echoed in the distance. A woman glistened next to him, and his hand rested on the hump of her swollen belly. Someone chopped wood in a forest nearby. The child screamed. An axe whined through the air, the belly split open, and a sack of kindling turned blood red...

The settler hawked and spat in the creature's face.

Realising it could do no more hurt, it shouted in an ancient tongue and leapt aside, out of his vision.

They carried him to the pit. A destiny he'd fathomed the moment he saw Isaac's malformed body. The dwellers shook him viciously, cursing and spitting, urged on by screeches and bellows from the spike-toothed horror sewn up in his son's decaying flesh.

The settler refused to shut his eyes to the pain, to the foul salivations spraying from their mouths, listening only to the soil squelching underneath. He felt a change in momentum as he was swung back and then forwards, thrown in a parabolic arc whose apex seemed to reach the canopy of the trees where the sky was purple with the threat of dawn.

Then the odious reek from the pit and he was falling down, down, down, into the hole of the world.

The first sensation was that of his flesh searing, as if he'd fallen into magma. The tar made ingress into every orifice, flooding him with heat and death. Billions of lives, their histories lost and forgotten, imbued him with their despair, knowledge finding space where flesh had burned away. The memories of the dead spun around him in a blur, every agonising moment replaying like a picture reel. The details mutilated him, branded his bones with anguish until it was as much his own as those who had suffered it.

He glimpsed his own past and path to that moment, and the onslaught paused. The recognition of himself, his life, and the memories therein had caused time to slow.

And that's when he realised he was not alone in the dark.

The pit's foetal offspring had found him. They clawed as he sank, their prenatal instincts nothing but mindless rage and desperate hunger, driving them to lash at the intruder trapped in the amniotic filth that was their birthplace. Death came slow, picking its way through sinew and muscle as he sank.

Near the end a humming began. A low sustained tone behind his head. The settler let his neck fall and it hit something hard and glowing. He could not see the glow but could feel it, could picture it in his mind's eye: a branch or root of some sort. He sought for it, blindly snapping until his teeth broke. When a rush of cool liquid flowed over the ribbons of his tongue the settler recognised the sap in its freshest and purest form.

There was no sense of relief, no hope, no gratitude. Just a blind instinct to drink.

The liquid sped down his throat and into his stomach, along his intestinal tract, rising to engulf his lungs and his heart, his ears, nose, and eyes. He swallowed and swallowed, each gulp larger than the last, until he could drink no more. Gradually, the darkness receded, and the forms and sorrow dispersed.

Sated, limbs thick with muscle, he pulled on the golden bough that had rejuvenated him, raising himself up through the tar until he breached the membrane and emerged gasping into the putrid gas flowing over the pit's surface.

With eyes preternaturally sharp the settler followed the branch's path out of the pit and to its source, surprised to see the splintered root he'd fallen on before – one of many swollen roots that spread from the base of a tree whose top was lost in the canopy.

The settler could see *them*, too. They were watching him, waiting, unsure of what they saw. He could feel their uncertainty, their caution. They'd never known anything return once thrown in. They wondered if he'd been reborn. They wondered what he was, what connection he had to *father*, whether he was like them or something else... something worse.

The settler writhed up the side of the pit on his

stomach like a pale snake. They were around him and he could see their hideousness. He felt no fear. After coughing up remnants of the pit from his lungs he stood and surveyed himself. He was naked, white, and hairless. The goosebumps covering his flesh tingled with new senses, senses that would need time to understand and practice to interpret. His mind pulsed with that same noise that had come to him inside the pit yet was subsiding slowly into the sounds of the forest, falling in tone until he could hear the whispered voices, their language now a part of him as much as the sap.

A group of the creatures parted to allow Isaac's gore to limp forwards, drooling black saliva. The others retreated into the shadows, padding the ground like bulls, curiosity whetting their appetites. This arrhythmic rumble was to the settler a call to arms: a violent drumbeat which echoed the powerful beat of his heart.

Isaac stopped a few feet from him. Raising the leg which served as an arm and pointing the toes, it said, "What are you?"

The settler walked forward a few paces and the creature shivered. The lower foot and hand stamped the ground.

"What are you?" the thing repeated.

The settler felt its agitation as that of a dog smelling a meal it cannot have. He took another step forward.

"Why have you come?" the creature wailed, bouncing up and down, the teeth protruding in a grimace so severe it seemed to lack jaws. "Why have you come?"

The settler grabbed Isaac by the throat and at once the forest erupted, the dwellers shrieking and clawing at the ground, banging their heads against the trees so frustrated were they by the confusion rendering them impotent.

The father lifted his son, unmoved by the boy's cries for clemency, and let him dangle, kicking and flailing, to meet his eyes one last time. Then, with his other hand, he gripped the top of Isaac's head and twisted it, slowly, until it tore free from the neck, causing black jets to spurt into the night as if fleeing the violence so rendered.

He listened with equanimity to the clamour of the others and tossed the head into the pit. It dissolved almost immediately and the settler did the same with the body and again watched it disappear below the surface.

The settler turned to face the rest of the creatures, but they'd fled deeper into the forest. Undeterred, he straightened his spine, rolled back his shoulders, and drew in a great lungful of air. The sap flooded the length of every nerve, shearing his former self to leave only the atavistic state common to all things, living and dead.

He was anathema to them now, the manifest underside of the forest, and he swore to rebalance the scales even if it took him an eternity.

"I will find you all," the settler spoke to the creaking of the forest, "and you *will* go back to where you came from."

The old woman was sat clutching the sides of her wheelchair when the tall figure came into the meek light of the bunker, approaching like a supplicant bearing alms. She took the offering and placed it in the chest, observing the visitor with a sardonic smile.

The stranger wore a long antique overcoat buttoned up to the neck, and a battered beaver hat pulled low upon the brow. The old lady watched threads curling away from the hat's brim and wondered if it were the foulness of the bunker that did it or if it was the other odour beginning to pervade the cramped space between her and the visitor.

The eyes were blindfolded, as was her custom when meeting those she had not met before, only this time the entire face was covered in black cloth. She motioned the figure to sit but was refused by the raise of a gloved hand.

She knew the figure then, had always known. And she knew the game, too. Perhaps was the only one who did.

"The first rays of sunlight will render the forest a wasteland until the return of twilight," the woman's croaky voice said. "But, you know this already. What you don't know and what I've come to know is that the sand of that barren place in the midday sun holds a small, gold pocket watch. If you seek it out and remove it from that place you may have your vengeance."

She picked up a silver cigarette case from her lap, opened it, plucked a stained cigarette and put it in her mouth.

She struck a match against the bunker wall and touched the flame to the end of the cigarette. "Let the other side have a go now, eh?" she said.

But the figure had already vanished, its black footprints disappearing into the air.

Chris Roper is a copywriter living in London. He writes as much as he can in his spare time, exorcising horrible thoughts and bad dreams by committing them to paper. When not writing, he's admonishing himself for not writing, which in turn leads him to red wine and Asian holidays.

Fake Internet Reviews and the One Time It Was Okay to Buy Them

Stephen Theaker

For most people, it comes as a shock to hear that any author would pay for a fake review. It is such a clear betrayal of the relationship between the writer and the reader, and it seems so pointless! Perhaps you can trick someone into buying your book, but it's much harder to trick them into liking it, and when they realise how ropey it is they'll be unlikely to give you a second chance.

However, on Red Nose Day, 24 March 2017, it was okay to pay for fake internet reviews. We at *Theaker's Quarterly Fiction* took your filthy backhanders and gave rave internet reviews to books we had never read. The money went straight to Comic Relief without ever passing through our grubby hands.

This idea was inspired by all the dodgy reviews I've encountered over the last decade or two. They come in many varieties. Some, perhaps the most benign, come from the author's friends and family, and I suspect that the two reviews from 2002 of my second self-published novel – one saying it had "truly altered the course of humanity", the other describing "the comedy of Douglas Adams and Terry Pratchett multiplied by the story-telling of Frank Herbert and J.R.R. Tolkien" – might possibly fall into this category.

The website Authonomy positively encouraged boosterism among its participants, as they voted each other up onto the editor's desk for potential publication, and unfortunately some writers carried that attitude over to Amazon and Goodreads, where they gave each other glowing reviews, while giving every impression, of course, that they were complete strangers who had just happened to have read each other's books.

One author used a pseudonym to cheerfully recommend their own book on Amazon whenever the opportunity presented itself, only coming unstuck when they used the same pseudonym to post a real review that they shared publicly. Lev Grossman wrote Amazon reviews of his own book, and then wrote a famous magazine article about it. When I interviewed him years later he was a bit annoyed that people were still bringing it up. "I was very inexperienced," he said. "Suffice to say I would never do a stunt like that now." Not all authors regret it so much, or even stop when they are caught out.

Although those reviewers weren't being honest with their readers, in that they concealed their relationship to the authors, at least they were writing reviews of books they had probably read. They were mere hobbyists of literary deception, trying to game a system that presumably they thought was rigged against them. It's irritating when you notice it, but it's unlikely to have a major effect, especially in an age where we can all read the Kindle preview of a book before deciding whether to buy it or not.

A bigger problem is the industrial production of fake reviews in large numbers. About five years ago I was on Fiverr, looking at the comments received by a vendor who offered a book reviewing service. They offered to review books on their blog and "all book sites". One author mentioned their pen name when thanking the "reviewer" for a job well done. Being the kind of irritant that I am, I brought this up in a comment on the Amazon review in question. That led to the author emailing me as follows:

> "I did not pay for a good review. I paid for an honest review on a blog spot. You did not see the private comment page. However, that isn't the reason I am writing. After I received terrible comments on [book title] I rewrote and reedited it. It is very hard to be an author. Every bad comment and review is like a knife through the heart. And the truth is, that I don't have a strong educational background. But I know that I have a great deal to say, so I write. … But it seems as if I have collected an entire group of haters who want nothing but to see me fail."

I replied to say:

> "Sorry, but regardless of how you feel about your book, paying people to review it on Amazon is wrong. It is against Amazon's rules, and what's more it is utterly unethical. I'm afraid you'll continue to attract 'haters' as long as you get up to such shenanigans!"

I think their remarkably honest reply explains a lot about why some authors do this kind of thing:

> "I was devastated by the reviews on [book title] and did not know what to do in order to get people interested in reading the new edition. Let me just backtrack for a minute. I worked on that book for five years. I researched and wrote and researched and wrote. Many times I came home

from working nights and stayed up just to work on the book. Then I paid an editor who screwed me. He knew I knew nothing about grammar and he took my money and told me the book was in great shape. It took me over six months to save the money to pay him. Then the book went live and got terrible reviews. Mostly on grammar, but a few on content as well. I was distraught. I rewrote the content and was blessed to find a good editor. I need help. I made a mistake."

The author in question repeatedly said things to me like "I paid for an HONEST review", as if that mattered or made sense. Did they really think five dollars would be enough to pay anyone for the time it would take to read their book and write a review of it? Whether they are still paying for reviews or not I can't say, but the book currently has 683 five-star reviews on Amazon.com.

The "reviewer" replied to me too. They wanted it to be very clear that they weren't paid to review the book on Amazon, oh no! They were paid to review it on their own blog, and the Amazon review was a bonus! The reviewer seemed to think I had disparaged how much work they were doing, rather than addressing the point that being paid by the author to review a book is wrong in the first place. They also explained how it was that they could read an 800pp book in two hours, and commiserated with me over the fact that no publisher or author had ever paid me for my reviews.

(Which, now I think about it, I realise might mean that there were publishers paying her to do it too. Ugh.)

The two of them didn't think they were doing anything wrong. Other authors may not even realise that they have paid for such reviews to be mass manufactured on their behalf. An author friend of mine paid a not inconsiderable sum to a book promotion company, the unexpected result being that hundreds of obviously fake reviews appeared on Goodreads over the course of a few days. The profile photographs of the "reviewers" looked like they had been grabbed from dating sites, and many of the profiles were locked. A quiet email to Goodreads got many of those accounts deleted, but not all. And before they were deleted, I saw just how many other books they had reviewed.

I wish authors wouldn't get ensnared in this kind of thing, but save my real anger for the people who take advantage of the desperation you can see in the quotes above. The so-called editor. The so-called reviewer. The so-called promotional company. It makes me ill to see those fake reviews sitting there, fraudulently persuading good people to part with their hard-earned money. And yet...

I'm fortunate to live in a country where there's a safety net of sorts. If my freelance work dried up, we could probably get by for a while. But if the only way I could feed my family was to write fake reviews, wouldn't I do it? Could I write enough of them in a day to make a living? I can certainly admire the craft of a well-written fake review. Being able to write a review of something you haven't read is a literary skill like any other; it's just not one you want to see in action.

Luckily, I don't need to do it to support my children, but I had the idea of doing it for a day to help other children, to some small extent, in the UK and abroad, via Comic Relief. And so, on Red Nose Day, we did just that on the Theaker's Quarterly Fiction blog. We raised money for Comic Relief by casting aside our scruples, our principles, the very core of our being, giving books glowing reviews – without reading them! – for people who donated five pounds, dollars or euros to Comic Relief.

It was quite a challenge. David Quantick, who made up lots of his music journalism, gave advice on how to do it in his book, *How to Write Everything*. Make it look convincing, he wrote. It's good mental exercise. If he hadn't been to the show or listened to the album, the review would always be nice. I tried to bear those things in mind. (And by the way, his fake reviews appeared in the *NME*, a magazine I *worshipped* as a teenager. I spent the money from my paper round on the albums and shows praised in those pretend reviews.)

Here are the reviews we wrote on Red Nose Day, raising £100 for Comic Relief. But keep an eye out for those fake reviews that are not so charitably minded!

This article originally appeared in slightly different form as a guest post on Ginger Nuts of Horror, and it led to some of our biggest donations, so a big thank you to Jim and his crew! If you still fancy donating, feel free: the page is still up at https://www.justgiving.com/fundraising/corrupt-reviews-for-cash

---

Professor Challenger in Space by S.W. Theaker

Professor George Challenger is one of the classic characters of science fiction, although he has perhaps not outshone *The Lost World* to the extent that fellow Arthur Conan Doyle creation Sherlock Holmes has thrown all the books in which he appeared into the shadows. This novel is by a writer I definitely do not know personally, S.W. Theaker.

I am definitely not S.W. Theaker writing under a different name to trick you into buying his book, because that would be wrong. I read on his website that this book was originally written in the nineties, in the course of a couple of weeks. Whether that is true or not I can't say, since, as I previously explained, I do not know him personally and am definitely not him writing under a pseudonym, but it is difficult to believe given how extraordinarily good this book is.

Arthur Conan Doyle's belief in spiritualism is shown to be mistaken by sheer dint of the fact that his spectre has not emerged from the grave to shake this author by the hand and pat him on the back, in gratitude at having done so much with the character. Granted, descriptions of the lead characters' physical attributes are few and far between, the author possibly having got halfway through writing this novel before going back to look up their descriptions in the Conan Doyle stories.

But would the creator of Sherlock Holmes, that master investigator, who famously said that when the impossible has been eliminated, whatever remains, however improbable, must be the truth, would the creator of that character ever have considered removing Challenger's head and putting it onto a robot body? Of course not, because it takes the imagination of a true genius to think of something so radical, and that is what we have here.

Some reviewers, the kind to which you shouldn't pay attention, the haters, the slaters, the Johnny-come-laters, might complain that here Theaker just recycles Grant Morrison's *Doom Patrol* idea of the chief as a head on a plate, but pathetic literary trolls don't realise how ingeniously that allows the good professor to travel through the vacuum of space! Complainers and moaners might also wonder why everything in the book is so lightly described, as if it was written in a rush and the author just wanted to write the dialogue, but that's simply to miss the point of this novel's marvellously pulpy fun.

This book gets five red noses from me! *Howard Phillips*

Children of Eden by Joey Graceffa

Joey Graceffa is a very famous YouTuber, well known for his exceptional talent for playing video games without a shirt on and being very good-looking. Mysteriously, this is something that greatly appeals to young women, and after they bought his first book in droves – *In Real Life*, about his unreal life as a YouTube star, made the New York Times bestseller list – he has now written a novel.

And it must be his own work, because his is the only name on the cover. He really is very, very good-looking, you know.

As we can tell from the cover, the book contains male characters and female characters, and while sometimes their interests overlap, sometimes they don't, and so their pictures are not completely aligned. This is very subtle.

Rowan is the girl, the second child of her family in a world where families are only allowed one child. After being hidden away for sixteen years she escapes for a night of adventure, but it's dangerous, because she has special kaleidoscope eyes.

She is a child of Eden, but cannot live there, and so the book asks us all a profound question: can it really be Eden if its own children are not allowed to live there? The answer must be no, because Eden should be a perfect place to live, and who could be happy in a place where your children are hidden away?

Although, if Adam had

been happy in the original Eden, would he have wanted an Eve? If Eve had been happy in the original Eden, would she have wanted an apple? So perhaps it makes perfect sense to call this unhappy place Eden.

Many adventures follow, and characters develop in interesting ways, some becoming happier, some becoming sadder, but always letting the reader see what is happening.

I would give this book five red noses. *Stephen Theaker*

(There is a real review of this book by someone who actually read it – and loved it – elsewhere in this issue!)

Letters to Barack Obama from Handsworth

Remember what it was like eight years ago? A new president was in the White House, but everything was so different. The mood was hopeful, we thought the future would be better than the past, and that is reflected in this book of letters and drawings that were sent from Handsworth, a gloriously multicultural part of Birmingham, to Barack Obama. The librarian who put the project together was nominated for the Chamberlain Award, and received a letter in reply from the White House (now framed and hanging on her wall), but the stars of the show are the local children, with their funny questions and quirky drawings.

"I wish I had all the power you have but I don't. That ain't fair!" said one. (Are we sure Donald Trump wasn't living in Handsworth back then?) "I wanted to tell you, you are a great man," said another in a matter-of-fact tone. "What is your favourite soccer team? I hope it's not a naff team like Wolves or Burnley," asked one pupil, with an admirable grasp of the most important issue of the day. "Was your name Barry when you were younger?" asked another, a question to which we now

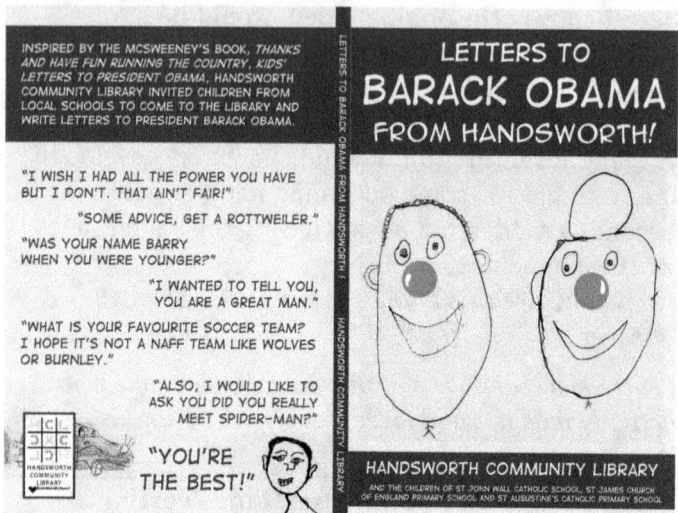

INSPIRED BY THE MCSWEENEY'S BOOK, *THANKS AND HAVE FUN RUNNING THE COUNTRY, KIDS' LETTERS TO PRESIDENT OBAMA*, HANDSWORTH COMMUNITY LIBRARY INVITED CHILDREN FROM LOCAL SCHOOLS TO COME TO THE LIBRARY AND WRITE LETTERS TO PRESIDENT BARACK OBAMA.

"I WISH I HAD ALL THE POWER YOU HAVE BUT I DON'T. THAT AIN'T FAIR!"

"SOME ADVICE, GET A ROTTWEILER."

"WAS YOUR NAME BARRY WHEN YOU WERE YOUNGER?"

"I WANTED TO TELL YOU, YOU ARE A GREAT MAN."

"WHAT IS YOUR FAVOURITE SOCCER TEAM? I HOPE IT'S NOT A NAFF TEAM LIKE WOLVES OR BURNLEY."

"ALSO, I WOULD LIKE TO ASK YOU DID YOU REALLY MEET SPIDER-MAN?"

"YOU'RE THE BEST!"

LETTERS TO **BARACK OBAMA** FROM HANDSWORTH!

HANDSWORTH COMMUNITY LIBRARY
AND THE CHILDREN OF ST JOHN WALL CATHOLIC SCHOOL, ST JAMES CHURCH OF ENGLAND PRIMARY SCHOOL AND ST AUGUSTINE'S CATHOLIC PRIMARY SCHOOL

know the answer to be yes, thanks to the Netflix original movie of that name.

The project was inspired by the McSweeney's book *Thanks and Have Fun Running the Country*, in which the letters were by American children. Here the letters are by British children, a crucial difference that perhaps explains the greater interest in association football shown within its pages. One of the most charming parts of the book was how often the children drew pictures of themselves with the new president, as on the cover. They trusted him, could imagine him hanging out with the class, buying them an ice cream.

It's hard to imagine any British children wanting to spend time with the current president, though if they did I imagine they would put him to shame with their maturity and interest in the world and its future. This book reminds us that it doesn't have to be that way, that we can have leaders we believe in, that give us hope, and even if they don't deliver on every single one of those hopes, it's better than the alternative. I give this book five red noses. *Stephen Theaker*

These United States by Clive Tern

I want to begin this review by telling you a story. When I was a young boy, our bedroom had a wide window, with a large fixed pane in the middle, and parts that opened on the left and on the right. I am not proud of what I am about to tell you, but I would exit on the left, walk across the exterior window sill to the right, then come back inside. It frightens me to think of it, now more than ever, as I think of all the joy that would have been lost if I had fallen to my death. No lovely wife, no beautiful children, and worst of all so many wonderful novels never written! Imagine if I had died then, never having seen *Game of Thrones*, never having used the internet, never having played an Elder Scrolls game!

It doesn't bear thinking about, so let's not, let's move on to another childhood memory. We lived near one of the (if not the) smallest train stations in Britain, Damems, on the Worth Valley Light Railway. We would walk down there to see the steam trains go by, and if that sounds like a scene from *The Railway Children*, well, parts of that film were indeed filmed there. I never took off my underwear and waved it at a train, but we did discover the ruins of an abandoned mill, with a huge enticing crack in one wall. The mystery of this entranced us for weeks, until we were able to take advantage of a Tandy special offer and get ourselves a torch.

I then led an expedition into the crack. This may all sound like an episode of *Stranger Things*, but let me assure you that this really happened. Following me into the crack were my little brother and a gaggle of other children, some of them probably as young as five or six. We shone the torch into the crack and made our way inside. It was terrifying, but we kept going, step by worrisome step, the light shining ahead of us into the darkness, but seeming to illuminate only more darkness. Before long the crack narrowed and I began to worry about being trapped in there.

I called a retreat, and had to wait, anxiously breathing as deeply as I could, while the youngest children at the back got the message and led us out. I think back to that often, and consider how easily we all could have died. No one knew we were there. No one would have looked for us there. If the walls of that crumbling mill had fallen, that would have been it for all of us. We would all have died, and it would have been my fault. I'd be famous for being the idiot that led a group of younger children into a hole in the wall of a abandoned mill.

All of which is by way of explaining how intensely you may be affected by the stories in *These United States* by Clive Tern. It's a collection that will make you gasp in horror at how easily you might have let it pass you by, changing your life forever, very much for the worse. He is not from the United States, but declares a strange love for them. He writes about a man who can't die, and another who is locked up all day, and aliens and sea-gods and dangerous cigarette lighters all while making you think and taking you to a different state of the union each time.

In thirty years time, do you really want to think back to this moment and rue the terrible mistake you made, or do you want to read this book right now? And it's only volume one! How many more can we look forward to?! I give it five red noses. *Stephen Theaker*

You can buy the book here: books.pronoun.com/these-united-states/

There Will Be Walrus: First Volume V

Military science fiction is a part of the genre that does not always get the attention it deserves, but thank goodness Cattimothy House is on the case, producing an anthology of stories and essays that ranks with the very best sf being produced in the world. Overrated social justice writerers such as John Scalesy and Jim B. Hinds might knock this kind of stuff and despise the fans who love it, but us real fans know the real deal when we see it, and here we do!

Like all the best books, this is edited by a gun-toting feline, in this case Timothy the Talking Cat, "one of America's foremost political philosophers and one of the aspiring leaders of the future". He has been assisted in bringing the book to publication by Camestros Felapton, and the contributors include such amazing stars in the science fiction sky as Timothy the Talking Cat, Straw Puppy, Mr Atomic, Flight Rear Admiral General Fortescue-Billinghman, Chilsed McEdifice, and the infamous Vax Doy, well known for his failed attempts to rig the Hogu Awards.

It includes five forewords, each better

than the one that came before, a guide to surviving a squirrel attack, self-publishing advice for indie authors, stories with names like "Clean Up on Gamma-6-Gamma" and "Behold the Valiants" and "The Dead Tell No Secrets of the Dead", and an FAQ for those people who just stubbornly refuse to get with the program and need a handout! Online, I get the impression that some people haven't taken the book seriously, but I bet those are just omega males, or even more embarrassingly, people who aren't even male at all.

The book contains twenty-two thousand, one hundred and eighty words, which seems like just the right length. Not too short that it has finished before you get going, but not so long that you will wander off to read something less walrussy halfway through. And it's free, the best price of all, so I have no hesitation in awarding it the maximum five red noses out of five. If it doesn't win any awards that can only be down to the machinations of those evil social justice weirdo cat hating squirrel lovers. *Stephen Theaker*

You can get the book here: www.smashwords.com/books/view/636378.

Sea-Girt Jungles by Cyril Collenette

This book, subtitled The Experiences of a Naturalist with the "St. George" Expedition, was written by Cyril Leslie Collenette, a naturalist (i.e. someone who studies nature, not someone who takes their clothes off in public) who lived from 1888 to 1959, and it was published in 1926 – the year my alma mater Reading University received its charter!

It describes the highlights of an 1924 expedition that went to Madeira and Trinidad, then through the Panama Canal to some islands in the Pacific that were at the time less frequently visited. After that came the famous Galapagos Islands, the Marquesas Islands, the Tuamata Atolls, Tahiti, the Austral Islands and Rapa Nui (Easter Island). On some of these islands were the jungles of the book's title, surrounded as they were by the ocean.

Collenette was a fellow of the Entomological Society, and so his professed interest was in finding examples of butterflies, moths and beetles, though rumour has it that he also took quite an interest in a rather more sophisticated lifeform: Cynthia Longfield! She went on to a glittering career of her own, becoming known as Madam Dragonfly for her research on that creature.

The book does not mention his reaction upon returning to the United Kingdom to discover that, during his absence from these shores, the *Sunday Express* had become the first newspaper to publish a crossword. One is left to wonder also how he felt about the news that Eric Liddell had won the four hundred metre gold at the Paris Olympics while setting a new world record, that fridges were now on sale, that fellow explorers George Mallory and Andrew Irvine had met their doom on Mount Everest, and that the first naturist (i.e. people who take their clothes off in public, not people who study nature) camp had been established in Wickford, Essex. We can only speculate.

Collenette was known for collecting pteridophytes and spermatophytes, and went on to publish books about the Ruwemzori expeditions of 1934-1935 and 1952 as well as the H.E.K. Jordan expedition to Angola. There had been hope that the 1924 expedition would discover buried treasure, which if it had happened would have made this already brilliant book even better. It did not, but Collenette was after all more interested in the bugs than the booty, and so this book remains a fitting legacy. It gets five red noses out of five. *Stephen Theaker*

Clovenhoof and the Trump of Doom by Heide Goody and Iain Grant

This is the latest in a series of hilarious short books about Jeremy Clovenhoof, the earthly incarnation of the devil himself, Satan! Now, you might be getting nervous, casting a concerned glance up at the crucifix hanging on your wall, worrying that this book is in some way blasphemous, but the bible doesn't mention the devil having any cloven hoofs so it's probably not the same guy. Or is it? What was the greatest trick he ever pulled, eh? We should be careful, lest we end up reading a book that leads us down the garden path. All that's waiting down there is the Cottingley fairies!

Back to the book. This is up to the minute hot off the presses satire: Nostradamus foretold the barmy presidency of Donald Trump and the barminess of Brexit. The Archangel Michael will try to undo Brexit through the power of song (though perhaps he would have been better off finding a decent candidate for leader of the Conservative party who was willing to oppose it) while Clovenhoof goes to the United States to stop Trump becoming president. You may watch the news and think, sorry, Clovenhoof, too late, but this book, published by Pigeon Park Press, gives us hope that it can still be stopped. If you believe Clovenhoof exists, it's not too hard to imagine he has time travel powers and can still undo all of this.

The book begins in Sutton Coldfield, which is a great place for a book to begin. When I was there I found the best ever discount book store, and spent about a hundred pounds buying virtually everything in the Virgin Doctor Who line that I didn't yet own, including several hardback non-fiction titles and paperbacks that have since become exceedingly rare. The shop shut down within a week or two, leaving me to wonder ever since whether it was really there. Back then the high street also had a McDonald's where I would have a cheeseburger and small fries while reading the *Independent*, before, in good weather, heading over to the bench by the church to read a book, or, in bad weather, going into the library to read a book.

It's terribly sad that the library is now closing, as I spent many happy pages there. If only Clovenhoof could have done something about that, as well as fixing Trump and Brexit, this superb book would have been even better, but it would be unfair to mark down an otherwise exceptional and hilarious book for something so far out of its control, so it gets a rollicking five red noses out of five from me. *Stephen Theaker*

You can buy the book here:
amzn.to/2mzLljc

This is the Quickest Way Down by Charles Christian

Charlie Christian was a swing and jazz guitarist who played an important role in bebop and cool jazz, and he was inducted into the Rock and Roll Hall of Fame in 1990, 48 years after his death. There is a street named after him in Oklahoma City, and he played with Count Basie and Benny Goodman, among others. He is seen as an influence on everyone from Eddie Cochran and Chuck Berry to Thelonious Monk and Miles Davis.

But this book is not by Charlie Christian, it is by Charles Christian. Whether they are related or not we can't say, but it's not hard to imagine the author of this book tapping away at his keyboard while the electric guitar of his namesake works some cool moves in the background. A book of fiction is a lot like a piece of jazz music. You might start off with a plan, you might even know every event that is going to happen, but the only way to get there from here is  by improvising every word as you go along.

You may have noticed the remarkably beautiful woman on the book's cover. I know this reviewer did. While I count myself lucky to have married a brown-skinned woman, and indeed would have counted myself lucky to have married a woman of any skin colour, I must confess to a particular fondness for blue and green-skinned ladies, such as the Asari from *Mass Effect*, and the Orions from *Star Trek*. In any video game where you can create your own character, my first impulse is always to recreate my wife, since who else would I want to spend forty hours staring at on screen? But there's a good chance her skin will turn blue given the opportunity.

So the book got off to a good start with me. Then, inside, it sprinted to an amazing finish, with stories like "The End of Flight Number 505", "Confessions of a Teenage Ghost-Hunter", "A Baretta for Azraella" and "By the Steps of Villefranche Station" showing just what a short story can do, and how it can do it! There are thirteen stories in this collection, but if that's unlucky for anyone it's not the reader. This book gets five red noses out of five from me. What's more, it's available for just 99p! Just make your next Amazon order a no-rush delivery and you'll get that much back in promotional vouchers to spend on this book!

If you've ever wondered what a book of short stories written by a former practising barrister and Reuters correspondent turned technology journalist and poet would be like, wait no longer. It's right here! And it can be read on an unlimited number of Kindle devices too, with text-to-speech enabled. What more could you ask for? *Stephen Theaker*

You can buy the book here:
https://www.amazon.co.uk/This-Quickest-Way-Down-Fantasy-ebook/dp/B00PCWBI0C

Three books by Howard Phillips

Just as time was about to run out on Red Nose Day, leaving us cruelly just short of our target of one hundred pounds, our frequent contributor Howard Phillips jumped in with a last-minute donation. So here is our last review of the day, of the three novels he has completed: *His Nerves Extruded*, *The Doom That Came to Sea Base Delta*, and *The Day the Moon Wept Blood*. For boring business reasons (Howard lost all copyright in his work to me in a late-night game of Adventure Time Fluxx) these were all eventually published under my name, but they are all Howard's work, unmistakably so!

His Nerves Extruded is not the first book in the series. That was *The Ghastly Mountain*, which was never finished. But despite that this remains a brilliant introduction—

—No, I can't do this. It's one thing to write fake reviews of books that I haven't read, but I have read these Howard Phillips books, and I know how ropey they are. Can I really pretend that they're any good? He did make his donation at the last minute, and so, as I write this, it's no longer Red Nose Day, so strictly speaking I'm no longer obliged to give everything a glowing review. In fact, I think you would be disappointed if I did. So let's get back to normal:

His Nerves Extruded is a book by Howard Phillips about his own adventures, which you may or may not choose to believe. Whether it really happened or not, the way in which he parades around England with a troupe of paid palanquinettes is undeniably sexist. That the writer includes a photographer in the group and promptly forgets about his presence says a lot about how much thought went into the book.

The Doom That Came to Sea Base Delta sees Howard take his meandering adventures down into an undersea base, after a baffling interlude behind the scenes of *Late Night with David Letterman*. The book wants to be *The Thing* in an underwater base, but never rises to the level of *Plan 9 from Outer Space* in a bucket. There's an important chapter towards the end that Howard never got around to writing.

The Day the Moon Wept Blood is perhaps the most preposterous of them all. It's all about a terrible writer (it takes one to know one!) who steals a book from the British Library and plots the assassination of the central figure in English literature, whose surprising identity I will leave readers to discover for themselves. It's clear throughout that the author made no attempt to research the book's various settings.

All three books share a level of self-indulgence that is almost impossible to credit, a belief in the power of poetry that makes a mockery of that noble art, and a tendency to skip over events because the author doesn't feel like writing them. All pretend to be true, but all were written in less than a month and it shows. Do not read these books unless you are a glutton for punishment.

They can have one red nose to share between them. *Stephen Theaker*

And that was our last fake review. Thank you to everyone who donated, helping us reach our target of £100! Not bad for a niche fundraising concept that couldn't be explained in under twenty minutes and massively limited the number of people likely to sponsor us!

You're going to love Anthony. You'd better.

SIRENS

SIMON MESSINGHAM

The authorities called it The Moment. Without warning, without explanation, two hundred huma[n] beings on Earth simultaneously gained a new mental ability that would alter the planet forever. They called the power The Glamour and its recipients Sirens. Alien invasion? Divine interventio[n]? Evolution? Before anyone could work it out, it was too late.

Anthony Graves didn't want to be a Siren. He just wanted to be liked. Once a shy, suburban Lon[don] office worker, five years on he is ruler of Europe and responsible for the deaths of millions. Sire[ns] is a dark comedy by award-winning writer Simon Messingham. It is satire on a global scale; a cautionary tale of absolute power and its inevitable consequences.

The Quarterly Review

Reviews by
Stephen Theaker,
Jacob Edwards, Douglas J.
Ogurek, Rafe McGregor
and Lorelei Theaker

Douglas J. Ogurek's work has appeared in the BFS Journal, The Literary Review, Morpheus Tales, Gone Lawn, and several anthologies. Douglas's website can be found at www.douglasjogurek.weebly.com.

Jacob Edwards also writes 42-word reviews for Derelict Space Sheep. This writer, poet and recovering lexiphanicist's website is at www.jacobedwards.id.au. He has a Facebook page at www.facebook. com/JacobEdwardsWriter, where he posts poems and the occasional oddity, and he can now be found on Twitter too: https://twitter.com/ToastyVogon.

Rafe McGregor is the author of The Value of Literature, The Architect of Murder, five collections of short fiction, and over one hundred magazine articles, journal papers, and review essays. He lectures at the University of York and can be found online at https://twitter.com/rafemcgregor.

Stephen Theaker *shares his home with three slightly smaller Theakers, one of whom is* **Lorelei Theaker**. *Her previous review for us appeared in TQF12, when she would have only been three years old!*

We don't have a policy on ratings, other than that reviewers use them or not as they prefer.

Audio

Children of Eden, by Joey Graceffa (and Laura L. Sullivan) (Simon and Schuster Audio)

This is the Audible edition of Joey Graceffa's first novel. I enjoyed his previous memoir and I was just as pleased with this book. Although it is published under his name, he didn't actually write it. He probably came up with the ideas, but I think that it might be written by Laura L. Sullivan because she is thanked at the start. He is more well-known as a YouTuber and this is why I was interested in the book. He is very funny in his videos and he comes up with very creative and exciting ideas. I'm a big fan of his.

In this dystopian future couples are only allowed to have one child because they don't have enough resources. Almost everything is artificial: the plants, the food, everything. The world was saved by Aaron al Baz. He made the Eco Panopticon which is what keeps the world (and the humans) alive. Rowan is a girl who has lived her life as a second child. Her parents didn't want to kill her so they kept her hidden and had the birth at home so that no-one would know they had a second child. Rowan is Ash's twin and they are very close but Rowan wishes that she could go outside the wall and make friends.

So she does. She goes outside and has an huge adventure. She meets Ash's crush and they fall in love and Rowan kisses Lark (Ash's crush). But then she gets found out and reported so she needs to hide somewhere. Lachlan takes her into the underground, which is a home for second children, and tortures her to check whether she was actually a normal second child. Second children can be identified by their colourful eyes. At birth all legal children have their eyes protected from the artificial air but people can survive a long time without getting their eyes damaged. They go on an adventure that will save the

second children but end up saving the world, solving a mystery and revealing secrets.

I really enjoyed the story because it was full of suspense; the writer managed to fit in a lot of other dilemmas while the main storyline was going on. The vocabulary kept me engaged and made me want to keep listening. I felt the panic in the parts with the wall because you never know whether she's going to get caught or fall. It is definitely open to sequels: it has an ending that could lead on to another story.

I am not really bothered that Joey Graceffa didn't write it because it's fun to know that it is based on his ideas, and even though it's not written by a YouTuber, it's still a great book. I enjoyed this so much and I would love to read more books by Laura L. Sullivan and listen to more books read by Sarah Grayson. I think that it is very well read by her. She really makes it feel like Rowan is speaking to you, and she also changes the tone of her voice to show different characters very well. If you are a teenager you will especially enjoy this book, as I did. ★★★★★ *Lorelei Theaker*

The Dispatcher, by John Scalzi (Audible)

This is a two hour twenty minute story, told in the first person and read with gusto by Zachary Quinto (Spock from Star Trek films eleven to thirteen). He plays Tony Valdez, the dispatcher of the title. We first meet him in a hospital, where his presence in the operating theatre is required by the insurers. He's quite cagey about the precise nature of his job at first, and we know the surgeon isn't happy about having him in there. Is he there to kill people if the treatment gets too expensive? Is the patient someone of such significance that the staff will be punished if he dies? Or is this like Nick Mamatas's *The Last Weekend*, where someone has to drill the deceased before they turn into zombies? We don't find out until the operation takes a turn for the worse and Tony has to step in to do his thing. His job is interesting, as is the reason it is needed. The story soon segues into a hardboiled search for a missing dispatcher, while exploring throughout the implications of the difference between Tony's world and ours. The two-hour length reflects how much this resembles the pilot for a television series, with Tony teaming up with a tough female co-star for an adventure that establishes a strong premise, while leaving plenty more to be investigated. It's good, and very well read. It was free to Audible members at the time of writing, but if it's not by the time you read this it is well worth one of your tokens. ★★★☆☆ *Stephen Theaker*

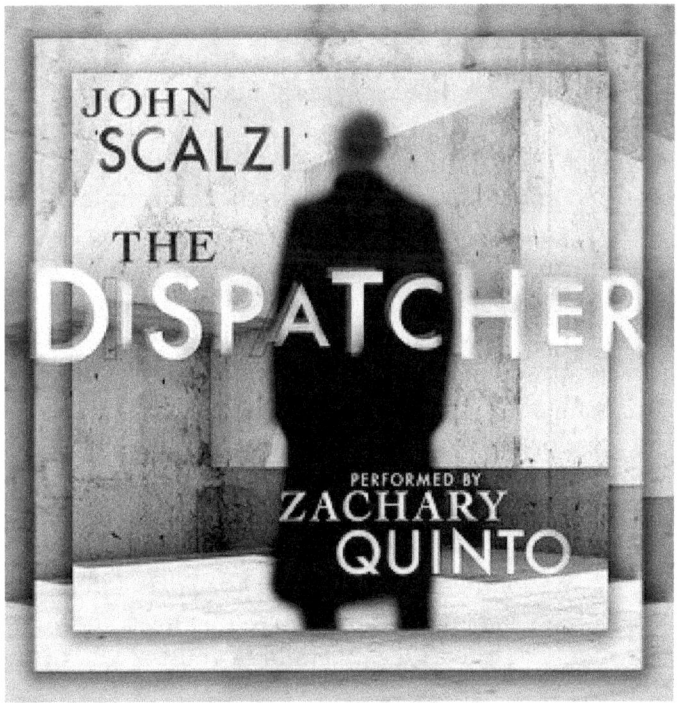

Books

The Cthulhu Casebooks: Sherlock Holmes and the Shadwell Shadows by James Lovegrove (Titan Books)

I've recently made several comments on the evolution of Sherlock Holmes from the cold criminal investigator who calmly rejected supernatural explanations of even the most outré circumstances created by Conan Doyle to a character who is probably most accurately called an occult detective in the twenty-first century. In my review of *Sherlock: The Abominable Bride* in TQF55, I mentioned that Holmes and several others who cross the threshold of 221b Baker Street are more akin to superheroes and supervillains, giving the series very much of a fantasy feel, and Guy Ritchie's *Sherlock Holmes: Game of Shadows* (2011) was served with a deliciously strong steampunk sauce. I recently responded to an article in *The Conversation* on the decline in the popularity of Doctor Who by noting that Doctor Who and Sherlock have become increasingly close in the last couple of decades and Steven Moffat is one of many writers who have written either official novels or screenplays for both the doctor and the detective. In my review of Simon Kurt Unsworth's *The Devil's Detective* in TQF56, I mentioned "the many failed and few successful attempts to combine Sherlock Holmes and the Cthulhu Mythos" of late, and the subject of this review is James Lovegrove's contribution to precisely that subgenre – a contribution that is by and large successful. The subgenre was launched with Michael Reeves and John Pelan's *Shadows Over Baker Street: New Tales of Terror!* in 2003. Re-reading my somewhat scathing review in TQF24, I stand by most of what I wrote (though not my dismissal of Neil Gaiman's "A Study in Emerald"). One of my main criticisms of this volume was that there had been little or no effort to recreate the atmosphere of Victorian or Edwardian London in most of the stories. The shadows are, after all, over *Baker Street*, not Angell Street or Clinton

Street. James Lovegrove's shadows are, as his title suggests, in Shadwell (the district between Whitechapel and Limehouse), and he has paid close attention to both the historical setting and the original Holmes stories such that the few anachronistic turns of phrase he uses are insufficient to distract the reader. It's the relationship between old and new where Lovegrove's contribution to literary pastiche is revealed at its most ambitious and most promising.

His intention is that the three volumes of which this is the first will "effectively rewrite the Holmes canon", peeling back the illusion of detection to reveal the reality of the Mythos. As such, *Sherlock Holmes and the Shadwell Shadows* begins in a similar manner to *A Study in Scarlet*, with Watson returning from Afghanistan with more mental than physical damage and meeting Holmes through Stamford. The location is not the Long Bar of the Criterion, however, but an unnamed public house in Limehouse which is a haven for illegal gambling, bare-knuckle boxing, cock-fighting, and prostitution. Holmes and Watson meet by making independent attempts to assist Stamford when he falls foul of a pimp and his henchman. Stamford flees in the ensuing fracas and it emerges that he is an opium addict and a suspect in a series of murders. The murders have been linked by Holmes but not Scotland Yard in that the victims are all of the unlikely-to-be-missed (in Victorian England) variety and appear to have been starved to death. Stamford quickly removes himself from play – after being found wandering the streets while raving about the Old Ones – committing suicide in a particularly gruesome manner. Lovegrove's writing is crisp and clean, lacking the laboured quality characteristic of so much pastiche and the narrative is fast-paced, more of a thriller than a mystery, but none the worse for it. Indeed, Lovegrove's Holmes and Watson are somewhat reminiscent of Ritchie's and his portrayal of Watson as a physically adept ex-soldier is particularly pleasing. The trail of the case quickly leads to Stamford's employer, a Chinese immigrant by the name of Gong-Fen who runs an opium empire in Limehouse. At Gong-Fen's bidding and under the influence of a cocktail of narcotics, Holmes undertakes a dream-quest where the existence of the world of the Elder Gods and Outer Gods is revealed to him. On his return to Baker Street, Watson discloses the truth of his experiences in Afghanistan and the cause of his wound. At the mid-point in the narrative, Gong-Fen, Holmes, and Watson are attacked by what appears to be the shadows of the title. This unequivocal manifestation of the supernatural in the present of the story, which is both gripping and otherworldly, marks the point of no return from crime to horror. The incident takes Holmes and Watson to the second layer of the puzzle, Gong-Fen's employer, whom they find following researches at the British Library, and thence to the Mythos itself, with a climactic battle underneath St Paul's Church in Shadwell.

My only real criticism comes compliments of Lovegrove himself. The novel is preceded by both an author's preface (where he employs a conceit based on the similarity of his own surname to Lovecraft's) and a fictional foreword by Watson and concludes with a brief epilogue in which Watson, writing in 1928, provides a teaser for the next instalment (due for publication in November this year), *Sherlock Holmes and the Miskatonic Monstrosities*. The first novel is set in 1880, the second in 1895, and the third (*Sherlock Holmes and the Sussex Sea Devils*, due for publication in 2018) in 1910. If Lovegrove is indeed reinventing Doyle's canon – and I think reinvention is the key to successful pastiche – then he needs to do a little more than rewrite the meeting of Holmes and Watson.

Given that this volume is supposed to tide us over until 1895, it covers the first two novellas and the first two collections of short stories but alludes to very few of the incidents or characters with which readers are familiar. Lovegrove has Watson explain that he wrote "one sort of story [detection] to deflect attention from another [horror], which strays into realms most ordinary people are incognisant of and are all the better off in their ignorance". Granted, but if the canon is being rewritten as opposed to Holmes and Watson simply undertaking an alternative set of adventures, then there needs to be a little more explanation or demonstration of the relation between Lovegrove's reinvention and Doyle's canon. Why, for example, did Watson write the particular stories that comprise *The Adventures of Sherlock Holmes* and *The Memoirs of Sherlock Holmes* rather than others? What happened in the reality of the Mythos that caused him to draw this particular veil of detection over it? If it weren't for Lovegrove's preface, this expectation would not exist, but it does exist and remains unrewarded at this point in the trilogy. Notwithstanding, the novel is an entertaining and accomplished contribution to the occult detective genre and an original and ambitious contribution to the Holmes and Mythos subgenre. *Rafe McGregor*

The Drowning Eyes, by Emily Foster (Tor.com)

The Windspeakers, weird weather wizards who have their eyes replaced with stones in order to gain control of their powers, have been attacked by the marauding Dragon Ships, and the seas are no longer safe. This means less work for sailors, since no one wants to travel. Chaqal, Tazir and Kodin, who sail on the good ship *Giggling Goat*, have found a job: Shina, a rich young woman who seems to be on the run from her family. They might be overcharging for their services, but she has secrets of her own, and they are all going to get in much more trouble than expected. Being a fan of short books in general, I like the Tor.com series of ebook novellas, not least for their diversity and for having original artwork on the covers (Cynthia Sheppard provides the art for  this one), and this is another fine example. It does feel like more of a novella than a short novel, covering for the main part just one journey, though it is an important one with serious consequences for their passenger. The ebook has a slightly annoying quirk – at least on Kindle, each incidence of italics is followed by a line break – but that wasn't anywhere near enough to spoil my enjoyment of a very entertaining book about a dashing group of characters. ★★★☆☆ *Stephen Theaker*

The Four Thousand, The Eight Hundred by Greg Egan (Subterranean Press)

In this tense science fiction novella, there is strife on Vesta. Back when the colony was first being established, each of the founding families contributed different resources. Problem is, attitudes to private ownership of intellectual property have changed so much since then that the family that bought into the project with its patents and inventions is now regarded by some as having stolen its share, and a proposal to have them pay it back is, unthinkably, passed, with 52% voting in favour. Some put up with this discrimination, some decide to fight back, and  some flee, either in passenger ships, or if the security forces are after them, via a space age underground railroad to Ceres, drugged, half-frozen, and hitching a ride on a rock slab. All of this will put Anna, only a week or so into her new job, in an impossible position, when a cruiser, the *Arcas*, is sent in pursuit of fugitives. It feels like a long short story rather than a short novel, but I enjoyed it very much, and it is of course remarkably topical, in that we too are experiencing what happens when a substantial minority of the populace is railroaded by a narrow popular vote rooted in prejudice and selfishness and hatred. The book does a terrific job of showing how that can happen, and how shocking it can be when it does. ★★★☆☆ *Stephen Theaker*

I Am Providence, by Nick Mamatas (Night Shade Books)

A horror book, or maybe literary horror fantasy. Lovecraftian fans, critics and writers gather in Providence, Rhode Island, at a hotel for a convention, the Summer Tentacular. To me it sounded very reminiscent of the first FantasyCons I attended (i.e. lots of blokes, lots of names familiar from the internet, and lots of poeple trying to sell their books; here, we almost immediately meet a chap hawking *Madness of the Death Sun* – which sounds great), while to newcomer Colleen Danzig it resembles a large Alcoholics Anonymous meeting, "except instead of alcoholism the

attendees had all sorts of other, subtler problems". Some of those people feel very familiar, but even if you aren't well enough acquainted with that particular scene to identify the people being parodied, you get the gist of why someone would want to parody them. We have two point of view characters – Panossian, an older writer who gets himself murdered, and Colleen, who wants to investigate his murder – and chapters alternate between them. The dead (or "posthumously conscious" as he puts it) man tells his story in the first person, and his view of this environment soured long before he was killed there. Fandom is the social network of last resort, he says. Lovecraftians are a bunch of misfits and social defectives. Literary critics and fans are two of the more ridiculous sets of people in the world. Ambition is a hell. And he admits to having been a jerk to a lot of people – a lot of very mentally unstable people. Asked for his thoughts on writing, his answer is, "Generally, I'm against it." He's rather brilliant and very entertaining, much like the book itself. ★★★★☆ *Stephen Theaker*

If Chins Could Kill: Confessions of a B Movie Actor, by Bruce Campbell (Aurum)

One of the first things we learn about Bruce Campbell in this partially updated autobiography is that he was quite an awful young man. He shoots a girl, peeps on women, and deliberately directs fireworks at a neighbour's house, almost hitting her. At least that makes it easier to laugh later on when we read about Sam Raimi putting him through hell while filming *The Evil Dead*, the film that put them both on the map – though not necessarily in the pink. One of the big surprises of the book is that even though Bruce Campbell was regarded by fans as a star, he wasn't always financially comfortable. "People often wonder why some actors fall off the face of the Earth for no apparent reason," he writes. "I've got news for you – there is *always* a reason, and frustration with the business is a huge factor." Makes you glad he had such a long run on *Burn Notice*, even if it never felt like we got the full Bruce on that show. We do now, in buckets (of blood), on *Ash Vs Evil Dead*, and this book shows us how that all began, in lots of detail, from the early films they made to show their friends, to raising the money to make the film, something in which Campbell was much more involved than you might have expected an actor to be. If raising the money was hard, filming it was a frozen nightmare, and that it turned out so well is a testament to the ingenuity, imagination and endurance of all involved. The book goes on to cover the rest of Campbell's career, in greater or lesser detail depending on whether he has a good anecdote to tell. The day he spent on the set of *The Quick and the Dead* turned up trumps in that regard, and it was also very funny to read about his work on the film version of *McHale's Navy*, where he launched Operation Screentime with French Stewart,

an attempt to beef up the roles of their underused characters. It's a book of short chapters, that's fun and easy to read. It's the first time I've read a book typeset entirely in a sans serif font, but there are pictures on almost every page so you can understand why the UK publisher probably didn't want to retypeset it.

★★★☆☆ *Stephen Theaker*

Letters to Arkham: The Letters of Ramsey Campbell and August Derleth, 1961–1971, edited by S.T. Joshi (PS Publishing)

This book collects the correspondence (or so much of it as remains) from the 1960s between the prolific writer and editor August Derleth and the young Ramsey Campbell. The latter would go on to be a titan of the horror world, and the former already was, his publishing of H.P. Lovecraft's work in hardback having done a great deal to cement that writer's reputation. The letters are often fascinating. Campbell, fifteen at first, is importunate, full of questions – reminding us that this was a time when you couldn't simply look things up on the internet – a virgin, somewhat testy and defensive. August Derleth, much older, is sexually omnivorous, patronising, encouraging, and exceedingly free with his opinions. One thing I had noted reading Derleth's pastoral *Sac Prairie Journal* immediately before this is that August Derleth's romantic life is completely absent from its pages, and these letters make it obvious why: he was having it off with whoever he could! Given that the letters are remarkably revealing, it's a credit to Ramsey Campbell and to the literary estate of August Derleth that their publication was allowed. That the book would be edited by Lovecraft scholar S.T. Joshi must have helped in that regard, and he provides very useful footnotes to the letters, supplying information about everything from incorrect film titles (there is a great deal of film chat) to whether planned titles from both writers were ever published, and if so in what form and under what titles. One of their favourite topics of conversation is films, and reading the book now, when so much of cinema's rich history is available for a few pounds and a couple of clicks, it's almost shaming to see the lengths to which the two of them go to watch really

good films, travelling for hours to get to a particular cinema on the one night that film would be shown. Since reading the book I've certainly been making more of an effort to watch better quality films. It's essential reading for fans of either writer, and very interesting reading for everyone else. ★★★★☆
Stephen Theaker

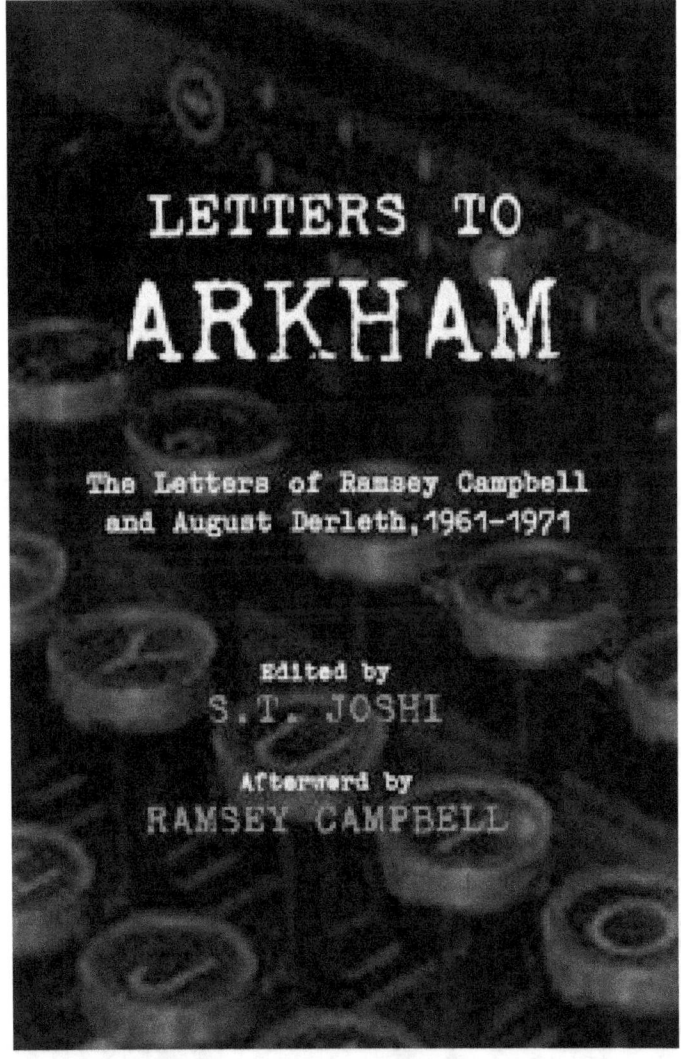

LETTERS TO ARKHAM

The Letters of Ramsey Campbell and August Derleth, 1961–1971

Edited by
S.T. JOSHI

Afterword by
RAMSEY CAMPBELL

Metronome by Oliver Langmead (Unsung Stories)

William Manderlay, an elderly man living in a care home, meets a Sleepwalker, March, a hunter of nightmares, in one of his dreams. March lends William his special dream compass, and tells him to go to the Capital of dreams, to chill out while March gets on with clearing out the bad dreams that are infesting his noggin. As well as helping him find his way, the

compass can show whether people he meets in this world are other dreamers or just figments. Unfortunately, he runs into June, another Sleepwalker who wants to get to Solomon's Eye, whatever that is, and for that purpose she needs a copy of the songs that William never got around to recording for his big hit album. They will provide her with directions. Eventually William gets involved in a rival quest, on board the *Metronome*, a clockwork-powered flying craft whose captain is willing to take him in pursuit of those stolen songs, because they happen to be the map to the centre of the storm where she lost the rest of her crew. This a nicely written piece of work, with plenty of ideas and a beautiful cover, but it didn't really excite me. It feels unfair to say that I feel like I've read plenty of airship stories now, when I wouldn't say the same thing about car stories or spaceship stories, but some of the beats did feel quite familiar from books like *Empress of the Sun* and *Clementine*. The portrayal of William in his old age is very touching, as his reaction to finding himself increasingly youthful again in the course of the dream quest. It was pleasant enough, and I'm sure there are people out there who will be more in tune with it than I was. ★★★☆☆ *Stephen Theaker*

Pirate Utopia by Bruce Sterling (Tachyon Publications)

This novella tells an alternate history story based on the anarcho-syndicalist republic that was declared in the formerly Italian city of Fiume, a city where "there were more great world causes to fight about than there were men to represent them", that was to become part of Yugoslavia after the first world war. In our reality the republic fell after fifteen months, but in this story a clever and capable engineer, Lorenzo Secondari, having been revived from death by a medical experimenter's "psychically advanced séance", arrives in the city in time to get its weapons factories up and running again. They had been taken over by female workers, including the formidable Frau Fifer, who becomes a companion of Secondari. As a result of his

BRUCE STERLING

PIRATE UTOPIA

INTRODUCTION BY
WARREN ELLIS

successes, Secondari rises to become "Minister of Vengeance Weapons", the original title of Pirate Engineer being rejected as not quite right. Eventually Harry Houdini shows up, a secret ambassador from the United States, accompanied by Robert Howard and a surprisingly chipper H.P. Lovecraft. I really liked one bit of dialogue from Secondari, when he says, "I don't have to believe any more, because it's the truth!" I've often thought that when someone says they believe in a thing, that can be a sign that they don't think it's actually true (or at least isn't true yet), whether they realise that or not. I enjoyed the book while finding it a bit hard to get to grips with, much like Michael Moorcock's Jerry Cornelius and Oswald Bastable books. The book also contains an introduction by Warren Ellis, an interview with Bruce Sterling, a useful afterword by Christopher Brown, and a note by the cover artist, all of which, while interesting and often educational, does make you wish the story itself was a bit longer. ★★★★☆ *Stephen Theaker*

Resurrecting Sunshine, by Lisa A. Koosis (Albert Whitman)

As human as it gets.

The rest of the world knew her as Sunshine but to Adam she was Marybeth, the love of his troubled adolescence. Behind the alter ego, beyond the music and the fame, Marybeth meant everything to Adam; and when Sunshine died she took Marybeth with her. Adam's life fell apart.

But what if he could bring her back? What if his memories could help resurrect Sunshine in a clone body? He would give anything, wouldn't he?

But will it really be Marybeth? Will having her back take the pain away?

The more Adam commits to the procedure, the more he starts to wonder if maybe Marybeth's death came a long time before Sunshine's...

I first happened upon Lisa A. Koosis when editing for *Andromeda Spaceways*. Her story "Soul Blossom" was sad and beautiful. As soon as I read it I knew hers was a name to look out for.

Resurrecting Sunshine returns to the same themes as "Soul Blossom" – loss; grief; hope beyond death – but gives them a book-length treatment, aimed at teens but no less profound in the telling. As an adult reader I found myself intrigued, drawn in and then taken by

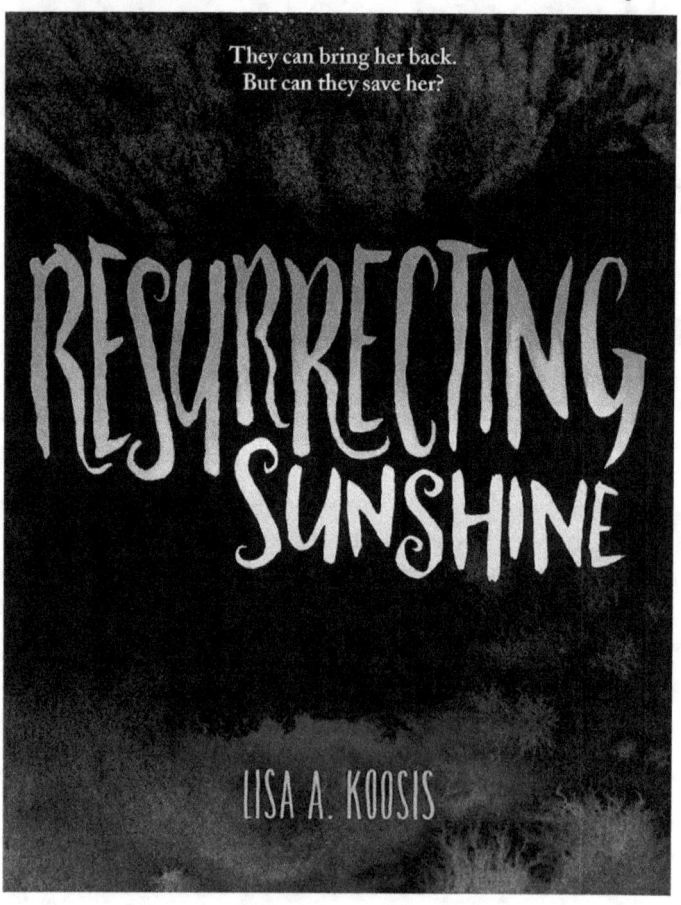

the story's flow. (As a reviewer I'd usually try for some kind of simile at this point, but it feels wrong; Koosis's writing calls out to stand by itself.) The novel is perfectly paced. I read it in three sittings, each longer than the last yet seeming to go faster. There was a sense of inevitability to the narrative, but not predictability. When the ending came, it brought closure.

In her acknowledgments Koosis describes *Resurrecting Sunshine* as "the book that would not die". This suggests also a book that didn't want to be born; a story that came but grudgingly into the world; and yet, whatever difficulties it posed the author, the end result is seamless. In fact, it is Koosis's obvious investment in her work that makes it so compelling. Underlying the spec-fic "now" tale is a heartfelt backstory whose gradual emergence brings a depth of emotion so lacking in most teen novels. All the characters feel genuine. They're not just there to tell a story; they're living through one.

Resurrecting Sunshine is written in the present tense from a first-person male perspective. Koosis handles this well, as does she that fine balancing act between keeping the reader guessing and allowing the book to retain its integrity. *Resurrecting Sunshine* is a profound, beguiling debut that transcends genre to resonate with yearnings deep within. Buy it for yourself and then buy a copy for someone you love. Because this is as human as it gets...

And wouldn't you do anything? *Jacob Edwards*

A Taste of Honey, by Kai Ashante Wilson (Tor.com)

An interesting and romantic novella, in which Aqib, a young and good-looking member of the Olorumi minor nobility with a special way with animals, falls for a rough soldier from the Daluçan embassy.

Forbidden and sweaty things happen, to their mutual delight, but it is important to his family that he makes the right marriage, and so when the opportunity for one arises he must choose between love and duty, happiness and family. As the story progresses we are

also shown episodes from progressively deeper into his future life, placing ever more weight upon the decision he will have to make. This was a very well-written, exciting and romantic book; the relationships of Aqib with both his lover and his other significant other are tender and believable. Using an extremely famous literary title for another book always seems a bit odd (see also *Signal to Noise* and *Journal of the Plague Year*), but the story works hard to justify it. A word for the evocative cover art: fantasy and science fiction book covers often feature great design, but it's brilliant to see that not every publisher has given up on illustrative artwork. ★★★★☆ *Stephen Theaker*

A Wizard's Henchman by Matthew Hughes (PS Publishing)

For those readers who have had the immense pleasure of reading several of this author's Archonate books, *A Wizard's Henchman* is simply unmissable. Over many short stories, novellas and novels we have been shown a universe on the point of collapse, rapidly approaching the point at which reality will flip, from being based like ours (one hopes) on scientific principles to being ruled instead by magic, or, to be more precise, by the will. Some books have shown magic bleeding through, and others have even taken us into the future for a brief glimpse of what is to come, but this is where it actually happens! It is very abrupt. Flying cars fall out of the sky. Buildings collapse. People starve. But not our protagonist. Knowing a little bit about what is going to happen, he gloms on to a promising candidate for wizardship and keeps him safe while he prepares and later learns to use his new powers. Less pleasant magic users are also making their play, and the denizens of other dimensional planes are also ready to take advantage of

the new status quo. The book offers a comfortingly familiar mix of science fiction, fantasy and mystery, while never being reluctant to offer a shocking image or idea when appropriate. It gives us a protagonist for whom self-preservation is at first a priority, but who grows in stature into a true hero, in large part thanks to his determination to adapt and learn. A brilliant book, probably my favourite new book of 2016.
★★★★★ *Stephen Theaker*

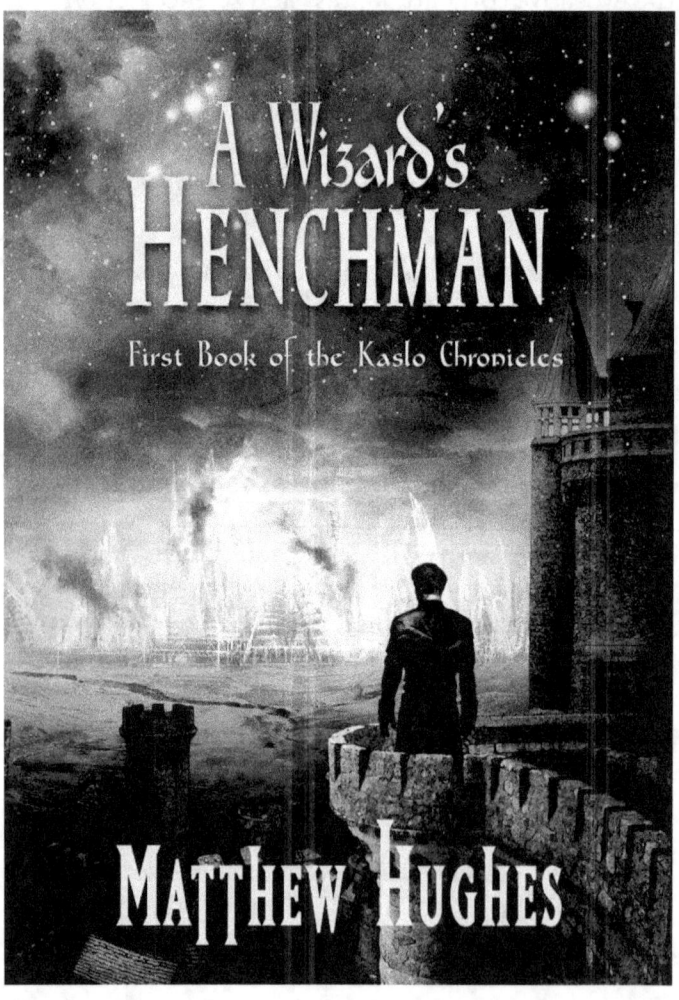

Comics

Adventure Time: Marceline Gone Adrift, by Meredith Gran and Carey Pietsch (Boom! Studios)

Following the successful tour recounted in a previous title, Marceline the musical vampire has lost her mojo. She's spent too long eating nachos with Finn the human and Jake the dog, and that's not enough to inspire her. While bemoaning this state of affairs she and Finn get walloped with a burst of electricity. When Marceline apparently goes on a rampage as a result, Princess Bubblegum feels she is  forced to shoot her off into space. The result is that both are left heartbroken, Finn goes feral, Cinnamon Bun declares himself king, Suspencer tries to cash in on Marceline's apparent demise, and Jake keeps eating nachos. *Adventure Time* has been one of the best shows on television for the last few years, and its art style translates perfectly to comics. As does its ever-changing moods, this story displaying all the whimsy, ebullience and melancholy fans of the show have come to expect, while focusing on the loving but fractious relationship between Marceline and Princess Bubblegum that has produced some of the finest television episodes. And it's clever and beautiful and funny. Ordered into battle by Princess Bubblegum, the leader of the banana guards declares, "All right dudes. Can't be ripe forever." ★★★★☆ *Stephen Theaker*

Bloodshot: Reborn, Deluxe Edition 1, by Jeff Lemire, Mico Suayan, Butch Guice, et al. (Valiant)

"Who was Bloodshot?" asks the first page of this comic. "Red Eyes. White skin. Guns... **Lots** of guns." He was a vicious, psychopathic killer manipulated by false memory implants, working for the government, presumably in previous Bloodshot comics, but that's all over now. At some point before this book begins he gave up his powers (regeneration, strength, aiming – basically Wolverine plus the Punisher) with the help of a woman he loved called Kay. That restored his humanity, but Kay didn't survive, and now, six months later, he's trying to keep calm and stay under the radar while working at a motel. Unfortunately, the nanites that provided his abilities are now taking over other people, civilians who aren't equipped to handle them, and they are going on murderous rampages. His

conscience gives him no option but to travel across the country recovering them, because at least he would be able to keep the nanites under control, but will it mean giving up his humanity once again? It's the archetypal story of the superhero who wanted to give up the powers that were ruining his life, but can't escape his sense of responsibility once they are gone. After that adventure is over, there's then there's an Old Man Loganish story set in a Mad Maxish future, where he teams up with other surviving Valiant heroes, which will probably be a treat for fans of those characters. Overall, I thought the book was a good read without being outstanding. It's as well-written as *Trillium* by the same writer, and there are plenty of ideas, it's just that it's about a character who doesn't massively appeal to me, and probably isn't intended to. ★★★☆☆ *Stephen Theaker*

The Complete Scarlet Traces, Volume One, by Ian Edgington and Disraeli (Rebellion)

Before the films, before the games, before Richard Burton and the brilliant album, and even before the book by H.G. Wells, my first version of *The War of the Worlds* was a comic strip. It was introduced by Tom Baker's head in *Doctor Who Weekly*, though my guess is that it was a reprint from Marvel's *Classics Illustrated*. It made a real impact, and yet this adaptation (and then sequel) was even better. I'm sure all of our readers know the story already, but anyway... The astronomer Ogilvy spots great flumes spouting from Mars, just as it is at its closest point to Earth. A great cylinder falls on Horsell Common, then unscrews, and from it emerge first the Martians themselves, and then their weapons, to incinerate humans with as little thought as we would give to swiping at ants on a picnic blanket. It's crucial for an adaptation of this story to get the horror of these scenes right, and here they are terrifying, Disraeli's artwork capturing brilliantly the fear on the faces of all those people realising that they no longer rule the world, they no longer even rule Horsell Common. This is pretty much a perfect adaptation to comics of the novel, in my opinion. After that the book moves on to a sequel, ten years later, by the same writer and artist. Again, this is well-trodden territory, though it hasn't always been trod with great distinction. There were books such as *The Nyctalope on Mars* (reviewed back in TQF31) and *The Space Machine* by Christopher Priest (described as dull by its own author), an awful television series, and the overwritten Marvel adventures of Killraven, born in the Martian pens.

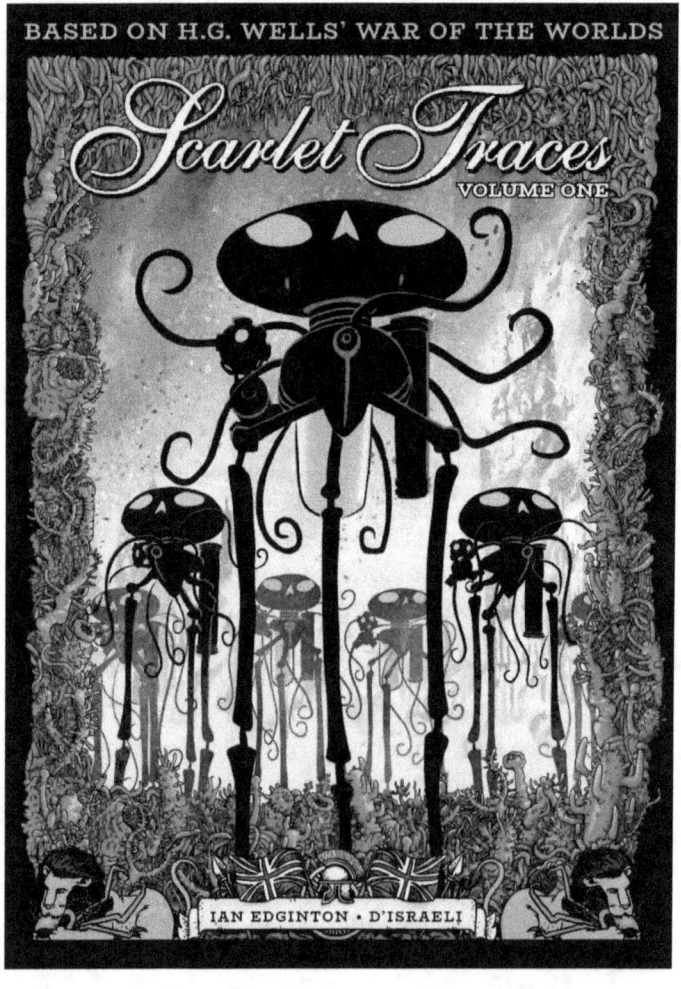

More recently, Stephen Baxter has written a sequel novel of his own, *The Massacre of Mankind*. The approach in *Crimson Traces* is to use new characters in a murder mystery story set in a Britain that has been greatly changed by the war between the worlds, the technology that was left behind by the Martian attack having been cracked open and repurposed to keep the empire running in tip-top shape. While delivering an action-packed thriller, the story also considers the results of automation without social equality. It's a problem that is likely to only get worse for us, and there's a warning here about how bad it could get. The sequel reminded me a bit of Bryan Talbot's equally excellent Grandville series, as it puts some tough, likable characters up against a mystery of national importance and a bunch of vicious villains. Definitely worth your time, even if you think you've probably had enough of the Martians and their tripods by now. ★★★★☆ *Stephen Theaker*

Groo: Fray of the Gods, by Sergio Aragones, Mark Evanier, Tom Luth and Stan Sakai (Dark Horse)

Groo is one of my favourite comics characters of all time, his idiotically violent behaviour a reliable source of chuckles since the day I first read an issue. He's better than Asterix, if you ask me, and the stories are better, and that he's not quite as famous can only be down to him being published on the whole in single issues in the USA rather than albums in France. The previous series, *Groo: Friends and Foes*, was the comic at its very peak, fabulously coloured and brilliantly drawn (not to mention wittily scribed), with some of the detailed double-page spreads being absolutely stunning. It set the bar very high for this follow-up, which tells the story of an upstart god trying to take his place among the pantheon, and was originally

announced as being twelve issues long, but by the time of release was down to four instead, with a new series to come soon. There's no mention of the change in the issues themselves, but it does feel like the story reaches a natural conclusion. It shows us something of how religion works in Groo's world (and ours too, for that matter) as the power of the gods waxes and wanes in proportion to how many believers they have. Groo causes the usual chaos, and there are plenty of chuckles to be chucked, and if it didn't quite hit the glorious heights of the previous run it's still one of the funniest things I read all year. ★★★★☆ *Stephen Theaker*

The Legion of Super-Heroes: The Great Darkness Saga, by Paul Levitz, Keith Giffen, Larry Mahlstedt and chums (DC)

This four-hundred page Kindle edition collects issues 284 to 296 (and the first annual) of the series that had previously been *Superboy and the Legion of*

Super-Heroes, from 1982 and 1983. This includes the introduction of the team's first brown-skinned human member (a new Invisible Kid) during an attack by Computo, and "The Great Darkness Saga", a lengthy story whose long-teased surprise villain is rather given away by his appearance on the front cover of this book. This is what I think of as the real Legion. Reading these stories again, all these years later, fully restored, colour reconstructed, in the right order, with no missing issues, was little short of joyous. The stories stand up. Saturn Girl, Light Lass and Shrinking Violet can be a bit drippy in these issues, but to be fair the boys cry a lot too, and they are all going through a rough time. It has a huge, imaginative and entertainingly fractious cast of heroes, a universe full of danger and adventure, and a knack for switching from jokes to deadly seriousness as the stories require. A lot of the comics I read last year were perfectly decent, but this was a startling reminder of what it was like to read a comic I had truly loved for decades.
★★★★★ *Stephen Theaker*

Princess Jellyfish 01, by Akiko Higashimura (Kodansha)

This 388pp manga collects episodes one to twelve in the story of an unhappily single Japanese woman, Tsukimi, and the geeky friends with whom she lives, and how her life changes completely when she meets a very glamorous young man. It's rather like *The Big Bang Theory* in reverse. She calls herself a fujoshi, which means (rather nastily) rotten woman – a woman who follows her enthusiasms rather than trying to fulfil her expected role as a mother or wife. There's no magical or fantastical element in this book, it turned out; it's called *Princess Jellyfish* because she is a jellyfish geek (a phase the author talks about going through herself in the biographical comments). That's what gets her talking to her gorgeous new friend: he brings his stylishness to bear in helping her save a dying jellyfish in a pet shop, just as later he will try to save Tsukimi and her friends from losing their home to property development. He's the first boy she's talked to since elementary school, and what gets her over that barrier at first is that she doesn't realise he's a boy: he likes to dress as a girl. It's a sweet and romantic comic,

with an adorable lead character and likeable love interests, and it's an eye-opening portrayal of gender fluidity in Japanese culture. The backgrounds are sketchy, but the character artwork is highly expressive . Unfortunately, at the publisher's choice, this Comixology edition can only be viewed a full page at a time (described as "Manga Fixed Format"). Not a problem on a tablet, but you'd struggle to read it on your phone. ★★★☆☆ *Stephen Theaker*

Superf*ckers Forever, by James Kochalka and chums (IDW)

A five-issue miniseries of the utmost puerility, this is very entertaining. The Superf*ckers are a Legion of Super-Heroes-esque gang of teenagers who live inside a club house and act like complete idiots. Even Vortex, who fixes up the universe every time the others destroy it, is willing to lie down on a sofa that has just been peed on by his colleagues Jack Krak the Motherfucker and Ultra Richard (it's better than weeing in the toilet, they decide, because you never have to clean it). The skull possessed by interdimensional super-villain Omnizod shows up, first getting turned into a lamp by stinky Grotessa, then encouraging Princess Sunshine down a megalomaniacal path. Orange Lightning is jonesing for his next fix of Grotus's slime, Computer Fist is struggling to get his robot fists working properly, and team leader Superdan returns from Dimension Zero just in time to lead a pointless new mission into Dimension Zero. The stories are sweary, rude and gross, and all the better for it. Kochalka's artwork is as brilliantly characterful as ever, while a series of backups by other creators show that these heroes look just as silly through their eyes. The entire series can be read in under an hour, but what a great way to spend an hour. ★★★★☆ *Stephen Theaker*

X-Men: Legacy by Simon Spurrier, Tan Eng Huat and chums (Marvel)

This twenty-four issue series, which ran from 2012 to 2014 and is available in its entirety to subscribers on Marvel Unlimited, as well as in four collections, tells the story of David Haller, the son of Professor Charles Xavier and an Israeli diplomat. He is known to the world at large as Legion, and though he isn't keen on that name (he'd be really annoyed that it's the title of the new television show based on the comic), it accurately reflects his powers: like Crazy Jane of the Doom Patrol, he has many split personalities, each of them with its own powers.

When he's in control, he can use those powers. When they're in control, the results can be disastrous. This series begins at the point in *Avengers vs X-Men* when something terrible happens to Professor Xavier at the hands of one of his friends, and that totally shatters David's control, as well as giving rise to a malignant and powerful new personality that resembles his father. Over the course of the comic David will try to re-establish control of his own mind, take a pre-emptive approach to mutant hate crimes, start astral dating Blindfold of the X-Men, and try to prevent an apocalyptic prophecy of his future from coming true.

It's interesting to see Marvel trying something like this. It is a bit like the original Vertigo comics – *Shade the Changing Man*, say – both in tone, and style, and in that a lot of the stories stem from David's own problems in keeping his powers in check; if he's not the big bad in each story, there's always the danger that he might be. The television programme will probably need to be less all about him, but it worked well for the comic. ★★★☆☆ *Stephen Theaker*

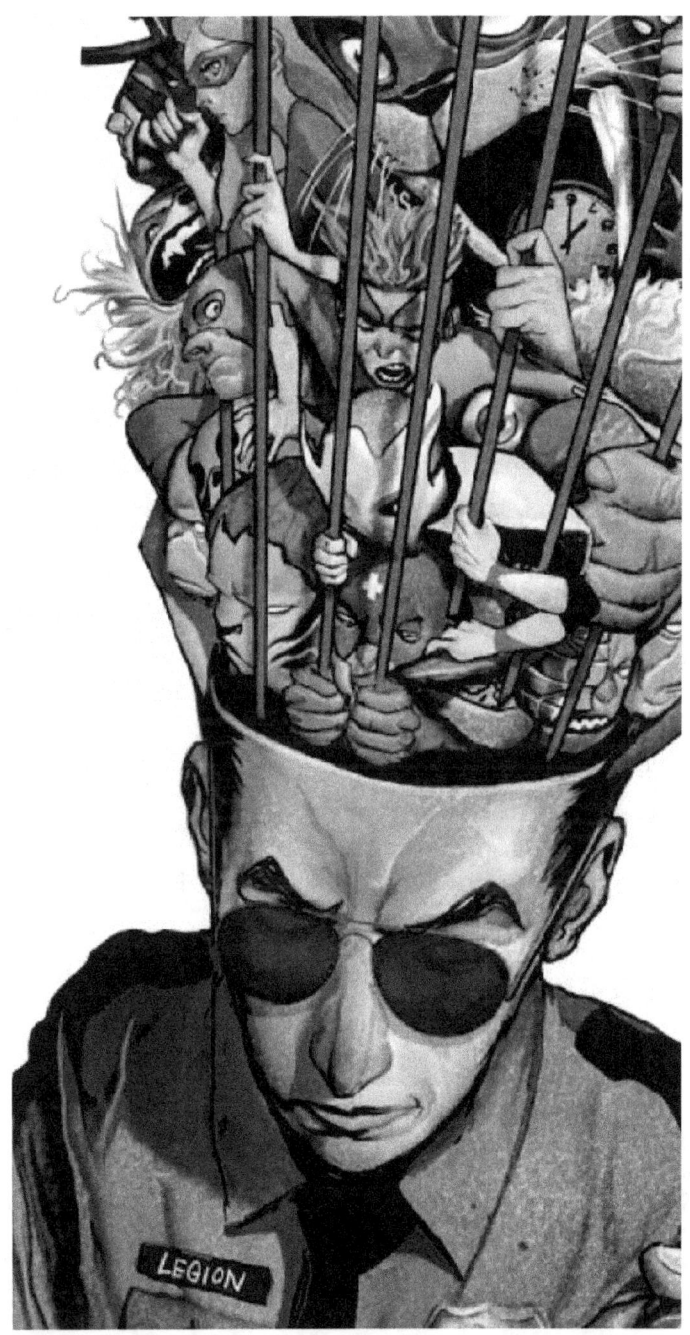

Films

Assassin's Creed, by Michael Lesslie, Adam Cooper and Bill Collage (Ubisoft et al.)

if you like eagles* flying
if you like lots of fighting
if you like people liable to jump from
the tops of high places
their options like eyelids, unbatted
surviving, unflappable, by means of –
[cut away]
why, i'd say this just might be for you

if you like falcons* flying
and jeremy irons
if you value high orders of god corporate
cluelessness, science divine
in its improbability
plots lines that spew from computer screens
proving the existence of game theory
really, this could be for you

if you like your hawks* flying
if you like your films stylish
if you like your macguffins quite rounded
your heroes brought low
but still bearded, gruff, cut from a mould
if you like all the conflicts to stay unresolved
'til the sequel that's stealing the plot
well, what ho! this'll do

if turkeys* are flying, if you stand to decry
but you find yourself writing reviews
with a semblance of rhyme
in the hope your denial won't show
and that no one will find out you didn't despise it
console yourself knowing the trailer with matt damon

blank-faced and fighting off dragons in china
probably gave you perspective (false positive)
rose-tinting all you'd expect to find dire

* despite prolonged opportunity, this viewer failed
properly to distinguish

Jacob Edwards

The Bye Bye Man, by Jonathan Penner (Intrepid Pictures et al.)

Their warning: "Don't think it, don't say it." My warning: Don't see it.

When I go to a horror film, I want to *feel* something. I want the jolt of a good jump scare, or the lingering unease caused by an unidentified malicious presence. I want to get grossed out, to be appalled by violence, or even to laugh with a good horror comedy. With *The Bye Bye Man*, a horror film whose primary intent seems to be to scare the viewer, I felt disappointed. Oh, it does occasionally incite laughter, but that's based on the bad acting and illogic.

The film warns that saying or even thinking "the Bye Bye Man" will unleash the monster that bears that name. He is a hooded figure with a penchant for using his E.T.-like fingers to scratch walls for no apparent reason.

Elliot, girlfriend Sasha, and friend John move into an old house off their college campus. After some dull introductions to Elliot's brother and his family, a dull housewarming party, and a dull séance – are you seeing a trend here? – Elliot stumbles upon the dreaded name and unwittingly resurfaces the figure after a near fifty-year hiatus. For the rest of the film, the Bye Bye Man infects the trio, casting them into a world of hallucinations, jealousy, and mistrust. Elliot's attempts to mentally expunge the name by chanting "Don't think it, don't say it, don't think it, don't say it" grow tedious and annoying. And isn't it true the more you try to fight certain thoughts, the more you have them?

Even the tensest scenes seem silly upon further reflection. For instance, one feels anxiety when Elliot and Sasha look at the black cowl hanging on their bedroom wall. But then, why is there a black cowl hanging on their wall? And why don't they just take it down? It's never explained. In another scene, Elliot heads down to the basement to investigate a scratching noise that could be the Bye Bye Man. If it is

indeed the hooded fiend, why is he scratching? Again, never explained. Then there are the coins dropping and the sound of trains to signal the Bye Bye Man is coming. But why?

Occasionally, the film flashes back to 1969, when journalist Larry Redmon, the last poor guy who tried to exorcise the name from the minds and lips of humanity, goes on a neighbourhood shooting spree. Not a bad way to start the film. But when a shotgun blows away someone at point-blank range and it just leaves a small smudge on the wall and no blood pool (presumably to meet PG-13 parameters), it seems inauthentic.

Once the Bye Bye Man is revealed in the (mangled) flesh, he loses a lot of his potency. As many of the scariest horror films in recent history have proven, the threat is most frightening when it hasn't manifested itself, when it's lurking and just as mysterious to the viewer as it is to the main characters.

If you can think of a horror movie cliché, it's probably in *The Bye Bye Man*. Sloppy sketches of frightening creatures, internet research, séances, creepy girl with eye shadow, character with eyes missing, and writing on walls. It's all in there. And how do the filmmakers substantiate the gravity of the research scene? They have Elliot wear glasses, of course! Additionally, when he searches "The Bye Bye Man", he gets zero results. That's surprising, since I just typed in some nonsense (i.e. "lke naea ene eare") and got 810,000 results. What search engine is he using?!

It says something when the film's most interesting character is the main villain's sidekick, a gigantic skulking hellhound with a huge head and skin that looks like toxic sludge.

The Bye Bye Man can't go bye-bye soon enough.
Douglas J. Ogurek ★☆☆☆☆

Get Out, by Jordan Peele (Blumhouse Productions et al.)

Brilliant directorial debut packed with eccentric characters and suspense.

Though comic genius Jordan Peele's directorial debut *Get Out* intrigued me, the preview seemed a bit silly. Particularly off-putting was a close-up of a teary-eyed Betty Gabriel saying "No. No. No no no no no no..." I almost decided not to see it in the theatre. What a mistake that would have been.

This tale of a well-adjusted guy in an unsettling environment steeped in racial issues offers a completely absorbing filmgoing experience from start to finish. Although it's billed as a horror, *Get Out* blends suspense, mystery, drama, comedy, and even a bit of soft sci-fi.

Budding photographer Chris Washington (Daniel Kaluuya) and white girlfriend Rose Armitage (Allison Williams) head out to the country to meet Rose's family. However, the carefree Rose has not told her family that Chris is black. Initially, the Armitages seem the perfect suburban family, but their oddities, along with those of their social circle and their housekeepers, gradually surface, leading to the discovery of a dangerous secret.

What makes *Get Out* so compelling is that *everyone* who Chris encounters displays some eccentricities, with Rose's family leading the pack. Despite his backslapping demeanour and his conviction that "I would vote for Obama for a third term if I could," surgeon father Dean (Bradley Whitford) makes comments that range from off-kilter to attacking. Rose's mother Missy (Catherine Keener), a psychiatrist, applies her specialty in hypnosis to attempt to stop Chris from smoking. But her intents may not be entirely beneficent – watch for Missy's menacing facial expressions. The most entertaining Armitage, however, is Rose's brother Jeremy (Caleb Landry Jones), a wild-haired medical student whose drunken banter highlights a tense dinner table scene.

The Armitages' idiosyncratic white guests, most of them older, watch Chris with a creepy fascination,

FROM THE MIND OF JORDAN PEELE AND BLUMHOUSE THE PRODUCER OF THE VISIT, INSIDIOUS & THE GIFT

JUST BECAUSE YOU'RE INVITED, DOESN'T MEAN YOU'RE WELCOME.

GET OUT

WRITTEN AND DIRECTED BY JORDAN PEELE

while housekeepers Walter (Marcus Henderson) and Georgina (Betty Gabriel) speak in a "golly gee" 1950s sitcom fashion. This strangeness isn't random; there is a reason for all of it, and when it surfaces, it's as jolting as what you would find in an M. Night Shyamalan film.

Comic relief comes in the form of Chris's friend Rod Williams (Lil Rel Howery), a TSA employee. Rod, Chris's lifeline to the outside world, offers a steady stream of humorous commentary.

Though everyone acted superbly, Kaluuya's performance deserves special mention. He achieves viewer empathy as our ally in this odd world. And when a hypnotized Chris reveals to Missy the circumstances behind his own mother's death, he transfers the emotion to the viewer.

Throughout the film, one can't help but ask oneself: Who are these people? And why are they so fascinated with Chris? What a phenomenal job Peele does of pulling the wool over the viewer's eyes.

Those of us who love horror films are constantly on the lookout for something completely original. This is it. ★★★★★ *Douglas J. Ogurek*

Kong: Skull Island, by Dan Gilroy, Max Borenstein and Derek Connolly (Legendary Entertainment et al.)

Out romance. Out cuteness. Out sentimentality. Make way for MONSTERS!

Lieutenant Hank Marlow (John C. Reilly) calls his cohorts' attention to a chirping. He says, "That sounds like a bird, but it's a [expletive] ant."

That the ants in *Kong: Skull Island* are so large that you can hear them says something about the size of the island's inhabitants, the biggest of which is King Kong. The famed monster has not appeared in a big budget film since Peter Jackson's *King Kong* (2005). That Kong was 25 feet tall. In *Kong: Skull Island*, the figure resurrects at an imposing 100 feet! Marvel at Kong's full-body profile before the setting sun. Now *that* is an iconic image.

Hats off to director Jordan Vogt-Roberts who, despite top-shelf acting talent such as John Goodman and Thomas Hiddleston, makes Kong and his supporting cast of colossuses the true stars of this film.

There's no buildup to this Kong: within the first five minutes of the film, his gargantuan (and realistic) head and hands burst onto the screen. Even if the rest of the film wasn't graced by strong acting, a solid story, classic rock, and an ecological message, *Kong: Skull Island* would be entertaining.

Threats Low, Threats High, Threats Right before Your Eyes
It is 1973, and the Vietnam War is winding down. Scientists Bill Randa (Goodman) and Houston Brooks (Corey Hawkins) head out to explore the undiscovered Skull Island. Joining them are Royal Air Force tracker James Conrad (Hiddleston), war photojournalist Mason Weaver (Brie Larson), and embittered Lieutenant Colonel Preston Packard (Samuel L. Jackson) and his troop of soldiers.

When the group drops bombs under the guise of a geological survey, Kong swats them out of the sky. Packard assumes an Ahab-like obsession with exacting vengeance upon Kong, while most of the others just want to get off the island, which is full of threats large and larger.

Some characters recognise that they are intruders on the island and advocate a nonviolent extraction, while others, particularly Packard, approach the situation with guns blazing. Packard is angered by the

ALL HAIL THE KING

KONG
SKULL ISLAND

outcome of the Vietnam War and upset that some of his men were lost during the initial skirmish with Kong, but his bloodlust seems to extend to the island as a whole. For instance, Packard doesn't hesitate to pick off a prehistoric-looking bird for no reason.

Comic relief comes with Hank Marlow, an inhabitant of the island since his plane crashed there during World War II. The Chicago native warns the visitors about the massive lizard-like creatures that live underground and threaten to surface and kill everything in their path. "I call them Skull Crawlers," he says. "I never said that name out loud before. It sounds stupid now that I think about it."

Again, though Marlow is entertaining, the most captivating players in this story are the island's animals, ranging from massive spiders and sea creatures to truck-sized yak-like beasts and winged man-eaters.

A Message of Planetary Proportions
Typically, King Kong develops a ridiculous relationship with a damsel in distress. This Kong exhibits toward his less hostile human visitors not necessarily a soft spot, but more of a not-as-hard spot. His relationship with Mason Weaver, for instance, is subtler. There are no crushes, playfulness, or snuggling. It's a mutual respect.

The film also imparts a timely message. Kong, protector of the island and almost like a god to its inhabitants, could represent the Earth's ecosystem. If you treat it with respect, it will support you, but if you hurt it, it might just hurt you back.

One soldier, Cole, says, "Sometimes the enemy doesn't exist until you go looking for one." In other words, leave it alone! Perhaps there are some places where mankind need not meddle. *Douglas J. Ogurek*
★★★★★

The Lego Batman Movie, by Seth Grahame-Smith, Chris McKenna, Erik Sommers et al. (Warner Bros)

Lego Batman was one of the funniest things about *The Lego Movie*, against strong competition, and the three Lego Batman games were all terrifically successful (and great fun to play), so it's no surprise to see him back in a film of his own. It doesn't refer back to his adventures in the previous film, but Batman is still a master builder who knows that he is made of Lego and can rebuild and reshape the world around him at high speed. This is in addition to his usual Bat-powers:

money, gadgets, fighting skills, acrobatics, and (in these films at least) the ability to shred on the electric guitar. For all his success, though, he's very lonely, and this really comes to a head when Commissioner Gordon announces his retirement. Barbara Gordon (Rosario Dawson) is going to take over, having cleaned up Bludhaven (this is a film made by people who have paid attention to the comics), and she's not so keen on vigilantes. Batman also upsets the Joker, by denying the two-way nature of their relationship, and that inspires the Joker to team up with some of the greatest villains of all time, some of them (not giving away any spoilers, because the identity of these villains was a wonderful surprise for those of us who didn't know in advance) British. A daughter of mine described this as one of the best films she has ever seen at the cinema, and it's hard to deny that it's a great deal of fun. Batman himself gets a little less funny as the film goes on and, as so often happens with comedies, the plot kicks in, but his brand new Robin Dick Grayson more than makes up for that, and that the two of them are played by Will Arnett and Michael Cera (a.k.a. Job and his nephew George Michael from *Arrested Development*), only adds to the enjoyment, as do many references to Bat-stories of old, including the Adam West film. The animation is gob-smackingly detailed, with dozens if not hundreds of characters on the screen at the same time, the cast excellent, and the script very funny, not at all the mess you would expect from a film with five credited writers. So much about this film made me happy, and a lot of it I wouldn't want to give away, but part of it is that Billy Dee Williams, who played Harvey Dent in Tim Burton's *Batman* and *Batman Returns*, finally played Two-Face. It's not the best Batman film there's ever been, but it might be the best one not directed by Christopher Nolan. ★★★★☆ *Stephen Theaker*

Logan by Scott Frank, James Mangold and Michael Green (Fox)

Decapitations and lamentations: Jackman and Stewart swan songs reveal human side of superheroes in violent, yet touching Wolverine threequel.

It's been 17 years since Hugh Jackman's rough and laconic Wolverine clawed his way into pop culture. Yes, Wolverine is strong, and he's great to watch. But can we truly connect with a guy who quickly heals from gunshots or stab wounds? In *Logan*, the final instalment of the Wolverine trilogy (and Jackman's final appearance as the character), we *can* connect. As its title suggests, the film offers a more intense exploration of the human and therefore, more vulnerable, side of the protagonist. It's not the all-powerful Wolverine, but rather the ageing Logan, a hard-drinking and world-weary has-been just hoping to retreat. Both he and Charles Xavier (Patrick Stewart), former head of Xavier's School for Gifted Youngsters (i.e. mutants), are deteriorating, and the feelings the film evokes captures this sense of loss.

But don't put on your bonnet just yet. *Logan*, directed by James Mangold, delivers all the skin-piercing, bone-breaking, head-lopping, full-throttle maniacal violence for which Wolverine is known. It even has the classic Wolverine roar.

The year is 2029, and the world is bereft of the original mutants, with the exception of Logan, nonagenarian Charles, and Caliban, a tracker with a severe aversion to the sun. They're shacked up in a remote Mexican outpost. Logan regularly takes his limo over the border into Texas to scrounge up enough money to medicate Charles with pharmaceuticals and himself with alcohol. He hopes to save enough to buy a boat and live out the rest of his days at sea with

Charles (and away from humanity). Then Laura, a girl with a familiar mutation, enters the picture.

Logan's initial response to Laura's guardian's pleas for help isn't the most heroic. He must overcome his demons to help Laura get to a place called Eden, where she can meet up with her fellow lab-manufactured escaped super-children. But there's a catch: Eden

might not be real. Thus the unlikely trio of Logan, Laura, and Charles embarks on an adventurous road trip filled with pain, discovery, and hope.

In the meantime, the lab has sent out bounty hunter Donald Pierce with his mechanical hand (never explained or used impressively) and his goons to retrieve Laura and the other child mutants. Moreover, the lab is cooking up something that's stronger than all these kids and that will, of course, be another of Logan's obstacles.

Hurt and Help
One character tells Logan that in her nightmares, people are hurting her. He says that in his, he's hurting others. He's not talking about the enemies he ploughs through, but rather those to whom Logan gets close. Pain is a constant companion to Logan. He has repeatedly dealt with physical agony, but the emotional turmoil has inflicted more damage. And what a remarkable job Jackman does, whether he's limping or grieving, in conveying both.

One of the most poignant aspects of this film is the relationship between Logan and Charles. Logan, worn down by loss, has no interest in helping others. And yet, in his own gruff way, he serves as Charles's caregiver. Sometime before the start of this story, Charles has, in his early dementia, used his mind powers to do something terrible on the East Coast. However, even in his intermittent mental fog, Charles encourages Logan to help the mutant cause, while always showing respect to the human race. Stewart, shedding his professorial demeanour and even dropping some f-bombs, offers a moving performance.

An Improbable Spokesman
If you look at the posters of the first three films in the X-Men canon, you will likely see in the forefront the same character: Wolverine. Of all the mutants, he

remains a favourite among the masses. Perhaps it's because he rolls his eyes at the whole superhero thing; he's not interested in capes and masks. With his outbursts and his pain, Logan reminds us of ourselves... minus the use of metal claws to hack off limbs, the indestructible adamantium skeleton, and the ability to withstand bullets, knives, explosions, fire and flesh-stripping winds.

Logan delivers everything that a superhero movie should have. You will feel exultation in the action scenes, and sadness in the dramatic scenes. Thanks to Hugh Jackman for giving the world a superhero with the ferocity of a wolverine, the grace of a swan, and the complexity of a human being. *Douglas J. Ogurek*
★★★★★

Rogue One: A Star Wars Story, by Chris Weitz and Tony Gilroy (Disney)

Some rooting, but more eye rolling... Rogue One *mostly no fun.*

Another group of sombre characters flying from planet to planet, another father-child relationship, another bad guy turned good, another sky swarming with spacecraft. Isn't all this Star Wars stuff starting to get a little old? I did root for the protagonists in *Rogue One*, but I also rolled my eyes quite a bit.

But then there's the guy at the theatre who told me he's seen the film four times. And what about all the critics and laymen who gave it glowing reviews? How can they look past the sappiness, the expository dialogue, the lukewarm characters? Could it be that they're all still under the spell of the first three films (Episodes IV–VI)?

Rogue One bridges Episodes III and IV. Like *Episode VII: The Force Awakens*, *Rogue One* features a female protagonist. This time it's Jyn Erso (Felicity Jones).

Accompanied by Alliance Captain Cassian Andor (Diego Luna) and reprogrammed Imperial droid K-2SO, Jyn undertakes a journey to find her father Galen (Mads Mikkelsen), a scientist forced by the Imperial Army to design a weapon of mass destruction. Then the heroes and their growing crew set out to get the digital plans for a flaw that Galen programmed into said weapon.

Rogue One isn't without strengths. A tense opening scene, for instance, shows a young Jyn escaping after chief antagonist Director Krennic (Ben Mendolsohn) and his Imperial henchmen capture her father. Krennic's spotless white uniform – it sets him apart throughout the film – flapping in the wind and his cocksure attitude propel the scene.

Moreover, a strong narrative arc follows all the conventions of a good story. Characters have clear-cut goals and rising obstacles impede their efforts. Still, an overly clinical approach to storytelling may have weakened the magic.

A couple of characters make a somewhat memorable impression. The verbally unrestrained K-2SO makes some rather snide remarks that may induce a chuckle. To Jyn, he offers this gem: "I'll be there for you," then, after a pause, "The Captain said I had to." And it's a pleasure to watch Chirrut Îmwe, a monkish blind warrior with a near-religious devotion to the Force, use his staff to speedily dispatch the bad guys. In the film's most emotionally stirring scene, Îmwe chants "The Force is with me and I am one with the Force" while walking through a battlefield. And it's hard to not perk up every time Darth Vader gets mentioned or appears. Though Vader's screen time is limited, he does regale the viewer with a demonstration of his fighting talents.

Still, the film offers no standout character, no Han Solo.

As usual, Forest Whitaker puts his all into his performance. Saw Gerrera is a mountain man type who saves and trains Jyn. However, his minimal screen time isn't enough to create an emotional connection with the viewer; anything that happens to him feels anticlimactic. It's like having a side dish from a five-star restaurant with a fast food meal: it just doesn't fit.

Another shortcoming of *Rogue One*: the opposition

never dominates, so the protagonists are never truly against the ropes. It all seems so easy.

The film builds to a major battle between the Rebel Alliance and Imperial Army. Yes, it's cool to see the Imperial Army's imposing structures amid sunny beaches and palm trees on the tropical planet of Scarif, but the chaos of the battle and the heavy reliance on special effects leave the viewer feeling a bit uninvested in what unfolds. Today's adolescent would surely scoff at the special effects of Episodes IV–VI, but didn't the lack of technology in the '70s and '80s propel George Lucas and company to create solutions that led to the timelessness of those characters and stories?

Though I'm far from a Star Wars fanatic, I (like just about everyone) think episodes IV through VI are brilliant and that *Episode VII: The Force Awakens* captures the magic. Also, that quiet Darth Maul (Episode I) is a blast to watch. It is hard to believe that, without the strength of its predecessors, *Rogue One: A Star Wars Story* would have received the same critical acclaim.

Remember what the 40-year-old Peyton Manning did after he led the underdog Denver Broncos to victory in Super Bowl 50 last year? He retired. Perhaps Star Wars should have followed his example. *Douglas J. Ogurek* ★★☆☆☆

Rogue One: a Star Wars Story, by Chris Weitz and Tony Gilroy (Disney) (take two)

The empire has ruled the galaxy since the events of *Revenge of the Sith*, but the Rebellion has been growing in strength, necessitating the construction of the Death Star, a weapon of planet-busting capabilities. Jyn Erso is in the Empire's custody, but she is sprung by rebels who hope her family connections can get them the information they need to destroy the Death Star (presumably so called because Death Sphere or Death Moon didn't sound quite as cool). She ends up going with a ragtag band of rebels on what may be a suicide mission. She's hoping to rescue her father (played by Mads Mikkelsen), while others in the squad have orders to kill him. Overall, this reminded me very much of the Dark Horse Star Wars comics. Respectful and serious in intent, lots of nods to the canon, well-made, but rather missing the mad invention of the six George Lucas films, which never stopped throwing new stuff at the screen even when the films weren't all that good. One real sticking point in the film is the appearance of a character from the original *Star Wars*, rendered with a mix of computer animation and a body double. If this were a CGI film, he would look fantastic, but standing in a room of human actors he sticks out like a sore thumb, and one wishes they had simply recast the character. It's not as jarring as the young Jeff Bridges in *Tron: Legacy* or the big brawl Keanu Reeves in *The Matrix Reloaded*, but at least in those films you could put the problems down to glitches in their electronic environments. Another problem it has is that the two lead characters are not quite as colourful as their fellow rebels. I wish I hadn't heard that Tatiana Maslany of *Orphan Black* was up for the role of Jyn Erso, since she would have been so perfect for it, but Felicity Jones does everything she's asked to do. At the last it over-reaches once again, trying for a special effect and just falling short, but if the film had ended thirty seconds earlier, one would have said it ended very well. ★★★☆☆ *Stephen Theaker*

Spectral, by George Nolfi (Netflix)

James Badge Dale (*24*, *The Pacific*) here plays Clyne, a

character quite similar to the chap he played in the underwatched spy show *Rubicon*. There he was an extremely intelligent analyst who grew concerned about the patterns he was beginning to see, and he stayed for the most part in his office. Here, on the other hand, he is an extremely intelligent engineer who gets pulled away from his usual work at a DARPA lab to address a problem in the field. There is a civil war in Moldova, at some point in what appears to be

the near future, and American peacekeepers on the ground have been seeing things through the special goggles he created: *spectral* things. And now the things have started to kill, leaving victims flash frozen. Once there, he meets CIA analyst Emily Mortimer and chap in charge Bruce Greenwood, and applies himself to the job. He confirms that whatever they are, they aren't glitches in his goggles, just in time for a massive surge in their numbers. As the city falls to their attack, Clyne must work with the surviving troops to track the spectrals to their source. This is a really good little film, with an excellent cast, sort of what you might expect the Syfy channel to produce if they weren't pumping out deliberate rubbish (enjoyable as that can sometimes be). It's directed very nicely by Nic Mathieu, and could easily have justified itself as a cinema release, although you know that if it had been, bigger stars would probably have been cast, their pay packets requiring the movie to be more of a traditional blockbuster, and it wouldn't have been the same. It never feels cheap (it feels not unlike a big budget Asian film), the spectrals have a interesting origin, and James Badge Dale makes a very likeable lead. It's great that the economics of Netflix made a film like this possible, and I hope there's more of the kind to come. ★★★☆☆ *Stephen Theaker*

Split, by M. Night Shyamalan (Blinding Edge Pictures et al.)

Shyamalan triumphs again in exploration of mind-body connection and victim empowerment.

By now, it's pretty much a sure thing. When I go to an M. Night Shyamalan film, I'm going to enjoy it. I'm going to get odd characters, interesting ideas, an intriguing setting, surprises, and a doozy of a climax, as well as a deeper meaning to reflect upon for years to come.

Split, the next jewel in the underappreciated director's oeuvre, delivers all these gifts. The film also proves Shyamalan's strong awareness of the filmgoer's role in the story. This time, he invites the viewer into the world of antagonist Kevin Wendell Crumb (James McAvoy), who has a diagnosis of dissociative identity disorder (DID) – they used to call it multiple personality disorder. Crumb imprisons three teenage girls for reasons that gradually come to the fore. It's a

KEVIN HAS 23 DISTINCT PERSONALITIES.

THE 24TH IS ABOUT TO BE UNLEASHED.

THE NEW THRILLER FROM
M. NIGHT SHYAMALAN

JAMES McAVOY

SPLIT

IN CINEMAS
JANUARY 20

WWW.SPLITFILM.CO.UK
/SplitFilmUK

fun story that keeps the viewer locked in for the entirety of the film, but also, in typical Shyamalan fashion, it's a tribute to those who face trials. This time, he takes on the broken and the abused.

Beauties and the Beast
The inciting incident happens a mere five minutes into the film: Dennis (one of Crumb's 23 personalities) abducts Marcia and Claire, along with chief protagonist Casey, a third girl he hadn't anticipated. He brings them to his hideout, then his other personalities, which are aware of each other's existence, begin to surface. Marcia and Claire try traditional escape routes, whereas the more pensive Casey attempts to manipulate the personalities. The scenes shift between the hideout, flashbacks to Casey's childhood with her father and uncle, and psychologist Dr Fletcher's interactions with Berry (a fashion designer personality of Crumb's).

Much of the film's tension stems from a villain the personalities refer to as "the Beast", who is supposedly coming for the girls. Shyamalan keeps the viewer guessing: Is the Beast a figment of Crumb's imagination? Another person? Some kind of superhuman creature? Or is it the antagonist's 24th personality that has yet to surface?

The Mind-Body Connection
The film introduces documentation of DID sufferers altering their body chemistry based on which personality is occupying them. For instance, one personality might need insulin whereas others don't, or one personality might have a different cholesterol level than the others. Shyamalan takes this mind-body connection to the next level, suggesting that Crumb *might* be able to use the power of his fragmented mind to achieve exceptional physical abilities.

Dr Fletcher doesn't give the viewer much

reassurance. She argues that the Beast is an impossibility, but also posits that those with DID could be more physically evolved humans due to their ability to manipulate their bodies. It's like a souped-up version of the philosophy that many of these self-help gurus espouse: if you think hard enough about some state of being, you can achieve it.

A Smash Split
One of the things I've always admired about Ozzy Osbourne was his willingness to step back and let his lead guitarists shine. Similarly, Shyamalan, despite his drive to impart a lesson and control his plot, lets James McAvoy do his thing and thus captures a truly riveting performance.

What a treat it is to watch McAvoy's facial expressions and vocal nuances as the camera lingers on him. Especially enjoyable are those pivotal scenes during which we witness, sometimes gradually and sometimes quickly, a character shift.

McAvoy's versatility is evident in Dennis and Patricia, the two vastly different "difficult" personalities that have enlisted the others in their "philosophy of the Beast". The most entertaining personality comes in the form of nine-year-old boy Hedwig. You know he's going to be fun the moment he utters his first words in the film: "My name's Hedwig. I have red socks." Watch for Hedwig's maniacal dance to Snails' "Frogbass".

Though his portrayal of DID is likely way off base, Shyamalan uses our Hollywood-instilled preconceptions about the mental illness to create a compelling story.

Remember that Shyamalan, the conscientious director, may be challenging you, the willing participant in this tale, to fill in the blanks. So as you settle into his dark world, look for the light that may just shine through. ★★★★★ *Douglas J. Ogurek*

Television

Ash vs Evil Dead, Season 2, by Craig DiGregorio, Cameron Welsh, Noelle Valdivia and chums (Starz/Virgin)

This is how you make a second season. It takes everything that was right about the first season – Ash the selfish jerk, buckets of blood, a teenagerish desire to shock, and an anything goes sensibility – and turns up the dial on all of it as far as it will go, then breaks the dial off, jams its own fingers into the hole where the dial used to be, and twists it even further. This reviewer and his night-time television buddy were constantly looking at each other in amazement, slapping our knees, and letting out howls at the grossness. It even led to a falling-out at one point when your reviewer was told to stop laughing so loud because it was going to stop the children sleeping, even though the thing on screen was probably the single funniest thing this reviewer had ever seen in his life.

After the events of season one, Ash and his two pals are living life large in a beach party town, but it won't last, and soon they are on their way back to where it all started: Ash's home town, and the original cabin in the woods. Ash meets his dad again, and his dad is played by *Lee Majors*. Episodes still last for half an hour, and there's even less filler this season, each part trying to top the blood, gore and ridiculous over-the-topitude of the one that came before – and largely succeeding. I'm still not a fan of the gendered language thrown at women when possessed by the evil dead – apart from not enjoying those terms being used by the heroes, it doesn't make any sense, because it's not the women who are evil, it's the monsters possessing them. It feels like a slander on someone who has already been unfortunate enough to die horribly. ★★★★☆ *Stephen Theaker*

Dirk Gently's Holistic Detective Agency, Season 1, by Max Landis and friends (BBC America/Netflix)

Elijah Wood plays a hotel busboy, Todd Brotzman, who discovers a bloodbath in a hotel room, just after apparently seeing himself (in pretty bad shape) in a corridor. He loses his job, but the universe seems to give him a new one, whether he wants it or not, as the assistant to Dirk Gently (Samuel Barnett – Renfield from *Penny Dreadful*, not I would ever have realised that without the help of the IMDB), a detective who doesn't rely on evidence so much as the fundamental interconnectedness of all things. The story involves an equally holistic assassin, the Rowdy Three (all four of them), two police officers, the FBI, the CIA, and Todd's sister, whose illness causes her to have hallucinations. Her brother's recovery gives her hope, but all the nonsense that's going on would be enough to make anyone doubt their grasp on reality. It's a long time since I read the two novels, but this seems from a reference to a sofa and Thor to be loosely a sequel to them. The first Dirk Gently novel grew out of what was once the unused script for *Shada*, and here Dirk Gently is very explicitly Doctor Whoish. He's a bit more useless and self-doubting than the Doctor, but you could put most of his dialogue in Tom Baker or David Tennant's mouth without it sounding at all odd, or at least, without it sounding any odder. I thought this was brilliant, a total delight, an unfathomably successful cross between *Who* and *Fargo* (the series), with perhaps a dash of *Psych*. Every change of scene takes us to a great character. Fiona Dourif is particularly spectacular as Bart Curlish, the holistic assassin who believes that the universe sends her to the people that she needs to kill, but has never slept in a hotel room or used a shower. If her father Brad Dourif ever retires from being cinema's favourite psychopath, there's no need to worry: the family business is in good hands. Jade Eshete is also terrific as Farah Black, a private security operative who is trying to rescue her old boss's daughter. If the show has any flaw at all, it's that it has a slight case of what I call Hellboyitis (after the first film), where we seem to spend less time with the title character than with the

chap who has just entered his world, but Elijah Wood is so likeable, even playing a bit of a jerk, that you can never resent the programme focusing on him. After the madness is over, just as the programme seems ready to settle into being *Psych*, it gets even better: the ending barges in and sets up season two very nicely. I would never have expected to be cheering just because someone was holding a rock, but that's where this excellent show takes you. ★★★★★ *Stephen Theaker*

Doctor Who: The Power of the Daleks by David Whitaker (BBC)

Seeing is believing – the BBC is your ser-vant.

Although most *Doctor Who* fans have a favourite Doctor, for many the choice is as much about era as actor. Style of story, and the broadcast years during which the viewer was of formative age, must go a long way towards shaping this preference.

Regardless of who comes in at number one, few people will rank the Doctors of the classic series without listing Patrick Troughton in their top two. Whatever the show itself was like, the second Doctor himself was exceptional.

Which merely adds to the tragedy of the BBC's junking policy. Fifty-three Patrick Troughton episodes are missing – the equivalent of two whole seasons of new series *Who* – and the word "missing" is itself a misnomer giving false hope. The master tapes were wiped, their content destroyed. When a lost episode miraculously turns up at a relay station in Nigeria or a rubbish tip in New Zealand, any celebration is tinged with cold comfort.

For many years one story particularly lamented for its absence was *The Power of the Daleks*. Not only was this Patrick Troughton's first full appearance (following the regeneration scene at the end of *The*

Tenth Planet), it also sounded like a cracking tale: Earth colonists on the planet Vulcan find and activate three daleks, which pretend to be subservient while repowering. Heedless of the Doctor's warnings, blinded by their own conflict, the colonists are turned upon and for the most part exterminated.

If this sounds oddly familiar, it is probably because Mark Gatiss pinched the idea – more kindly, homaged it – when writing the Matt Smith story *Victory of the*

Daleks (2010). And why not? The concept is far more chilling than the daleks' usual mindless blather; and after all, it wasn't as if new generations of *Who* fans had the opportunity to watch the original...

Not until 2016, fifty years after *The Power of the Daleks* was first broadcast, when the BBC, in celebration and atonement, released the story in full animation. All six episodes!

Animation was first used to reconstruct episodes one and four of the eight-part Cybermen classic *The Invasion* (1968), synching the footage with audio recordings of the original broadcasts. It was employed in similarly stopgap fashion for several other stories, but never had fans expected it to pull a wholly missing serial from the hat. Who would have thought? Half a century on, the chance to watch (and review) *The Power of the Daleks*...

Beyond its mere existence the animation is in many ways extremely good. Granted, the characters often stay front-on when moving sideways, resulting in an odd shuffle reminiscent of paddle pop stick puppets; true, there's a fair bit of bobble-about background acting; but this is entirely understandable. Remember, we're not watching a multi-million dollar production for cinematic release! More importantly, each person is well portrayed. The movement of mouths matches their speech. The characters are facially expressive. They have personality.

The backgrounds too are superbly rendered (and expertly lit), capturing the sinister moodiness of the story at large. Reconstruction producer-director Charles Norton has handled his job well, drawing from camera scripts, no doubt, but also conceptualising the action to complement a soundscape that features long sections without speech; passages that in audio alone would be quite bewildering. The first episode in particular sees the Doctor behaving erratically post-regeneration, and Ben and Polly wracked with uncertainty. From the patchiness of dialogue it seems the original broadcast version must have relied heavily on nuances of movement and expression, which the animation to some extent captures.

And so, to the story itself...

The Power of the Daleks is something of an oddity: yes, in part due to the nature of its reconstruction; but also because Patrick Troughton is feeling his way into an (at the time) unprecedented situation; and because there's a deliberate intention to obfuscate from viewers in 1966 whether this new Doctor really *was* the Doctor (a neat parallel with the newly submissive daleks); and indeed because it's the only second Doctor adventure not to feature steadfast companion Jamie McCrimmon. Add to this some obvious flaws – such as why Lesterson believes a single dalek, armed with a sink plunger, will double the colony's mining output; and why he and Bragen go unnecessarily stark raving mad – and one might start to doubt the "classic" appellation bestowed upon this so-called great lost serial...

And yet, it really *is* very good. The Vulcan colony, with its scheming factions, has a complexity that more or less justifies the story's six episodes. The Doctor shows newfound fallibility and a sorrowful, Stan Laurel-like expressiveness, the acting is impeccable (until Lesterson goes to pieces), and through much of the story there resonates that unnerving dramatic irony of the viewer perceiving an impending doom of which most of the characters aren't cognisant. All told, we have here the blueprint for the classic Troughton-era "base under siege" tale, kick-started by the daleks in a more frightening and cunning manifestation than seen so often before or since.

And of course the big point now is that we *can* see it. Just as portended by that final scene where the

TARDIS departs and a shattered dalek raises its eyestalk, the destruction wreaked upon *The Power of the Daleks* turns out not to have been total. All in all, it's a most admirable un-junking. *Jacob Edwards*

The Expanse, Season 1, by Mark Fergus, Hawk Ostby, Robin Veith and chums (Syfy/Netflix)

James S.A. Corey's novel *Leviathan Wakes* was one of the first books I ever requested from NetGalley, back in 2011, but I never got around to reading it. This excellent television version suggests that was a big

mistake. As the series begins, humans have not yet left the solar system, so far as we know. There is a good deal of tension between Earth, Mars and those who live further out. Julie Mao, a young woman with connections to the Outer Planets Alliance, has gone missing, and a freighter is attacked while investigating what we know to be the ship she was on. Our protagonists are a group from the freighter who survive, led by James Holden and Naomi Nagata, trying to find out what happened and why, and a cop on Ceres, Joe Miller, played by Thomas Jane, who also has a very groovy haircut, and has been hired to investigate the young woman's disappearance. It may not be a surprise to discover that there is a lot of shady stuff going on, but that's not to say there aren't plenty of surprises. This is a proper science fiction television series with a really good series-length plot that feels perfectly paced and still makes each episode feel like a significant chapter in the story. The effects are at times absolutely excellent, and never less than needed to tell the story clearly. The cast is excellent, and seem to be taking it all very seriously. I'm very much looking forward to season two. ★★★★☆ *Stephen Theaker*

---

iZombie, Season 2, by Rob Thomas and chums (The CW/Netflix)

Liv Moore is a zombie, after being scratched by one at a *really* wild boat party a couple of minutes into season one. Luckily she won't go "full Romero", as they call it here, as long as she keeps snacking on brains. Since the brains work just as well if the owner is already dead, she got a job in a morgue, where she works with lovable Englishman Ravi Chakrabarti (Rahul Kohli), who soon learnt her secret and began to work on finding a cure. In season two Liv continues to use her brain-visions to solve murders with Clive

Babineaux (Malcolm Goodwin), a grumpy detective. What she doesn't know is that Vaughn Du Clark (Steven Weber), the owner of Max Rager, the energy

READY FOR SECONDS?

iZOMBiE

SEASON PREMIERE | OCT 6 TUES 9/8c CW DARE TO DEFY

drink involved in kicking off the original zombie freakout on the boat, is experimenting on zombies and has ensnared someone close to Liv... At nineteen episodes this series is perhaps a bit longer than it needs to be (season one was a tidy thirteen), and having a couple of arch-enemies in the main cast means that (like the second season of *Terminator: The Sarah Connor Chronicles*) we check in with them very frequently, even though the meat of the programme isn't the ongoing arc, it's the stories of the week, where the humour of Liv dealing with her new brain-given personalities make it come close to being the replacement for *Psych* that I really, really want. This season includes episodes where she eats the brains of a fraternity brother, a real-world vigilante, a librarian who writes erotic fiction, and a country singer, always with amusing consequences. The funnier it is, the more I like it. ★★★☆☆ *Stephen Theaker*

The Man in the High Castle, Season 2, by Frank Spotnitz and friends (Amazon Video)

Philip K. Dick's *The Man in the High Castle* (1962) is one of the most disappointing books I've ever read and it's no spoiler to say that the novel simply doesn't end. It's not even as if Dick deliberately withheld closure to fascinate or frustrate his readers, but more a case of found himself in a narrative corner from which he saw no escape, stopped writing, and moved on to the next project. He could have used a disappointing device like that employed by Sarban (the *nom de plume* of John William Wall) in his similarly dystopian *The Sound of His Horn* (1952) or declined to publish, but left what I suppose is a rare artefact in itself, an unfinished novel published during an author's lifetime. What is even more baffling is that it won the Hugo Award for Best Novel in 1962. The work is of course rich in Dick's trademark complexity, weaving several subplots together and combining literary themes with genre conventions, transporting the reader to a strange and very unpleasant world where the Axis powers were victorious in the Second World War. It was perhaps the careful crafting of this alternative twentieth century that won Dick the award, although that world is not represented with quite as much verisimilitude as the subsequent efforts of Len Deighton in *SS-GB* (1978) and Robert Harris in *Fatherland* (1992). I mention the novel in such detail for two reasons: first, as a spoiler alert (alert: Dick spoiled the novel by not finishing it), and second, because the suggestion that there are two different realities in season 1 (that of the story world and the real world revealed in the films of the real world that appear in the story world) was cause for concern that season 2 would follow Dick in failing to explain the very question it had raised.

Season 1 managed to capture many of the finer points of the novel and Dick's writing more generally, including his use of multiple and often apparently unrelated subplots. Viewers were introduced to a host of characters without knowing which of them the overarching plot would coalesce around or who would live or die, all of which added to the suspense. The narrative appeared to focus on the two characters used to advertise the series, *Obergruppenführer* (SS-General) John Smith (Rufus Sewell), based in New York in the Greater German Reich, and Juliana Crane (Alexa Davalos), a young woman who has remained remarkably free from prejudice in the San Francisco of the Japanese Pacific States. The two are linked by a third, Joe Blake (Luke Kleintank), a young American who is employed as an SS agent by Smith and meets Juliana on a mission in the Neutral Zone between the two empires. The main problem with season 1 was that Sewell stole the show. (I must interject here to berate

AMAZON ORIGINAL
THE MAN IN THE
HIGH CASTLE
STREAM NEW SEASON DEC 16
amaz▸n
Prime

the BBC for cancelling *Zen*, which featured Sewell in the title role, in 2011 and reducing the best British crime series to date to a meagre three episodes.) Granted, Smith is head of SS-US, has previously participated in genocide, and keeps his fellow citizens under the jackboot, but he is also fiercely loyal (to his family and the *Führer*), very shrewd (in outwitting the various Nazis jockeying for power as Hitler's health declines), and pretty much un-killable (whether the assassins be fellow-Nazis or enemies of the Reich). In contrast, the heroes, including Juliana, are continually wavering between joining the Resistance and accepting their status as a colonised people and when the Resistance in either the (Japanese) West or (German) East does take action it is either pointless, useless, or both. What is perhaps most disappointing is the heroes' general selfishness and lack of interest in sacrificing their personal safety for a greater cause – unlike Smith, who has devoted his life to service, albeit it to a completely reprehensible cause.

Producer and writer Frank Spotnitz wisely decided to change the book that was written by Hawthorne Abendsen (the man in the high castle), *The Grasshopper Lies Heavy*, in Dick's novel to a series of film reels. This adaptation both enhances the film and reveals a further weakness in Dick's story. *The Grasshopper Lies Heavy*, the book within the novel, is a representation of a world where the Allies won the

Second World War (i.e. the real world) and naturally banned by the authorities. But the fascination with the novel is never quite explained nor is there any need to explain how the author came up with the ideas – that is, after all, exactly what authors do, make things up. In contrast, the existence of documentary film reels seems to show an actual alternative reality, particularly in an era where special effects were extremely limited in scope. The films immediately suggest a science fiction element in addition to the alternative history and the presence of Blake and others therein at the end of season 1 creates a compelling mystery that is largely absent in the novel. At the beginning of season 2 it is revealed that these films do not depict what has happened, but possible futures – events that have not happened yet, but might, and Abendsen is cataloguing them year by year in order to attempt to change the future of the story world.

The main plot of season 2 revolves around geo-political events, specifically the escalation of the jockeying for power within the Greater German Reich as Hitler's health takes its final turn for the worse and the rush for the Greater Japanese Empire to build a nuclear bomb in order to maintain the Cold War peace. The events in the two empires are exacerbated by the presence of jingoistic elements on both sides: Germans who are attempting to pre-empt a war with Japan before she is capable of nuclear retaliation and Japanese who want to build a bomb as a precursor to declaring war on Germany. In the midst of these momentous world events, the various subplots in season 2 focus on five main characters, the three from season 1 and: Frank Frink (Luke Evans), Juliana's boyfriend and newcomer to the Resistance, and Nobusuke Tagomi (Cary-Hiroyuki Tagawa), the Trade Minister of the Pacific States. This narrower focus sees all five characters, including the heroes, pursuing clear goals as Juliana and Frink commit fully to the Resistance, Joe commits to the Nazis, and Tagomi finds himself capable of moving between the story world and the real world. The tension and action are heightened for all five and the revelation of the relevance of their own stories to the apparently inevitable Third World War makes for exciting viewing. In a reversal of the way in which I was amazed at Dick's novel winning a prize, I am amazed to see negative reviews of this series, which – if watched as intended, as the sequel to season 1 – is really outstanding in terms of plot, acting, cinematic production... it really is difficult to find a flaw. Perhaps the most satisfying aspect of the series is the way that season 2 ends. The films and, more importantly, the two realities between which Tagomi can move, are explained in full. There is a resolution with respect to both Smith and Juliana's plots and the geo-political situation reaches a milestone rather than a climax. The contrast with Dick's original is stark: where the novel terminated without concluding, season 2 has been perfectly-judged, such that the narrative concludes in a satisfying manner as-is, but could continue in future seasons. Where Dick's novel failed to provide any closure, Spotnitz's closure is unusual – if not unique – in working equally well as both an interim and final conclusion. *Rafe McGregor*

Sherlock, Series 4, by Mark Gatiss and Steven Moffat (BBC One)

Like Conan Doyle, who famously tired of his creation, the BBC seem curiously reluctant to represent Sherlock Holmes on the small screen. Compare *Sherlock*, which began in 2010, with CBS's *Elementary*, which began in 2012: the former has a total of thirteen episodes across four seasons (I'll use the American term to distinguish an individual season from the series as a whole); the latter is, at the time of writing, in its fifth season and will have aired a total of 109 episodes by the time this review is in print. In addition to the British tendency to disguise mini-series as series, writers Mark Gatiss and Steven Moffat seem intent on frustrating our enjoyment of the Benedict Cumberbatch (Holmes) and Martin Freeman (Watson) partnership in a way that Robert Doherty does not with Jonny Lee Miller (Holmes) and Lucy Liu (Watson) in *Elementary*. Season 1 ended with Holmes and Watson about to blow up, season 2 with Holmes' faked suicide leaving Watson bereft, and season 3 with Holmes exiled to certain death. Ominously, the final episode of season 4 is called "The Final Problem" and it is telling that Doyle's story of the same name – his half-hearted attempt to kill off Holmes after 26 episodes – is the only original case to have inspired two of the TV adaptations.

In my review of *Sherlock: The Abominable Bride* (the 2016 Special, which bridged the gap between seasons 3 and 4) in TQF55, I was clear that the conclusion of Holmes' drug-fuelled investigation is that, whatever appearances to the contrary, Moriarty is dead. I'm pleased to say I was right. Moriarty is dead and he did commit suicide in the finale of season 2, "The Reichenbach Fall". Season 3 was Moriarty-free and the overarching plot across the three episodes was the discovery of the real identity of Mary Morstan (Amanda Abbington), whom Watson married in "The Sign of Three", interwoven with Holmes' struggle against Charles Augustus Magnussen (Lars Mikkelsen), a very nasty blackmailer of people in high and low places. The third season ended with "His Last Vow" (based on the Conan Doyle story "Charles Augustus Milverton" rather than "His Last Bow" as the title suggests), where Holmes was sent on a suicide mission to Eastern Europe in lieu of standing trial for the murder of Magnussen. The episode finished with Moriarty (Andrew Scott) apparently returning from the dead, being broadcast on every television screen in the UK and asking "Did you miss me?" The Special began with Holmes being recalled only a few minutes after his exile and its purpose was to confirm Moriarty's death and establish his revenge as posthumous. Most of the Special takes place inside Holmes' Mind Palace (AKA his drug-addled brain for this case) so the time elapsed between the end of season 3 and the start of season 4 is a matter of days rather than the three years the tormented audience has had to wait. Once Holmes reassures the

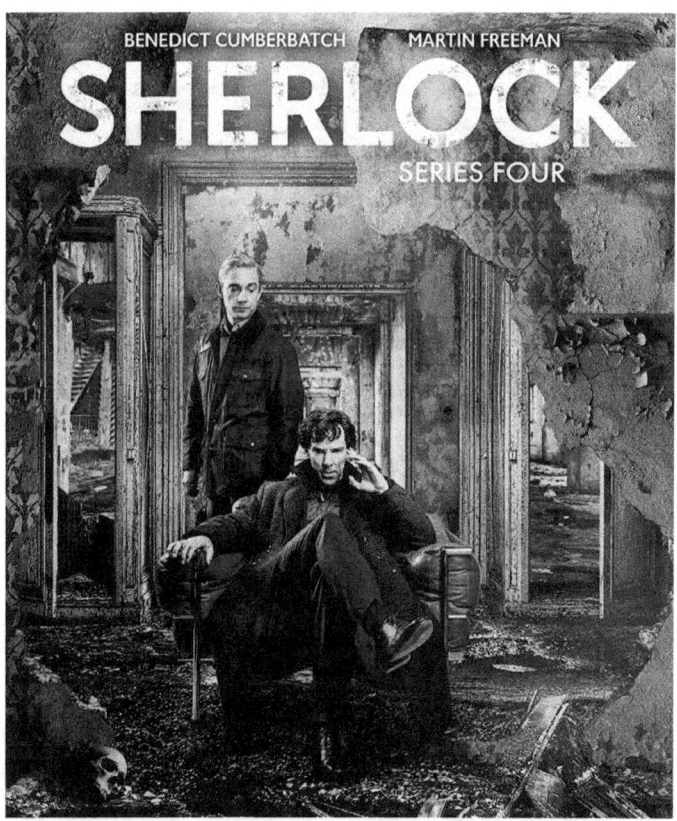

authorities that Moriarty is dead, his murder of Magnussen is covered up, and he is reinstalled in Baker Street to await the unfolding of Moriarty's retribution.

The three episodes in the season all take their titles from original stories – "The Six Thatchers" ("The Six Napoleons"), "The Lying Detective" ("The Dying Detective") and "The Final Problem" – and succeed in both paying homage to them and creatively reinventing them for viewers who have and have not read them. Following the segue from the Special to season 4, "The Six Thatchers" sees Moriarty's machinations fade into the background as a link emerges between two of Holmes' new cases. The focus of the episode is actually Mary's past catching up with her (she was a freelance military contractor who worked for the CIA and the British government amongst others). Mary decides to leave John and their child for safety's sake and is persuaded to return by Holmes. The episode ends with Watson blaming Holmes for the consequences and demanding that he never darken his door again. Watson's reaction is completely unfair, but provides the writers with an opportunity to deprive audiences of the beloved partnership without the threat of death to one or both of them (par for the course by now).

The series as a whole has been a mix of crime, fantasy, horror, and humour, but took a sinister turn after the confrontation with a really unsettling villain in Magnussen. The events of the first episode and the Holmes-Watson rift that results set an even grimmer tone for "The Lying Detective". The villain of the piece, millionaire entrepreneur and philanthropist Culverton Smith (Toby Jones, whose performance inspires a perfectly-pitched combination of fear and disgust) makes Magnussen pale in comparison. In fact, after Magnussen and Smith one begins to wonder what all the fuss about Moriarty was. The case becomes a descent into hell for Holmes and his return to excessive drug use following Watson's departure is employed as a device to blur the line between reality and hallucination, giving the story a surreal edge that marks the change from fantasy to horror for the last two episodes of the season. I was completely gripped and saw the episode as the highlight of season 4, although I wasn't surprised to see it was the least popular – it is *very* dark in tone and Toby Jones' Smith may be too much for many viewers. I do wonder, however, if Holmes' drug addiction hasn't become definitive of the character in a way that marks a complete departure from the original. Holmes' occasional use of cocaine and morphine were only mentioned a handful of times by Doyle and were indicative of his desire for mental stimulation rather than addiction. They were also introduced at a time when both drugs could be bought over the counter in department stores. In contrast, Miller's Holmes is a recovering heroin addict and Cumberbatch's Holmes an addict in denial. I also wonder if Cumberbatch's Holmes doesn't glamorise drug abuse. Unlike Miller, whose day-to-day battle with heroin makes his life more-than-miserable, Cumberbatch emerges from his binges with barely a hair out of place.

"The Lying Detective" ends with the revelation that the third Holmes child, to which there has been previous allusion, is a sister rather than a brother and that she – Eurus (Sian Brooke) – is the instrument of Moriarty's revenge. "The Final Problem" sees Holmes and Watson not only reunited, but joined by Mycroft (writer Mark Gatiss) in a Freudian excavation of the shared childhood traumas of the Holmeses. Eurus is a psychopath who shares the superhuman skills of her brothers and has spent most of her adult life in a maximum security prison on an island off the English coast. Mycroft allowed Moriarty to meet Eurus and when Holmes and Watson arrive on the island they find the tables turned and the inmate running the asylum. Eurus sets the brothers, Watson, and the prison governor a series of tasks to achieve in order to survive and the narrative is nothing short of harrowing, maintaining the grim atmosphere of the previous episode. The plot is quite similar to the final episode of season 1, "The Great Game", but this is to be expected given that both involve Moriarty's prolonged torture of Holmes. As there is currently much speculation about a fifth season it is no spoiler to say that the episode (and season and probably series as well) ends with Holmes and Watson back in practice in Baker Street.

There is no little irony here. Holmes is now free of the three supervillains that have dominated each season and he and Watson can, well, just get on with solving crimes and stuff (plus a bit of child-rearing, let's not forget baby-Watson). Indeed, the ending is reminiscent of the first story in *The Return of Sherlock Holmes*, "The Empty House", which sees a miraculously resurrected Holmes and conveniently widowed Watson set up shop once again, ready to resume business for another 33 episodes over the next 24 years. In a strange way, then, *Sherlock* ends where *Elementary* begins. The American series has been far less concerned with overarching plots and links between episodes than the British one and this, combined with the American focus on crime rather than fantasy or horror, has made it more rather than less faithful to the original stories, despite appearances to the contrary. Given the predilection of Gatiss and Moffat for frustrating the desires they have stimulated, I feel I can almost guarantee that the only season that does not end with the Cumberbatch-Freeman partnership teetering on the brink will be the last. At least there are 25 episodes of season 5 of *Elementary* to ease my withdrawal... *Rafe McGregor*

Westworld, Season 1, by Jonathan Nolan, Lisa Joy and chums (HBO/Sky Atlantic)

In the future life is too easy (good to know they fixed that whole global warming thing!) and so people jazz up their lives by coming to Westworld, a live action roleplay version of *Red Dead Redemption*, with robots playing the parts of all the non-player characters. The original film didn't spend a great deal of time thinking about how any of this would work, simply showing people having a gunfight and bedding girls in brothels before setting Yul Brynner off on his famously terrifying rampage, but this new series is all about life in Westworld, and specifically what life is like for the robots who live there. For reasons best known to the park's founders (one of whom is here played by Antony Hopkins, bringing his usual gravitas to a show that really appreciates it, since it is trying its hardest to be taken seriously), these robots, rather than being all run by some central computer system, have individual minds of their own, some of which have been operational for over thirty years, and they are beginning to have strange thoughts. They start to notice the glitches in their matrix, they start to remember their mistreatment at the hands of the park's patrons, and they start to get angry about it. Thandie Newton, Evan Rachel Wood and James Marsden portray brilliantly some of the androids as they react to their dawning knowledge of their unconscionable situation, and here the show is at its best: how should we treat non-human people, and how will they react to that treatment, it asks. The programme's problems come when you think too much about the park itself, and how it is supposed to work, and why people would want to go on holiday in such an unpleasant and horrible place. Yes, we're happy to play *Red Dead Redemption*, but when you fall off your horse in that game you won't break your actual neck. Westworld guns may not work when pointed at a human, but a knife will kill you just as quickly if a visitor decides to kill you and there aren't any androids around to stop them. Would anyone want to go to dinner in a place where your fellow holidaymakers could start sexually assaulting someone right in front of you? And would the people who liked the idea of doing that kind of thing be happy to be filmed doing it? The programme does show one chap being blackmailed, so it's unclear why this doesn't bother everyone else. Equally odd is the way the quest lines work. They seem to proceed whether any players turn up or not, which leads to a great deal of damage being done to the scenery and the androids, all of which (it's a major plot point) needs to be repaired, apparently pointlessly. Hard to understand why they don't just use squibs for the explosions of blood, rather than wrecking the androids every day. And why use expensive androids rather than cheap human actors, as, for example, in *Austenland*? Plus, if you're a guest who rolls out of bed a few hours late, how happy would you be to find that all the storylines have gone on without you? Would you be happy paying $40,000 a day to twiddle your thumbs? The important new storyline being created by Hopkins doesn't seem to have any role for a human at all – though that might foretell a twist to come in season two, showing that the new storyline is not actually the one we're shown; there do seem to be some metagames going on. (Though there's nothing to suggest this in the first series, I wondered if it will eventually be revealed that the Earth faces disaster and so the park is an attempt to accelerate the evolution of post-humans who might survive it.) It's an HBO programme, so there's a requisite amount of nudity. Most of it is degrading and unsexy, in the course of the androids being repaired, reprogrammed and analysed; you're supposed to feel bad for the androids, as demonstrated very clearly by a scene where Antony Hopkins' character rips away the clothing a lab technician has allowed one robot, but you feel bad for the actors too. That doesn't stop it being an interesting programme, though, and it

EVERY HERO HAS A CODE

WESTWORLD

rewarded the time it took to watch it with some later developments making clever sense of what had previously appeared to be storytelling non sequiturs. I would never go there on holiday – at least in Austenland the food looks nice! – but I'll be happy to watch more idiots risk it. Here's hoping for Roman World in season two. ★★★☆☆ *Stephen Theaker*

Notes

Also Received, But Not Yet Reviewed
Notes by Stephen Theaker

The Collapsing Empire, by John Scalzi (Pan Macmillan). "In the far future, humanity has left Earth to create a glorious empire. Now this interstellar network of worlds faces disaster..." Reviewed for *Interzone* #269. I liked it a lot.

End Times: Rise of the Undead, by Shane Carrow (self-published). Zombies in Perth!

Kingdom: Aux Drift, by Dan Abnett and Richard Elson (2000 AD). "Genetically modified dog-soldier Gene the Hackman wages war against giant insects in a Mad Max future."

The Order: Die Mensch Maschine, by Kek-W and John Burns (2000 AD). "The Expendables meets H.P. Lovecraft as knights and robots take on a dark, hidden power in medieval Europe!" For a long time I had thought for some reason that Kek-W was a pseudonym of D.F. Lewis; apparently not!

The Penny Dreadfuls, Vol. 2: Macbeth Rebothered; The Odyssey; The Curse of the Beagle, by David Reed, Humphrey Ker and Thom Tuck (BBC Audiobooks). Audible edition of the BBC

Radio 4 plays; features Susan Calman as the Narrator and Robert Webb as Odysseus. Review next issue.

Raven Strategem, by Yoon Ha Lee (Rebellion). The sequel to *Nine Fox Gambit*.

The Searching Dead, by Ramsey Campbell (PS Publishing). "Dominic Sheldrake has never forgotten his childhood in fifties Liverpool or the talk an old boy of his grammar school gave about the First World War. When his history teacher took the class on a field trip to France it promised to be an adventure, not the first of a series of glimpses of what lay in wait for the world."

Thrill-Power Overload, by David Bishop and Karl Stock (2000 AD). The revised and expanded history of the battle-scarred survivor of the post-apocalyptic wasteland that is British comics.

Waking in Winter, by Deborah Biancotti (PS Publishing). "On a far, frozen desert world, Muir the pilot discovers an ancient artefact in the ice. She sees a mermaid at first, but later comes to wonder if it is Ningyo, a fish god from her homeland in Japan." Review next issue.

Windcatcher, by A.J. Northfield. Book I of the Stone War Chronicles: "Far away from home, under the command of his brother, Raylan and his squad must retrieve an ancient relic ... Raylan learns that the ancient relic holds unexpected life; a creature buried in legends..."

The Wrack Line, by Robert Edric (PS Publishing). "A man arrives to spend the overheated summer in an abandoned chalet. Adrift in his own faltering life, he slowly embraces the failed and struggling world in which he unexpectedly finds himself..."

About TQF

Copyright

ISBN (print): 978-1-910387-24-5
ISBN (epub): 978-1-910387-25-2

ISSN (print): 1747-6083
ISSN (online): 1747-6075

Website: www.theakersquarterly.blogspot.com

Email: theakersquarterlyfiction@gmail.com

Lulu Store: www.lulu.com/silveragebooks

Feedbooks: www.feedbooks.com/userbooks/tag/tqf

Submissions: Submissions are very welcome! See website for guidelines and terms and reading periods.

Advertising: We welcome ad swaps with small press publishers and other creative types, and we'll run free ads for relevant new projects from former contributors.

Sending material for review: We are happy to look at anything that's fantasy-related. We prefer to receive books for review in epub or mobi format, and comics in pdf. Feel free to send ebooks without querying first, but it's fair to warn you that we've only reviewed about 15% of items received since 2011, and even then that's often been stuff we've actively requested from places like NetGalley.

Mission statement: The primary goal of *Theaker's Quarterly Fiction* is to keep going. If you're wondering why we do something a particular way, our primary goal is probably why.

Copyright and legal: All works are copyright the respective authors, who have assumed all responsibility for any legal problems arising from publication of their material. Other material copyright Stephen Theaker and John Greenwood.

Published in Theaker's Paperback Library during March 2017.

Other Publications

Theaker's Quarterly Fiction
Douglas J. Ogurek (ed.) *(#58)*
Stephen Theaker (ed.) *(#1–54, 56–57)*
John Greenwood (ed.) *(#9–54, 56–57)*
Howard Watts (ed.) *(#55)*

Space University Trent: Hyperparasite
Walt Brunston

There Are Now a Billion Flowers
The Hatchling (forthcoming)
John Greenwood

The Mercury Annual
Pilgrims at the White Horizon
Michael Wyndham Thomas

The Conan Doyle Weirdbook (ed.)
The Adventures of Roderick Langham (forthcoming)
Rafe McGregor (ed.)

Professor Challenger in Space
Quiet, the Tin Can Brains Are Hunting!
The Fear Man
His Nerves Extruded
The Doom That Came to Sea Base Delta
The Day the Moon Wept Blood
Stephen Theaker

Five Forgotten Stories
John Hall

Elephant
Harsh Grewal

Elsewhere
Steven Gilligan

New Words #1–4
John Greenwood, Steven Gilligan
and Stephen Theaker (eds)

Forthcoming Attractions

Expect **Theaker's Quarterly Fiction #60** in June. We are open to fiction submissions for it from April 1 to May 31, but we may close early if the issue fills up. Reviews are welcome any time.

Our blog can be read here:
www.theakersquarterly.blogspot.com

Stephen tweets every few days or so at:
www.twitter.com/Rolnikov

The zine has its own Twitter account too:
www.twitter.com/TheakersQrtly

Our email address is:
theakersquarterlyfiction@gmail.com

If you've enjoyed this issue, and especially if you haven't, please consider giving it a rating on Goodreads, or LibraryThing, or wherever you keep track of your books. We don't need to sell any copies to keep going, so that's not a concern: it's just nice to know you're out there!